A PLAY OF PASSION

A PLAY OF PASSION

David Holbrook

W. H. ALLEN · London
A Howard & Wyndham Company
1978

Printed and bound in Great Britain by
Butler & Tanner Ltd, Frome and London,
for the publishers, W. H. Allen & Co. Ltd,
44 Hill Street, London W1X 8LB

ISBN 0 491 02282 9

The actual name of Nugent Monck has been used
because it would be absurd to try to disguise him.
A few others keep their real names. Where invented names are used, the characters bear no relation to living persons.

The author acknowledges support from the Arts
Council of Great Britain.

The quotations from the Passion Play are from
The Norwich Passion Play published by the
Wherry Press, 1939.

For Kate

What is our life? A play of passion,
Our mirth the music of division.
Our mothers' wombs the tiring houses be
Where we are dressed for this short comedy.
Heaven the judicious sharp spectator is
That sits and marks who still doth act amiss.
Our graves that hide us from the searching sun
Are like drawn curtains when the play is done;
Thus march we playing to our latest rest,
Only we die in earnest: that's no jest.

Sir Walter Raleigh

I

The little man put his left thumb and forefinger to his bald head, squeezing the skin of his forehead into wrinkles. His face was rather like a clown's mask, pale, with watery grey eyes and a small expressive mouth. His eyebrows were strongly marked and comical, a little like George Robey's, but more subtle in shape, like commas with points, that put everything in ironic brackets as he responded to it.

'We haven't even got the curtains up yet, and I must start the run-through at eight o'clock. It would help enormously if you could all stay on or come back at six.'

He was talking to three awkward boys of sixteen, in grey school suits.

'Can't we just go on with it now?' asked one of the boys who was struggling with a long mass of stiff painted hessian, trying to fold it.

'I'm all gratitude, ducky, but unless I am here . . . and I *must* go up to the Crypt!'

Nugent Monck gave his dribbly kind of chuckle, modest and rather arrogant at the same time—the chuckle of the artist who, whatever else he would give up, would never relinquish his standards. But he always seemed to slobber a little bit as he chuckled, and then suck the spit up to make his mouth neat again.

'Unless *I'm* here,' he said with determination, 'it won't be done properly. In any case, since I have no char, I have to go home, do the washing-up and make the beds. I shall even have to empty my guest's chamber pot, I have no doubt. And then prepare the supper.'

He gave a stagey sigh and a wave, and illuminated them all with his impish and feminine smile, fluttering the long pale lashes around the light grey eyes in his rather plain face.

'There's no rest for the wicked, and God doesn't love me.'

I

'Can't *we* help ? At your home I mean ?'

Paul Grimmer was one of the three boys struggling with the heavy curtains. He had only just been elevated into the lower sixth form of his school. He was one of three pupils sent by his headmaster to help at the Maddermarket Theatre in Norwich. The theatre happened to be putting on one of the set plays in their English paper for the Cambridge Higher School Certificate examination, *Much Ado About Nothing*. It was 1940. Monck's theatre was a replica of an Elizabethan 'apron stage' auditorium but with a roof, created in a building which had been a Salvation Army citadel, before that a baking-powder factory, and before that a Catholic church. A dull square little hall, it was hidden behind a paved courtyard, down an alley, a footwalk which descended through the arch under the flint mediaeval tower of St John's, Maddermarket, to Charing Cross. All around was a huddle of ancient buildings, slums and crowded alleys, between the Market Place in Norwich, the Guildhall, and the River Wensum. Below the theatre was a cobbled open space with a horse trough, where madder dye had been sold since the Middle Ages until the last century. The little market place spread in a triangle below the wall of a raised ancient graveyard—raised, it was said, by the mass burials during the Plague. Across the road from this was the old Public Library, a dull municipal building of red brick which inside, however, displayed an astonishingly up-to-date intake of books, and held vast files of reference material behind and above circular iron staircases in its recesses.

Paul had been to the Maddermarket Theatre once, to see *Othello* with a school party. The theatre company created in their little bare house an art of elegance and charm. Even the unruly boys of fourteen, all bum and giggles, had been overawed by the old theatrical play-bills in the little foyer, with its coir matting, the smell of coffee, the pink and blue lamps throwing their soft beams onto the rich costumes of the actors and the painted sets. The great advantage of the little theatre was that everyone could hear every word. Nugent Monck used to recount how when he first went into the gloomy empty warehouse he said aloud: 'What awful blue paint!'—and at once realised the acoustics were perfect.

But when on this Saturday the boys arrived to 'help Monck' the romance was gone. He was wearing a rather threadbare grey flannel jacket and trousers and a pullover. Without introduction he handed them two dustpans and handbrushes, a broom and a hessian sack.

'The place is *filthy*, after the spinet concert,' he said. 'I should *never* have let them have it. I *know* they took at least fifty pounds, and they paid me *five*. Those women never clean the place afterwards. They are *much* too *"artistic"* to sweep up properly.'

His eyebrows swept up, Robeyish, to emphasize each italicised word.

So the schoolboys, somewhat subdued, crouched down on the floor under the rows of tip-up seats upholstered in red rexine with cast-iron legs and frames, banging their brooms against the cast-iron frames, sweeping up tickets, fluff and leaves brought in on people's shoes. Stephen found a woman's glove and Paul a man's silk handkerchief.

'*Quite* a good one,' said Monck, holding it up to the light, spinsterishly. 'I hope nobody claims it, and then we can put it in Scutcheons.'

'What's Scutcheons?' asked Paul. He was rather afraid of the little man, and yet fascinated by him. A shy boy with a lanky body to which he was not yet used, he felt gormish in strange company and clumsy: his mouth was dry. And yet he felt he must talk, must break out of his oafishness, of his adolescence, into the 'world'—if this was the world. He found the little man provocatively mysterious, especially with the names he would throw out: 'Veronese', 'Holst', 'Fiesole', 'Pirandello'.

And now 'Scutcheons'.

'Scutcheons is our wardrobe workshop. Perhaps I should explain something about the Maddermarket?' Recovering his public manner, he perched on a dark square wooden stool, a 'Jacobean' prop, and waved his hand at the floor covered with straw-coloured woven matting. The boys stood awkwardly, embarrassed, leaning against a pillar or the end of a row of seats.

'I built the theatre in 1908, and it was the *first* theatre to be designed on the lines of the Elizabethan Globe, with an apron stage and a simple fixed set, in this country. As you see, it has *no* proscenium arch.'

None of the boys knew what a proscenium arch was. They had been to the Theatre Royal (pronounced 'thēē-étter') and to the

3

Haymarket, which had a glorious interior, all plaster garlands, gilt and cupids. Paul had been to the latter for Christmas pantomimes as a child, his eyes riveted on the curved sweeps of plaster as the rose-coloured lights touched it, and his heart beating as the stage maroons flashed and banged. But they were acquainted with none of the technicalities, so they looked blank and the sensitive little man was immediately aware of their discomfort and ignorance and turned fatherly rather than spinsterish.

'What's a proscenium arch?' asked a boy called Jack Brown doggedly.

'No one ever seems to learn anything at school these days! I had to learn *everything* myself. In Shakespeare's time the actors used to be able to come forward, right *above* the audience, do you see: some of them even sat *on* the apron, that's this bit that sticks out in front of the stage—and that, of course, makes sense of the soliloquies, and many other stage conventions of the time. You can talk gently into the front row's *ear*. And there was no frame. 'Look!' With astonishing agility for someone of sixty, the little man placed one hand on the edge of the stage and swung himself up. He acted terribly badly, in fact, and this was a great joke with his company. He was a producer of great skill and taste: but he fluffed any part he undertook, though when he forgot his lines he made up lines that sounded almost as good. Once, after being prompted twice—his memory was terrible—he came angrily down to the prompt corner and declared, 'I don't *need* a prompt, Maudie!' The schoolboys, however, knew nothing of all this: they were only astonished and deeply embarrassed. Moncklet drew his mask-like face into an expression of tragic foreboding and hissed behind his hand:

> If it were done when 'tis done
> Then it were well it were done quickly:
> If the assassination could trammel up the consequence
> And (er) catch with his surcease, success . . .

Streams of spit shot in their direction. The lights were being tested and the droplets soared into a white beam.

'You see, I spoke very quietly, but you felt I was actually *confiding* in you, didn't you?'

'Yes,' mumbled the boys weakly.

4

The fluting voice of an elderly man came clearly and plaintively from the shadows.

'Moncklet, do stop showing off to those boys and come and help me with these back cloths . . . He spits too much, don't you think?' it added to the boys.

The tall grey-haired figure, who moved as if he were strapped in whale-bone stays, with an even more feminine manner, threw down a long roll of painted curtain material. Paul Grimmer gave a grunting kind of laugh. The boys didn't know how to behave at all, as the theatre people play-acted at one another. Coming from ordinary suburban homes, they had never come across anything like it. They tended to nudge one another and retreat into their little herd, suppressing their sniffs and giggles behind their hands. But they were awestruck, too.

'This is *Peter*,' said Moncklet, drawing back his spit with another chuckle. 'Peter Taylor-Smith. He comes from the Old Vic. He is the *only* person in the theatre allowed to talk to me like that, because he's been here as long as I have. He's really the chief *needlewoman* of the place, and a great craftsman—he makes all the costumes and props, and looks after Scutcheons, which I just told you about. It contains many genuine period costumes, swords and jewellery, and is insured for ten thousand pounds.'

'Do you think you ought to tell them?' asked Peter cynically, with the casual drawl they were getting to know as the 'Maddermarket voice'.

'They have no vice,' asserted Monck. 'Unlike you.'

'I'm not, however, too lady-like,' drawled Peter, drawing himself up with a certain silvered magnificence like Prospero, as Paul imagined him, 'to sew on two hundred bloody curtain hooks ready for tonight's rehearsal.'

'Well done,' said Moncklet. 'These boys will help us hang them. They've been sent by the City of Norwich School to help in the theatre. I am introducing them *gently* to their tasks. They've been sweeping up.' He seemed obsessed with impressing upon the boys the need to recognise that art was hard work. 'I must tell you the rest of the history of the place another time. It has a *ghost*! . . . he is seen at matinées: and sometimes in rehearsals he sits at the piano.'

Paul had helped his father with a few household tasks, but

5

nothing as daunting as the theatre jobs. The enormous painted hessian curtains were as heavy as carpets. Across the back of the stage was a bridge, so that, by the use of curtains, a balcony could be created above and a cave or indoor scene below. Then, at the fore-edge of the frame in the ceiling, there were further rails so that a front-of-stage scene could be played on the apron before them. A curtain on a curved, concave rail was used to cover the whole bridged rear to make a large interior scene: and again straight curtains could be pulled across half-way, painted with street scenes or forests or palace interiors. Each production required at least ten enormous drapes to be heaved out of their cupboards, some painted after hanging, some to be painted as they lay on the stage, with pots of water paint smelling strongly of glue, and hung when they were dry. A few flats could be fixed, some folded over from sides to middle, like picture scenes in a book. But there was no elaborate machinery and no space above for flies: the curtains were often pulled back or drawn by the actors themselves at the close of a scene.

To Paul Grimmer, who was beginning to enjoy Shakespeare at school, it was fascinating that everything they did down in the little warehouse theatre was in the service of the imagination. Lugging a spinet off the stage into a room at the side of the platform, struggling with a folded grey velvet curtain, carrying stools or swords and hangers about, he was working for imaginary things, events which happened only in people's minds. He understood that gladly. As an idealistic adolescent of sixteen he was deeply distressed by the materialism of his world, its attachment to things. He couldn't articulate it, but he knew that what went on 'inside' him, in his feelings and his imagination, was what was most real in his life.

'Rose too deep!' Monck would cry of the stream of rose-coloured light striking the stage. The flood-lights were lanterns fixed to the pillars which held up the balcony of the auditorium. Up there were seats for about seventy people: downstairs another hundred could be accommodated. The lights hung just above the heads of people in the stalls. Frames of coloured transparencies would be lowered and raised by strings from the lighting box, clacking as they did so. At rehearsals Monck would call: 'Pull up No. 5 and put rose pink in 8!' and the strings would clack.

6

'Everybody's nose will look *red* and the *women* quite *apoplectic*. Boy—what's your name?'

'Paul, sir,'

'God, Peter, he's calling me "Sir". Am I so frightening?'

'Moncklet, you know you always wanted to play Napoleon.'

'No, Peter, you're wrong—I want to *be* Napoleon.'

He crouched down, in a spasm of self-mocking laughter, showing his eye-tooth and gleaming brightly at the boys with a sardonic look. Paul Grimmer found his clownishness deeply attractive. He had never known such a fun-loving adult.

'Paul—get the steps and change the rose jelly to pink in No. 6 Pollitt will give you a pink jelly.'

Pollitt was the electrician in the little room called the lighting box at the back: he gave the whole of his spare time to the theatre.

So it was all moving towards the rehearsal: but there were still curtains to be hung, and no one to do it but the three boys. Everything was behind-hand and Monck decided he must refresh them.

'I must *feed* you,' he declared. 'I will give you some bread and cheese at the Crypt, and we will buy a *cake*. Many hands will make light work, and we shall come back in time to have everything ready.'

The producer put on his blue trilby hat and rather old and shabby overcoat. With his determined vigour he stumped off, leading the three boys out of the maze of alleys up into St Giles and along the street where the trams ran down to the Guildhall Hill. At St Giles he suddenly turned left crossing Bethel Street and dived through an opening in the red brick wall into a dark inner space labelled 'Ninham's Court' in black and white. Monck always moved with his arms and legs working like pistons, his elbows sticking out doggedly; the boys had a job keeping up with him. Once he threw his face into a toothy smile and raised his hat to a plump woman, who bobbed at him deferentially.

'Good evening, Mr Monck.'

To them he whispered, stagily: 'She keeps the fish and chip shop on the corner going the other way. She and her husband *never* miss a performance. We have nearly a thousand regular patrons with season tickets.' He tossed his head proudly. 'True converts to the faith!' And raised his comic eyebrows.

The little court, dark and dank, might have belonged to Dickens's

7

time. It hadn't changed for a hundred years, and at the other end loomed steep wood gables of derelict timber-frame houses, black and carved with scrolls, evidently Tudor or Elizabethan, but in bad repair, with leaded windows burst and gaping, and plaster hanging away. Yet they were inhabited, as was clear from the glow of lamps behind drawn rags of coloured curtains. In front of these at the end of the court were some untidy shrubs and a ragged laurel. A fence ran along the valley with wooden gates in it: the nearest one opened with a click into a small garden, mostly cobbled, but with a few wallflowers and shrubs. This was Monck's house, 6 Ninham's Court. It was called the Crypt because it had a great vaulted cellar. It had been the first home of the Norwich players, and had been left to Monck for his lifetime by a gentlewoman admirer of his art. The City Corporation was Trustee.

Above the grim court it rose, a rambling Elizabethan house with big timbers and leaded windows, uneven and weathered. It immediately impressed Paul with its long-settled benignity. The front door was made of heavy oak, like a church door, with long black iron hinges. Above it there was a strange little protruding window glazed on both sides. The timber-framed windows ran along the whole court side of the house, those upstairs on the first storey being the largest. They consisted of tall panels of leaded glass between strong oak bars, leaning out slightly at the top. There were three storeys. There was a mullioned window in the end of the attic space and the gable ends were carved with a scrolled pattern. The roof sagged a little under the weight of its deeply weathered red tiles, some arranged in patterns of dark and light red. A big black and white cat sidled out to mew at Monck, who drew a big iron key from his overcoat pocket and thrust it into a hole in the massive oak door.

'Oh, Tib,' said Monck, 'what *are* we going to give you?' The huge door creaked open, and the little man clicked on a light, swept up the cat and nuzzled it against his face, removing his hat. He could never resist an 'entrance'. Turning to the boys, he held the cat up to his face with his hand under its bottom, like a Madonna holding the infant Jesus:

'Mother and child!' he declared, posing.

The fire was soon raked up into life, and Paul Grimmer stared round at the big living-room as the flames glittered on the polished

8

dark wood furniture. Everything seemed to belong to the Elizabethan room: they were good cottage things, like old domestic furniture he had seen in the period rooms at the Bridewell Museum. But it was simple, too: the floor was yellow and red brick, covered with coloured rugs: there was a sofa and armchair upholstered in a patterned chintz, a low oval gate-legged table in dark polished oak, and a grandfather clock clunking gently. Against one wall was a tiny green-painted ottavino virginals on a stand and the bookcases contained mostly play scripts and poetry in red, black and cream bindings. One of the boys, Stephen Blake, was despatched with a pound note for a cake and a bottle of milk for the cat. The little man pounded up the curved oak staircase which creaked: he held on to a thick rope handrail as he heaved himself up.

'I must go and pee. Can one of you fill the coal bucket? The coal is in a little shed in the back yard through the kitchen.'

Paul took up the heavy copper bucket and groped his way through to the back. He found the light switches by fumbling, one by one. First there was an open space at the bottom of the stairs with a polished brick floor. Here stood a large wooden dresser in a warm pinkish wood, covered with fine china plates in green and white, displaying their ivy-leaf patterns. In this room, called the scullery, there was an oak refectory table and benches, and it was here that snatched breakfasts and suppers were taken. Then, behind this, there was a primitive kitchen with an earthenware sink and a scrubbed beech draining board, on which a pile of washed plates and dishes were draining. There was a plain old-fashioned enamelled gas-cooker, and a big white refrigerator. A back door with a brass knob led out into a tiny yard. On one side was a fig tree with tangled branches, and on the other the coal store, where Paul fumbled at the black rock in the dark until he had filled the bucket. Certainly it was all very different from his semi-detached home life in the suburbs. At home, his father and mother did all the chores. It was very unusual for him to do anything. At home, as a sixth former, he was treated like a kind of privileged intellectual. Perhaps at Christmas he would fill the coal bucket. But normally, he didn't do the chores: his mother wouldn't even let him peel the potatoes. She didn't like people 'interfering'. Monck's chores were completely new to him, and strange: he

9

knew what to do, but fumbled at doing it, banging his knuckles, spilling the coal.

The boys all took household management for granted at sixteen, as boys do. The fire was lit, the breakfast prepared, as if by those gnomes and pixies for whom housewives left cream by the fire in the old stories. In fact, of course, Paul's mother, like all the other boys' mothers, scrabbled the coal out of the little coalhouse under the stairs, among the sacks of potatoes and the bundles of garden tools, with the smell of mouldy earth and tar. It was mum who rattled the grate to sieve the ashes from the cinders, and sneezed as she shovelled out the pinky-grey ash. Perhaps now and then the adolescent son would take a hatchet to some firewood: but mostly that too was done by the mother, whose hands grew more ingrained with dirt, and creased with harsh application.

The adolescent boys weren't exactly indifferent: they were simply unaware of the way their mothers laboured at the buckets and tubs. Occasionally, as they lay in bed warm and relaxed, they would have a twinge of conscience hearing their mother chopping sticks on the back doorstep in the keen frosty east wind. But the enormous lethargy of adolescence would overcome them, and they would sink back into a guilty oblivion. They simply lived with boiling coppers and clouds of steam, the copper-sticks and mangles on wash-day. So it was a strange and novel experience for all three, to be so busily organised by the theatre director, to do chores like adults. Stephen and Jack were soon wiping the dishes: Paul was collecting the scraps of peelings and emptying wastepaper baskets all round the house. Monck laid the gate-legged table with blue willow-pattern plates, glasses and cutlery. It was obvious the man insisted on every detail being properly carried out, just as he did in his productions. Paul, at one point, brought in some simple kitchen knives and forks from a drawer in the scullery: the little man swept them all up and trotted back into the washing-up room with them, where he rattled them, sighing, into a drawer. Everything they did was wrong, it seemed. Everything must be right: not in any genteel way, but absolutely to the highest standards. 'I will not allow slovenliness!' he declared spittily.

'The proper cutlery is *here*,' he declaimed, drawing a little baize-lined basket out of the dresser, containing plated knives and forks, with reeded handles. 'The Woolworth ones are for use in the kitchen. And the knives go on this side, and the forks on the left. Spoons we shall *not* need—as there is *no* pudding.' He banged everything about, to underline their uselessness, and how he was forced to do everything himself, with a weary upturn of his big watery eyes, and a devastating extension upwards of his comma-like eyebrows.

In fact, as they had already scented, it was to be better than the promised 'bread and cheese': there was an earthenware pot of stew cooking in front of the fire.

'Of course, *I* made it,' he said, '. . . at *six* o'clock this morning, before it was *light*. I had to come home at lunchtime to make up the fire. Someone here is *always* hungry. This house used to cost me six shillings a week from Norwich Corporation: since they mended the roof and cleaned out the drains, I have had to pay thirty. The garage at the end wants to pull it down, but they never will, because it is mine for life. When I am dead, pray God, the Forty Thieves will have to maintain and let it.'

The three boys ate nervously if ravenously, watching the little man to see how he used his knife and fork, and how he ate every-thing. Actually, though he ate in a delicate and feminine way, he made a crumby mess as he did so, chiefly because he got excited and talked too much. Before they sat down he had made them go to wash their hands, and charged up and down the stairs for a towel for them. They were overcome with his energy: it shamed them to be so outrun by a man as old as their own grandfathers. Nor could they understand the glee with which he took such a paternal pleasure in trying to 'civilise' them. At home, people asked for things to be passed, listened to the radio, reported hap-penings and quarrelled, all in a continually flowing chaos of simply living on top of one another. Monck obliged the young people whom he invited into the Crypt to have 'conversation'—though these bewildered boys didn't yet recognise it as such, and felt it was all quite artificial to do more than grunt and ask for the salt.

'The problem is always Beatrice's "Kill Claudio!"' said the little man, his mouth full of stew and bread. His careful manners never prevented him from talking with food in his mouth, often so that crumbs would fly out with his sentences.

'It's a chilling moment in the play which on the whole is to be taken lightly. And one has to be careful she doesn't forfeit the audience's *sympathy*.'

'Does she really *mean* it ?' asked Paul.

'Well, of course, it could be that she is trying him, and doesn't really want the order to be taken seriously. I did think I would get her to play it with icy seriousness. But once we began rehearsals Cicely made me think otherwise: she plays it as if everything was a whim—rather like Leperello—so I think I'll get her to play that like a whim too. She could put a finger on his shoulder, so: arch her eyebrows: "*Kill* Claudio ?" Perhaps that's it ?' He mimicked her expressions and movements, in his feminine way.

'Who's Leperello ?' asked Stephen, determined not to pass the whole meal in silence.

'Don Giovanni's manservant in *Don Giovanni*.'

'That's an opera by Mozart, isn't it ?' asked Jack, the third boy, a ginger-haired lad whose father was an engineer at the power station.

The little man patted his lips with his napkin, rose, and stepped over to the bookcase.

'Don't get it greasy,' he said. 'On second thoughts, I'll *hold* it and show you the pictures.'

It was a superb folio edition of the score of *Don Giovanni* with plates from a performance at the State Opera in Vienna. The boys stared at it, wide-eyed, never having seen such an opulent book, and certainly not such a one devoted to a whole area of experience of which they had heard nothing. Even the paper of the book, rich and hand-made, was beyond Paul's awareness: he had never seen or felt such stuff. But it had never struck him before that there could be anything exceptional about paper. Paper was just paper. But this was like rich petals. The little producer seemed a wizard, who could conjure a stew out of the hearth, an interpretation of a Shakespeare scene out of the air, a segment of European culture out of his bookcase. With the delicious stew warming his inside, Paul felt a great benignity infusing him from the man and his simple, lovely old house.

'The secret,' said Monck, 'is a spoonful of *Pan Yan pickle*.'

There was a creaking in the boards of the house.

'Ghosts !' laughed Stephen.

'It could be *the* ghost,' said the little man, not turning a hair, as

12

he munched his last piece of bread with which he had mopped up the last of his gravy. 'But he doesn't *often* walk, and it isn't his anniversary.'

'Is this place haunted, too, then?' asked Paul. He was beginning to treat every episode of Monck's life like a turn, a scene, making himself a feed to the man's demonstrations.

'There's a sad, lost creature in the attic who appears every year. I think he must have *hanged* himself on one of the beams.' The boys winced and sniggered. 'I feel he has to do it again, every day on that date at about 1 am. I've slept there, and asked him what it is he has to tell me: but he never *says* anything. He simply glides towards that end beam . . .'

Gazing like Macbeth at Banquo's ghost, the little man stretched out one of his rather ugly hands at the end of one of his short arms towards nothing, with his jaw fallen. He's a clown, thought Paul. Moncklet seemed to grasp the air, to let the thing go, then his arm fell.

Now, to the boys, sitting at the table in the ancient room with its pools of lamplight on unfamiliar objects like silver inkwells and the tiny portable virginals, there was a distinct sound of creaking footsteps. Actually, as Paul soon discovered, it was a feature of the house: as anyone walked across the floor, their feet pressed down the huge loose oak boards. A few minutes later, perhaps even as much as five minutes later, the boards would start back into place, sounding as if feet were walking across the room. Stephen had been to the lavatory across the study floor upstairs five minutes ago: they had forgotten that. They didn't know the rational explanation, and a cold trickle flowed down each back.

They cleared away and washed up, feeling creepy now in the dark Elizabethan house with its many shadows. Just before they left Monck remembered the cat, and tore round the house seeking Tibby, who was unearthed at last curled up on a bed in the haunted attic room.

'Out you go, darling,' said the little man. 'I'd hate you to *disgrace* yourself!'

'I think I should *warn* you,' he said, once he had his trilby hat and overcoat on, and a grey and white woollen scarf wound round his neck, making himself look for some reason like a small elderly detective about to go out on a case. 'I'm a *homosexual* . . . I'm not

13

an *active* one, so there's no danger. I don't seduce people—and in any case I believe *sodomy* is too painful. I'm a bachelor, as you see, and—despite my work—I'm often very lonely.' He paused, and one had a feeling the lights would turn to rose pink, while his face softened its mood.

'*Some* people are fond of me, and I have some very close friends. Perhaps one or other of you may grow to be fond of me. But don't be afraid, and don't believe anything anyone says if they are malicious about me. I never do anything over which I could be blackmailed. "I'm not that sort," ' he quoted, ' "and if I were, a *shilling's* not enough . . . besides, there's no *place*." '

He chortled, rather sadly.

'Above all, let me give you good advice: *never trust a bugger*. But I—' he turned the heavy key in the lock—'will never do anyone any harm. I have suffered too much myself.' He turned: 'I am too busy with my theatre.'

He stuck his chin out nobly.

In the light of the street lamp in the alley, Paul could see his eyes were full of water: and he had adopted, for this moment, a pose from one of El Greco's paintings of scenes around the cross.

Monck's eyes were easily tearful: it was all part of the continual drama. But it was also part of the old man's magic—of making the imagination alive. Paul's head was a-whirl with the day's experiences already.

That evening he had his first sight of the little man at work. The couple on the stage, he knew, were Mark, a master at the grammar school, and his rather effervescent wife Cicely: all the players were amateurs, though for some it was the primary interest in their lives and their devotion was total. The Maddermarket was no place for amateur theatrical standards: Monck would not put up with anything second-rate or sloppy. His standards were professional, and he would put the actors through their paces again and again until he was satisfied. None of them was allowed to be known under his or her name: all the programmes were anonymous.

'*No, no, no!*' he cried. 'Cicely, you are being too *soft*, too . . . oh, God, what is the word?'

'Diaphanous?' suggested an actor in the stalls.

'Cicely could *never* be diaphanous,' said Mark, her husband.

14

They were big-limbed people, tall and powerful, with a lively and affectionate relationship in which they continually teased one another, indeed rather like Benedict and Beatrice.

'You are revealing too much of your soft *vulnerability* to him,' said Monck. 'At this stage.'

'How awful!' giggled someone.

'Please!' said Monck. 'Please can we be *serious*? This is the most important scene in the play. Now, can you turn passionately to him, and yet apart, and say with parted lips, almost as if frightened at your own will and whim: "*Kill* . . . Claudio!" '

The woman responded perfectly to the direction, and her man responded with a slow, horrified gesture. Paul saw the little man's eyes filled with tears again. His eyes shone with hawk-like intensity of attention. There was nothing off-hand about Monck's creative devotion to the play in hand. He threw himself into the work with long, cunning experience of how to make beauty by drawing potentialities from ordinary people. And in the way he grouped them, moment by moment, he obviously had in mind the great paintings he had seen on his trips to Italy.

'Very good,' he cried. 'But will you *remember* it?'

'We'll practise in bed, Moncklet,' said the husband. Laughter echoed round the theatre, from Barbara painting a pillar on canvas, from the lighting mechanic, from Peter—they were all fond of Mark and Cicely Smith.

'The problem,' said Monck, 'will be to get the others to respond properly when they turn up. They stand there like dummies. "*Ow!*" '

He made a face like an idiot.

' "*Ow!*" It's their only response! I can say it because they're not here.'

'Except to mutter sausage and rhubarb, Moncklet.'

'Sometimes I despair. But it's coming: I have a good Beatrice and Benedict at least.'

The blacked-out streets were dark as the three boys walked home after the rehearsal, weary but excited. They had the familiarity of school mates, of belonging to the same class at the grammar school out at Eaton Road. But outside school, Paul Grimmer thought, contemplating his companions, they hadn't much in common. This became clear as they walked up St Giles towards the Newmarket Road side of the city. Under the tower of St Giles church which loomed into the darkness a party of helmeted police and air raid wardens passed them in navy blue uniforms, clumping along in boots; otherwise the city was almost deserted: it was nearly midnight.

'Slush's bloody ideas,' said Jack. 'Slush' was their cruellest nickname for their headmaster, who had a slight speech defect.

'Why? Whatever do you mean?' asked Paul.

'Lugging yer guts out for that old homo.'

'I didn't mind the work,' said Paul. 'I liked all the talk.'

'N't going there again,' said Jack, grimacing. He wore a smart pale raincoat with a tartan lining. He came from a very respectable engineer's home: they all exuded ambition, and gave off a professional, scientific feeling about the future. Mr Brown had a science degree.

'Why ever not?' asked Paul, really surprised.

'Don't want to get mixed up with types like that.'

He wriggled his hips, insultingly. Stephen guffawed.

'That old bloke Peter was a right old pansy. Bloody old woman.'

'So wuz old Monck. Cor! Blast!' said Jack. He mumbled something incoherent and hostile in broad Norfolk. All the boys lapsed into Norfolk from time to time.

Paul was silent, really angry with them. They had lapsed into their family prejudices, instilled by the popular newspapers. The evening had opened a new world to him—not so much of homosexuality, but of European culture. He had been surprised by the homosexuality but also found its otherness fascinating and amusing: he knew already, from reading if not experience, that the world of arts was full of such extraordinary people; but it had never touched him, except perhaps as a distant anxiety about his own sexuality and whether he was 'normal'. But he had taken an instant liking to the little man, not because of his femininity, but for his energy, his wit and the world of culture to which he pointed.

At one point Monck had said: 'I am an atheist; but I believe there is something beyond us, something'—his eyes filled again—'to which we must submit ourselves.' Paul's heart leapt: he had no one to whom he could talk of such things. Yet he thought about them, all the time. The clergymen he met simply avoided such subjects. It was amazing, suddenly, to come among a company which regarded them as normal topics, as if they were everyday matters.

Secretly, as his schoolfriends peeled away into the night at the Catholic church, calling goodnight, he knew the Maddermarket Theatre would be a major influence in his life. There was something in the air, even in the dust-motes floating in Moncklet's lilac and rose flood-lights, that offered to transcend the existence in which he felt now so imprisoned, just coming up to seventeen. About the sexual problem, he couldn't help feeling one was what one was. As a tall young man had walked awkwardly onto the stage, he had heard Moncklet murmur: 'My God! Once . . . always!'

'What does that mean?' Paul had naïvely demanded.

'Was I talking to myself?' asked the little man. 'It means "Once a lady, always a lady". You'll understand it, one day. Only it will never apply to *you*,' he added, almost sadly. Paul felt already very fond of the older man with whom he seemed to develop an easy, comic empathy. He already felt part of the Maddermarket world and knew it would be important to him in his life.

2

His mother was in bed having her afternoon rest. Every day she went up to her bedroom at two o'clock with a cup of strong brown tea and went to bed, sleeping for two hours. She had difficulty in sleeping, because of her 'nerves', she said. She lived in a strange world of her own, his mother, a world of her rituals for sleeping, her sleeping tablets, her glass of Guinness before going to bed at night. Her intense obsession with her 'insomnia' prevented any detached conversation with her at times. This dinner time it had been difficult, because Paul's head was full of his new experiences of the Maddermarket Theatre, while her thoughts trod the weary old path of her own afflictions. So they had sat at her browned and bubbling cottage pie together, not really talking to one another. Paul thought his own thoughts while she talked at him, and he grunted answers without really hearing her. Outside, a few orange crocuses glowed on the little lawn and on the air raid shelter mound. It was a showery March day, with clouds and bright moments rushing past.

'Oh, boy, I did have a bad night last night. I felt so full of wind. I wonder if thass that new Guinness? Do you think I ought to have Guinness at night?'

'You know you can't give it up, mother.'

'Oh, come you on now. Anyway, why should I give that up? I've worked for it. Thass been my work that's kept your father steady, so he could get on and get where he is. Surely I'm entitled to one little treat in life? I work hard enough for you and your father.'

'I don't know that the Guinness is really any different, mother. It's just that they've put a new label on it.'

'Oh, no, thass *quoite* different. Thass sweeter, I think. And that give me wind, now. I heard every stroke of the hour until three, last night, before I took three more aspirins.'

'Perhaps it's the aspirins that give you wind?'

'How could they? They're *medicine*, aren't they?'

'I don't think aspirins make you sleep. I read a thing in the paper.'

'Well, I need them to make me sleep. I can't do without them.'

'I don't think aspirin is a drug that sends you to sleep. It isn't a *soporific*.'

'Sop-or-piffy,' she cried contemptuously. 'Squit! You don't know nothing about it,' she declared against his reasoned judgement, with all the suspicion of a woman brought up in the close peasant life of a North Norfolk coastal village. Eleanor was born in East Runton in the eighties, and so much of what she believed was dogged village prejudice.

'Well, I'm sure aspirin is bad for you. Rots your stomach.'

Paul sighed. He didn't want to talk about aspirin and Guinness. The whole question of his mother's ailments bored him. He loved his mother, and would have been glad to have been able to influence her, and to try to encourage her to take a more sensible attitude to her health. She read voraciously: she continually read her way through the whole of Dickens. But why could she not take in 'non-fiction' advice on her health problems? He felt sure she was doing herself serious harm by taking so many aspirins to try to make herself sleep; he wished she would simply enjoy the Guinness and not pretend it was a sleeping draught. And he felt that if she went for a walk in the afternoons instead of going to bed, she'd sleep better at night. But they had been over and over this ground, ever since he had turned fourteen or so. What was the good? It wasn't really a *debate*, or a proper *argument*, he said to himself: it was just an anxious treadmill of words. The poor woman had a face that was always puffy with depression, big swollen bags under her deep brown eyes. But he tried again.

'It's not at all a bad day, mother: why don't you go for a walk instead of lying in bed all afternoon? I'm sure you'd sleep better.'

'Huh!' she replied. 'And where would I go? Round that boring old Eaton Park? See a lot o' old mud and grass?'

Her voice went up at the end, in that Norfolk country singsong way. He wondered if she ever went along that broad open beach at Runton as a child? Or did she skulk indoors then, helping her mother run a boarding house single-handed? Her father, he knew, had run off' in her childhood. He had apparently become an alcoholic, after the failure of his wheelwright's business, and home life became intolerable.

They ate some prunes and custard in silence. Paul gave up. Inwardly, he felt a rage against his home. Oh, yes, they housed and clothed and fed him, and he was grateful. But he felt guilty for being so snobbish, so ungenerous, as to criticise his parents' tastes and their ways. In truth he was in the throes of adolescent revolt, hating his home, feeling guilty for doing so, and loving it, *needing* it, at the same time. None of this could be explained to a 'nervous' old woman obsessed with herself. So he simply sulked.

It doesn't have any shape or meaning, this home, he thought; I feel suffocated, in this terrible muddle. He had looked at his home in a new light since he had moved into the sixth form and started preparing for university scholarship work, in which the wider perspectives of civilisation began to open up to him. He went to other people's homes, to museums, and now to Monck's home. He came to feel ashamed of his parents' little semi-detached house with its muddle of patterns and its nondescript furniture. But as he did so he felt disturbing pangs of unrest and guilt. He had to throw his mother and father off; but the ties were very close too. So the conflict had become a terrible self-laceration. As a child, as a young boy, he had done things for his father and mother in the home: he had put up a shelf in the bathroom with Rawlplugs, and had painted out the little lavatory at the top of the stairs. But everything about his home now irked him: he hated the colours, the patterns, the cheap quality of things. He had whitewashed his bedroom pure white, and had hung up a reproduction of Van Gogh's yellow chair, and some Cézanne apples. He loved the book *Lust For Life* and wanted to be swinging along on a road in Provence or cutting off his ears, rather than sitting in Lowland Avenue swotting for Higher.

He looked round now at the little living-room. There was a fireplace, of beige-coloured shiny tiles with a porridgy pattern, pink and earth colour, with stepped sides and a flat top on which stood a cheap brown wooden clock with a curved body. In front of this glossy ceramic fireplace was a clumsy tiled hearth over which everyone tripped, and in front of this a rug, made in the evenings by his father, by pulling tufts of rug-wool through a net of fibres. It had an ugly ziz-zag pattern on it: now he remembered a patch of tufts he had done himself, to help his father. They had been working one at each end of the strip of backing and Paul had loved his new, orangy-red tufts and the way you clicked them into the rug-making tool, and drew them through the holes. He could feel the firmness of the knotted tufts in his hands. He had loved working at it with his father, who had kept laughing and pulling his end, and who worked with his big tongue stuck out.

'Oh, bugger, boy, thass goin' to be the cloosest wool rug ever made by hand, there y'are!'

But the end-product was a mess—ugly, shapeless, kicked up into ridges over the underlying carpet, which was itself a cheap factory square with a dull 'abstract' pattern. And their rug-wool cuttings kept coming untied and falling out, despite what his father had said.

On the hearth was a large kind of round coal box made of sheet metal with a hinged lid, pressed into a scrolled leaf pattern. It was always a terrible nuisance to fill, falling over when you were least prepared, or its lid falling on your fingers as you dug into it with the tongs. He hated that, too, though his mother filled it ten times to his once.

The table! he exclaimed to himself. Mrs Grimmer had a strange way of cluttering a table, first placing cork mats at the place-settings, covering these with a cloth, on which she had embroidered coloured flowers in Sylko. Then, on top of the mats, she would put further pieces of embroidered linen, on which she would lay the knives and forks.

She always made the table look rather like the uneven surface of a desert, on which used plates and dishes would look, after a meal, like the debris of a retreat by an army in Africa, Paul thought. The food was always good, countrified and wholesome: his mother was at her most creative in the kitchen. But it was always served in such a muddle, of discoloured baking tins brought straight onto the table, of rickety vegetable dishes, and spoons and carving tools lying higgledy-piggledy around on the uneven table.

Paul's reaction to this muddled nature of his life at home became obsessive in itself. In the living-room were two brown 'leatherette' armchairs with loose sprung cushions. These would tend to become littered with old newspapers, his mother's basketwork sewing basket, her steel needles and wool half-way through knitting a sock, and an electric torch, come unscrewed. Underneath the cushion would accumulate half a dozen copies of *The Radio Times*, *John Bull*, and a quantity of seed catalogues. It took several minutes of effort before anyone could tidy up the chair enough to sit in it, and from time to time in desperation he would have to have a blitz on the chairs, to throw out all the rubbish accumulated in them. And the same with the dark oak-faced plywood sideboard; the gramophone cupboard that no longer contained a gramophone; and the piano stool, full of torn scores of old operatic songs from *Il Trovatore* and *The Yeoman of the Guard*.

With a good book, and a warm fire, it was possible to forget the muddle. But at times of crisis, he found it intolerable. There was nothing to which he could attach any sense of meaning, unless it was his father's black and white pen drawings of Norfolk churches, which were really devoted, often beautiful, in catching the forms they studied. They had a lovely quality; but, to Paul's irritation, the man never took his drawings seriously.

And in this atmosphere, even in the home he loved, he could not take those things seriously which were most dear to him. He felt he was dying, even in the dear place which had given him life. He was bursting with inner distress, a terror of meaningless. A little later in that spring of 1940 he had had a terrifying experience which he could not explain to himself: but it was a crucial sign of change in him. He had had flu, and had been lying a few days in his mother's bedroom, the best front bedroom, facing the little street. Anyone who was ill was put in that room because it had a fireplace. There was no fireplace in his little single bedroom, and one of the rules of the household was that if you were ill enough to stay in bed, you had a fire. So he changed beds with his mother: she had the white walls and the Van Gogh; he had the muddled patterns and the sepia photograph of his mother dressed for Haddon Hall, leaning on a garden urn, and a bad painting in oils of two oranges in a gilt frame by one of her mother's lodgers.

Paul was weak and had had a fever; he could not read and his mind was full of dread. He had missed the Maddermarket *Much*

Ado. For hours he ran his eyes over the shape of the bed rails, which had brass knobs screwed onto an old-fashioned frame all rods and metal tubes. In the corner there was a wardrobe of solid dark oak, a rather art nouveau kind of shape with be-ribboned metal handles, and in the window a dressing-table with a round mirror on pivots. The floor was a mottled linoleum and there was a brown hairy rug in front of the fire. The walls were covered with a wallpaper on which were printed wreaths of roses and leaves, in a criss-cross trellis shape. These all seethed in front of his eyes as his temperature rose during his bout of flu.

His whole relationship with the world, with reality, suddenly seemed threatened. But no one else knew: no one could know. In his sickness, Paul had lapsed back into his childhood re-lationship to his home, glad to be nursed and waited on, his mother bringing his meals up on a tray, and jugs of the lemon-juice she made from fresh fruit and sugar. But as he recovered his rebelliousness returned again, just as he grew weaker. He became incapable of playing, in his eyes and mind, half-asleep, with the silly shape of the wardrobe and the ugly form of the dressing-table. The wallpaper roses, instead of being the vehicle for fantasies, came to look like a crazy joke, badly printed bad drawings, on paper which was beginning to turn yellow. Now all this muddle seemed to menace him, as his self felt weak and disintegrated, dissociated.

Gradually, one morning towards the end of his convalescence, the process of his seeing through all the absurd and meaningless shapes of his home accelerated. Everything collapsed into its components—stretches of cellulose fabric, stained plywood, torn wood pulp cells, decaying shellac, cheap mortar. It all seemed to explode. He could hold nothing together, and could play with no more shapes or forms; and he too became a crumbling assemblage of matter, a confused mass of flesh atoms menaced with decay. It was as if he had come to the end of all the playful, half-serious, half-dreaming activities of the consciousness of childhood. No longer could he hold off the recognition of death, of his in-evitable mortality, of the progressive mutability of all stuff. New emotions—strong and strange—poured in upon him. In a sense, it was his first moment of adulthood, which was also the first taste of brutish mortality. It seemed suddenly to lunge at him from the top of the ridiculous wardrobe, and all life suddenly seemed to him meaningless, as nothing ever had done before.

So rapid and catastrophic was the collapse of all playfulness in his perception of his world, that everything in the room now seemed to threaten him—to menace him with solid, brutal reality. The wardrobe seemed to lean over him like a cliff; the cheap wooden picture-rail seemed to cramp down on his head. The patterns swirled and gyrated until there was nothing in the room except a chaotic mass of molecules, striving to return to chaos, to dust, a black shadow overwhelming him. It was as if all the muddled, meaningless objects of his childhood home had thrown off their nursery-rhyme fantasy existence and were breaking through to him with a fundamental brutality of unredeemable matter. He was nothing, and his mind was nothing: he could perceive nothing in any way which charmed or transcended it. The things themselves had broken away and were grinding him and his consciousness into ashes and darkness. He suddenly lost all hold on his consciousness and felt he was sinking into a vortex of nothing.

He actually cried out and lay, exhausted and in a cold sweat, striving at the shadows behind the dark wardrobe. He couldn't even hide his face under the bedclothes; he knew that old childish trick would never work again. It was as if he was finally thrust into a threatening world, into a doom from which he could not escape, enchained in his own flesh: reborn, but condemned.

'Why, boy,' cried his mother, who had stumbled upstairs, in her floral Woolworth's pinafore, hearing his cry, 'whatever is the matter with you, Paul, boy?'

'I . . . I felt . . .' He reflected on the impossibility of ever telling her—ever telling anyone what the problem really was. '. . . I had a kind of nightmare, awake. I . . . felt as if I was going to die . . .'

'Why, *blast*, don't be so silly!' she said, tut-tutting at him like a hen and putting her arm behind his head and punching his pillow up for him. 'Why, boy, you look right white and lantern-jawed. I'm going to make you a nice cup of tea.'

He laughed. 'I meant,' he said, 'I suddenly realised what it means to die.'

'Ah, well, thass that nasty old flu, Paul. That get into your brain, I reckon. Shall I stay up here with you a bit?'

24

He responded gratefully to the rising note of love and care in her voice. He was glad of her company, very glad, and held her work-worn hand for a bit, looking up into her troubled dark brown eyes. She was a sturdy woman, still handsome, though depression had lined her face, and her eyes had those big droopy bags under them. But her hair was still dark brown, glossy and full, and her eyes were brown and deep. She wore a rather ill assortment of clothes, saggy woollens and shapeless tweed skirts, so that she looked untidy and tubby. She had been lovely once, with an almond-shaped face and a heart-shaped mouth. Paul saw her like that, like her photographs in operatic performances in her youth—before she had even met his father. On the back, his father had written 'Lovely!'

'Thass silly,' he said, lapsing a little into broad Norfolk. 'Thass silly a great felloe of sixteen should be waited on and nursed by a poor old woman who've got enough to do on her own account!'

But he was glad when she came up grunting a little, as the afternoon darkened, with a tray of tea and chocolate biscuits, and tried to comfort him with talk about the early days of her marriage.

'If that hadn't been for that little old pony cart that used to come round, old Abbs, I don't know what I should ha' done. He had noice rabbits, and on Sunday we'd have a hen, you know, a boilin' fowl, and a bit o' his farm butter now and then. I never bought that International muck,' she added with pride, 'and as fer *margarine.*' She made a wry face. That was the best thing about his home, he decided, as he listened to her, its links with country life. His mother's father had been a wheelwright, and so had his grandfather William on his father's side. One grandfather's business had gone bust: the other went to work on the railways. But both had lived in the country. He heard the street vendor's bell as he listened to her, and the fish man's cry: 'Kippur! Haddock, smoked haddock and bloat-ah! Kippur!' The man sang it like a piece of recitative, falling in fourths, lah-mi's.

'There was a man used to come round with a muffin bell, and a tray on his head with a white cloth over it, and all hot muffins and crumpets inside.'

'Thass right—up at Eversley Road, Mile Cross. He used t'remind me of Dickens, and them old times. Thass all gone!'

I'll read Dickens, he thought. His mother loved Dickens's

novels, and they had them all in the house, in cheap editions produced by one of the newspapers. She loved *David Copperfield* because old Peggotty reminded her of her father, who had worked in Cromer before he left his family.

So Paul climbed out of his terror, his new dread of the tyranny of the cheap and ugly objects in his home, by reading his way again through *David Copperfield* and *Nicholas Nickleby*. By doing so, as he paused between chapters, sipping the delicious lemon drink his mother brewed him, he regained a perspective on his home.

But despite the reminiscences of a former past, his home now was so lacking in meaning to him, he must break out to find new meanings and vision, to throw over the terrifying menace of mere things. There was no doubt now in his mind from his science teaching that everything was only matter in motion, and meaningless. How could he ever feel anything he did had any point?

As soon as he felt strong enough he took a tram to St Giles and called on Moncklet. The older man was as pleased to see him as if he had been his own son. 'I *heard* you were ill,' he cried. 'I'm so *sorry*! And you've just come at the right moment. I've got to go to a *funeral* and you can support me!'

'I'd be glad to,' said Paul. 'And I'm glad it's not mine!'

'It's very bad, this flu. Our poor Peter Taylor-Smith nearly died of it: he was rushed to hospital with pneumonia. Benny, my Man with a Load of Mischief next month, looks like death. Mercifully, *I've* escaped. But the cathedral organist has died of it, and I must represent the theatre at his funeral. I *hate* funerals, and I would be most grateful if you could come and hold my arm.'

He held it out in such a way that it couldn't be refused. They walked through the city, and even the little man was rather grim.

It was a sung service and, since Paul never knew the elderly musician who had died, he could pay attention in a detached way to the music. At first he dreaded entering the huge empty space of the Norman cathedral with its great circular pillars and the carved geometrical patterns twisting round them. He felt appalled by the spire reaching desperately into the sky and by the immensity of the long nave, on whose roof bosses were told all the stories from the Bible from creation to the last judgement. But if his convalescent mind was at first appalled by the dreadful massiveness of the stone building, its immense cavern-like space, its cold stone mass, he soon became caught up in its meanings and reassured. Looking up, although the carved bosses were faint in the shadows, he could see figures suffering there—the raised sword, the spreadeagled figure on the cross—and the individual death was swept up into the universal suffering of man. And so too the echoing sound of the organ wove the individual life into the unfolding lines and structures of a Bach fugue, or the flowing polyphony of a sung requiem cantata. The very gleams and shadows of the April day seemed a cycloramic background to the magnificent music.

So from this detachment, Paul could watch the others dispassionately—the relatives of the deceased, two rows of elderly, bowed people in pews towards the front of the nave. The men and women stood side by side confused and bent in their dark clothes, shifting uncomfortably from foot to foot, and looking round furtively. One woman burst occasionally into sniffs and sobs, cringed in her body, and was comforted by a tall grey-haired man who put his arm round her.

'Poor things!' whispered Moncklet, clutching Paul's arm. Together, not daring to speak above a murmur, they opened their prayerbooks, with their shiny black covers, at the burial service. The little man read the first page over to himself, his lips moving.

'It's so *dramatic*,' said Monck, in his stagey whisper. 'The Church was always so good at *staging* things,' he hissed through his teeth, his eye-tooth sticking out rather, with nervousness and excitement.

At once, the long fugue on the organ came to a magnificent close, and there was a silence in which steps echoed at the back of the great cathedral nave. Glancing back, they saw the light streaming down from the immense multicoloured east window, bathing the stone with rose and blue, like the theatre lights, and beneath it the priest bearing a cross, leading in the pale oak coffin slowly carried by six bearers.

'I am the resurrection and the life!' cried the preacher, in a ringing voice. Moncklet gripped Paul's hand, trying to convey to him his profound appreciation of the drama and the tension. Paul's heart beat, and he heard Moncklet give a little chuckle of sadness and delight.

Once the coffin was placed in position below the altar the choir burst into the Bach Cantata, *Es ist genug*. The focus was on the yellowish wooden box with its brass handles, conveying the dead-weight of the body, the crouching figures of the bereaved, the shadows around the stone tombs, all bearing down on them with a weight of loss and grief. But even as the voices uttered their lovely columns of sound, their vibrations in the air, weaving and drawing together into structure and form, the whole ritual entered into another dimension: and the people there became transcended. The drooping figures in the pews drew themselves up, actually stood straighter. What could barely be borne, the reality of the stiff corpse in its long box and the pain of loss, all that weight of the awfulness became distributed—the load being taken by the form of the ritual, spread over the great squat pillars of the Norman nave, spread over the lovely shapes of the music. Paul looked up at the ribs of vaulting soaring into the roof with its depiction of the long story of the world according to myth. How much friend-lier than the bleak view he was being taught in physics! The music absorbed the actual death moment into a scale of time which transcended the individual mutability. It was painful, tragically painful, but it relieved the personal confusion by translating the death into the common terms of human experience, so that it became Everyman's death, and Christ's death: our death. Paul's thoughts ran along on these lines, as if telepathically prompted by the intelligent little man beside him, who punctuated the service by pointing at telling words in his prayerbook or by tugs at Paul's sleeve as the anthems rang out.

The service went on with the magnificent passage from St Paul, about how the corruptible will put on incorruption. Paul glanced at Moncklet, whose eyes were full of tears again, while he dabbed at them with a dazzling big white handkerchief. 'I ironed myself four large hankies,' Monck whispered during the subsequent pause, and then: 'If only it were *true*,' he moaned—'I should *love* to become *incorruptible*!'

The hymns were bad. 'Let me hide myself in thee!' They had the opposite effect to the great cantatas, bringing back a bewildered grief, and messy emotions. Monck hissed 'Awful!' and Paul nodded.

'Once,' said the little man, 'I played Lechery in a morality play, and was led in to dinner by the Archbishop of Canterbury. On another occasion it was said I was easily recognisable as Satan. But I have *never* been able to *believe*!'

As they left, and Moncklet put his gay trilby hat on his ir-regular-shaped, domed head, Paul felt strangely enriched, despite the gloominess of the ceremony and the big shiny black hearse rolling away from them now through the gravelled Close to the crematorium.

'It's just like coming out of the theatre!' he said.

'Exactly. Of course, I should have been a priest. It's the *one* thing the Church can offer—the drama, the ritual.'

'The hymns are terrible, as you said.'

Monck sighed. Popular bad taste distressed him: he wanted beauty for people.

'Yes, dreadful. They're either Victorian and morbid, or else they go back to Wesley, to the guilt and the ecstasy. I can't believe either in the guilt or in the ecstasy: I am *not* black with sin, and I *don't want* to die. I don't believe Christianity, despite its marvellous stories about Jesus and the Book of Job. But yet I cannot believe the world . . . that life . . . is meaningless!' He blew his nose, gasping in the open air. Paul pulled him back from walking into a car, blind behind his handkerchief. 'Mind you, Bach could be in ecstasies about dying because of his belief. But we've *lost* it,' said the little man with a wide gesture of his arm. 'It's a disaster—the loss of the next world, and the loss of the Devil. Modern man believes in neither, and so he has no rewards or punishments. I can't read philosophy, but I believe Nietzsche . . .'

The word made him spit and show his tooth.

'Nietzsche believed that the effects would be catastrophic, and I feel he may be right! Indeed, I'm *sure* he's right. Of course,' he added, with a Robey mask, 'he was *insane*!'

'I'd never realised before, the value of funerals,' said Paul.

'If the thing is done *well*,' said the theatre director, 'it trans-forms everyone and turns the private pain into universal tragedy. In one of the great Russian novels—is it in Dostoevsky?—a dying man who is an un-believer asks for a Christian burial. "Why?" asks his brother. "Why, you wouldn't fling me into the ground as one flings a dog!" '

He grinned mischievously, spitting vigorously on the 'flings', chuckling moistly and gesticulating with his arms.

They had reached the bus stop by the Erpingham Gate on Tombland and the waiting passengers were amused by the middle-aged man's emphatic speech and gestures, especially as he wore a black tie, which lent an added zest to his clowning. From their seats on the top deck as the bus rose up the hill Monck pointed out the Golden Ball Inn which, he said, had been saved by the intervention of the Norwich Society, of which he was a member. The Corporation was to help the brewers to do it up, instead of pulling it down to make a car park.

'But *all* that area,' he said, waving a hand at the cattle market behind the castle, 'will become a *car* park. The cattle market will be put out at Trowse, and the city will lose all the trade associated with it—the shops will lose the farmers' wives and the pubs the farmers and stock men. The city is dying, and the Forty Thieves—who should be called the Forty Fools—are killing it.'

The Forty Thieves, in local parlance, were the city councillors.

'Everything will become a car park in time, no doubt,' said Paul. He found it exciting to enter into this criticism of the provincial bureaucrats from an educated radical position.

'And so *dead*! The centre of every city, empty and dead. How unlike my dear Florence! There, there are bake-ovens flaming away, in the centre, and people live there, right in the centre, thriving—or they used to be,' he added gloomily. 'Of course, it's a *slum*. And will probably now be flattened by the RAF anyway.'

'What can we do?'

'You must stop it! After the war, you young people must *stop* it.'

'Huh!' said Paul angrily. 'Much notice they'll take of us.'

Monck got off at St Giles, but Paul stayed on along Unthank Road. How strange, he thought to himself. All I've done is to waste a morning, giving old Monck some support at a funeral: and yet I feel cured—cured so that I feel everything is a great stagey joke. Is that insincere? He had felt swamped, suffocated at home and didn't know why. With Monck, every moment was taken up with an energetic attention to the nature of the world, what it could teach one, how one could interact with it and change it. That was how one should live, not in a passive muddle, day to day. He went over what Monck had said, about Bach, about Florence, about mediaeval architecture. He always had a reference beyond . . . beyond.

They had been alone for a moment after the stop on Castle Meadow, and Monck had said in a low voice: 'One of the problems is that people don't notice life. The world simply passes them by. You watch them. They come onto a bus, and sit down, and simply look straight in front of them.' He made his idiot face, the jaw dropped, the eyes unseeing. "*Ow !*" I often wonder if they'd notice if the conductress was stark naked.'

So they had been in fits of giggles, all along Gentleman's Walk and up Guildhall Hill, as people came onto the top deck, and sat staring featurelessly into space, or scowled down at their ticket, and over the conductress, who was so ample in figure that the idea of her clipping tickets naked was rapturously absurd.

3

Going with old Monck to the funeral, he thought, was rather like going to church that time with Annie. He enjoyed her company in a not dissimilar way: she too had a mocking, ironic attitude to everything. They were always having the giggles together. After that visit to her church it was about the priest sloshing everyone with holy water, using a brush. When they saw anything like it, such as a man pasting up advertising bills, or a man brushing the pavement outside his fishshop, they would call out 'Kyrie Eleison! Slosh! Slosh! Tinkle! Tinkle!'—and everyone would think them mad, as they swayed about guffawing on a bus or in a shop.

Annie was plump with an open, pleasant, smiling face with large, rather silly brown eyes and long lashes. She worked as a window-dresser and was warm-hearted and generous. Paul's mother obviously suspected her of seducing her son and found it a shock that Paul had now brought home a girl who used lipstick, and wore silk stockings—when she could get them—like a woman. Mrs Grimmer was older than his father, and she hadn't had time to be courted until she was thirty. So she was envious of her son's emerging sexuality. She asked him questions, uneasy.

'Do you like girls that wear lipstick, Paul?'

'I don't like it when it comes off.'

'Oh, Paul: do be careful.'

'Whatever do you mean, mother?'

'I think you young people go too far, nowadays.'

He remained silent, smirking.

'Is Annie a nice girl?'

'She goes to church.' He wanted to ask her how far 'too far' was.

'Ah,' said the woman. 'So do plenty of people who are no better than they should be.'

'Annie's a Catholic.'

'Ah,' said his mother darkly, 'that don't mean nothing, boy. They're some of the worst, once they get a-goin'.'

'Now, mother, I'm fond of Annie, and I shouldn't have brought her home if I'd been ashamed of her.'

But, he thought, I'm lying, because I know perfectly well she would be horrified if she knew how we hold each other's bodies under our clothes in the cinema, and I'm certainly not going to tell her about that. What I'm really concerned about is how to keep all that from a mother who knows me so well.

His mother noticed he was blushing.

'Well, now, I trust you, Paul, not to do anything wrong. You young people, you know too much nowadays. When your father and I got married we didn't know nawthin'.'

A pity you didn't know a great deal more, thought Paul. On his part, he knew without really being conscious of it that his parents' marriage had really ceased to be a marriage, and had sunk to mere tormented companionship.

'I'll be all right. I tell you, I'm fond of Annie. And you like her, too, don't you?'

'She seems a nice girl to me. But you're both so young, Paul, and thass a wicked world.'

Nelly Grimmer looked deep in his eyes with her brown full irises, possessive and envious, yet in loving care for her only child.

They were fencing, of course, walking a long way round the truth. Paul felt both deeply fond of his mother and grateful for her care. But yet he had become as resentful of her concern for his emotional life as he was of all the face and pattern of his home.

With Annie, at sixteen, Paul had broken through to an easy and warm companionship. They loved being together, and their sexual adventures were happy and mostly guiltless, though Annie was afraid of what her father would say, and she was in dread of getting pregnant. This, however, was most unlikely, as they did no more than hold and touch one another with their hands, kiss, and have rather lonely, separate relief by petting.

But for Paul Annie was the most comfortable of the few girls he took out in adolescence. She had few wiles: she was guileless. Most girls he had been attracted to had tormented his emotions. They didn't seem to understand how a boy feels. They had dropped their eyelashes at him, and smiled enchantingly, and had even lured him with those movements of breast-pride that a girl can use, only to hurt him in the end. Marion Molton, for example. He had been so deeply in love with her for three days that he had composed a piano sonata for her, the 'Marion' Sonata, a thin and repetitive theme, but with some passion in it. She had played duets at the piano with him in her respectable Victorian villa in Judges' Walk, dressed in a tight provocative pullover, her firm little breasts projected at him. They made his head swim, and there had been sea-noises in his ears: half-way through some piece by Grieg one afternoon after school he suddenly left off playing, with a pain in his belly, and placed his hands on her breasts. At once she had unwound herself, saying 'Please!' and becoming coldly respectable, 'cooling him off' and bringing the moment quickly to a close; but what did she expect pushing her pretty bosom in his face like that? However, that was the end of the affair, and after that she only smouldered at him as he passed her on his bicycle, smouldered with defensive virginity, yet some-how triumphant, too.

The truth was, neither the girls nor Paul knew what to expect, or what to do. Who tells the truth about adolescent experience? In later life people idolise it, and are even envious of the young. The truth is that much adolescent experience is painful—painful with bewilderment, with confused and not understood feelings, and with physical distress. After joking with a couple of girls, as they stood at a street corner with their bicycles, Paul would fancy himself in love with one or the other; but more distressingly, he would come away, simply because of the intimacy, with a bad pain in his groin. Or, rather, it wasn't really in his groin, but in his pubic region, right inside. Sometimes it felt like a constipation pain. But—and this was so sad—it didn't go if one relieved one-self, however one tried. He would sit on the lavatory to try to get rid of his pain, or he would try to bring relief to himself; but the physical pain doggedly remained, and he thought there must be something wrong with him. Then he became frightened, in case his desire hardened into some horrible disease. There seemed no solution: there never is. He was certainly far from being able to cope with complete sexual love with a girl.

He yearned for a girl's intimate company; but then this body

34

desire would rise, and she, instead of being naturally sympathetic when he was embarrassed by his body swelling in his trousers, or his desire pain, she would become cold and frightened, and brusquely get rid of him. Some of the girls enjoyed leading a man on, and then enjoyed as much his discomfort when they refused to go any further. They seemed so cruel and foolish.

Annie was as kind as could be. They never ever went as far as actual coition; and yet Annie wanted them to be as easy as they could be.

What they longed for was just to have their private intimate time together, exploring their bodies and their capabilities for joy. And it was here that Annie was so comfortable and comforting. Instead of removing his hand, she would help him remove her brassière: instead of going rigid, she would nuzzle him and kiss him warmly. It was sheer inexperience that kept them from making love fully: he dared not be bold enough, and she was too afraid of pregnancy. They knew nothing of contraception—except that they saw the packets in the barbers. Once Paul bought one, blushing and furtive. Annie laughed at it with her full mouth: 'Whatever do you do with that silly thing ?' she cried.

Yet their relationship never felt unsatisfactory. What they did was what they wanted. They made love on country walks, in the cinema, and in an air raid shelter at the bottom of Annie's street, a brick building standing above ground on the wide pavement, damp and airless.

Making love in the cinema was awkward. Annie had to wear dresses that opened up at the front, and could be quickly done up if there was a power cut. In wartime the current was likely to fail at any time, and so too, of course, were the projectors, for which there were few spares. Sometimes the siren went: the show went on, but some people would go out. When either happened, the emergency lights in the auditorium would go on, and you only had a short while between the blackout and the emergency lights going on, to take your hand out of a girl's dress and button up.

On his part, Paul allowed her hand in his trouser pocket, and she would caress him like that. But one day, without telling her, he wore a pair in which the pockets had been torn out, and for the first time he was held nakedly by a woman's hand. The daringness of it made his heart throb wildly, and the delight of her touch made him have an orgasm almost at once. But this was the problem with loving in the cinema. Annie grunted, and then snorted with amusement, and they had to begin struggling to clean up with handkerchiefs in the dark, trying to hide everything from people round them. And even so, when they came out Paul was cold and wet and uncomfortable.

Later that year, in May, when it was warm enough to lie about outside for the first time, Annie had been persuaded to come out with him into the marsh countryside he loved, behind Eaton Park, down by the little River Yare.

Paul's happiest childhood days had been spent here on long and timeless Saturdays with other boys, but he had never taken a girl down there. With 'Rosy' Johnson, a girlish boy of fourteen with pink cheeks, he had spent day after day in the summer holidays and even evenings in term-time in a leaky old rowing boat on the small winding river, rowing and swimming in the reedy water, while big swans glided menacingly past, eyeing them with beady eyes. Footsore, burned all over by sun and nettle stings, cut, bruised and muddy, Paul would lie afterwards in the bath at night glowing and stinging with satisfaction as the sun went down. In the weary depths of his boy's relaxed body he would recall the sensations of the day, how they had chased a water rat or circumvented an angry swan, breathing the smell of bruised mint and watersedges, been dived at by green and blue dragonflies like jewel tubes or run barefoot among the clumps of warm wiry grass.

There were days when he was seized with an overwhelming desire to be alone, and he sought this solitariness on the little river. Like a bee, when the spring comes and the sun comes out, he was impelled to leap out onto a bearing, and pursue it to a goal. The goal was often indefinable, and must remain indefinable, only half-conscious, but must be ruthlessly pursued. Yet what was hunted was nothing—he was simply, idly relishing being alive in that silent, remote world of the River Yare.

One morning that May he felt this urge, and got out of bed before his parents were astir. He was intensely anxious that no one should speak to him. A thrush was calling loudly in the garden, in the early sunshine, and he wanted to keep his consciousness in that dimension, hearing the natural call. Of course, he did not know what it meant: but it spoke of a natural life to which he also belonged, under the surface of his social life, his ego, his relationships, his work. Who was to say that natural life wasn't primary ? At any rate, he would hunt it. So he quickly ate some bread and butter and apricot jam, and drank a glass of milk. He cut some slices of bread and wrapped them in greaseproof paper with a slice of red cheese, and stuck this in his pocket with an apple and a couple of his mother's home-made oatmeal biscuits. That would keep him going until teatime, he thought.

He had to ride his bicycle up the hill and along the side of Eaton Park down to Bluebell Road, where he turned left along the river to Cringleford. At Cringleford, he turned right into a lane along the other side of the river, until he reached a field gate. Half a mile down the side of the field between the hedge and the tall, tough grass, he reached the boat-house: and in there was the little rowing boat, *Phyllis*, which his geography master allowed him and one or two other pupils to use. The oars were tucked away in the roof of the boat-house and the rowlocks were tied up on a hook.

There was no one about anywhere, except the odd milkman with his pony and cart, and he went through all the motions of getting to the river in a blank impatience, as though those minutes did not exist. Yet the morning was glorious—it had rained in the night, and the air was clear, with that East Coast brightness. The trees, in their tender May green, sparkled, and the gardens were fresh, bright with irises which had unfolded their fragile purples and whites, with their furry tongues, and the as yet bloomless roses were dark and shiny with new growth.

At Cringleford Mill huge horsechestnuts towered, covered with white flower-spikes, and the foaming weir glittered in the sun, as the beech trees with their small pale green leaves sparkled against the blue sky, in which small grey and white clouds rode across in the breeze. The wind swirled across the surface of the water as he pushed off, his feet clunking on the boards, his oars put ready in the rowlocks.

Whenever he pushed the boat out into the river he felt he had broken away from the everyday world, and had entered another country altogether, a country belonging to nature, to a different rhythm and a different dimension. In fact, of course, at any time he could pull to the bank, walk up to Bluebell Road and catch a bus.

37

But it never felt like that: he felt totally freed from all his ties. He rowed a short way, towards a group of trees and a stretch of water covered with water-lily leaves, brownish red, pushing their circles across the surface.

Then he stopped, and simply sat in the boat, the sun on his face, being quiet. The heavy little rowing boat, its worn green paint revealing the wood in places, floated slowly downstream, and the water tapped gently against its clinker boards. There were reeds along the banks, and a few willows: on each side of the river were marshes, uncultivated and ungrazed, all frothy with tall white weed, Queen Anne's lace, tall white umbelliferae and banks of young nettles. But most of the water was clear, and he gazed intensely into the river. Strips of waterweed stirred lazily in the depths, and every now and then the boy would catch sight of a fish, muddy green in the deeper water, still, and then perhaps darting, as the shadow or sound of the row boat disturbed it. Looking up at the bank, he saw the bright yellow flowers of the king-cups, and here and there the sword-like leaves of green flags rising. In one little muddy inlet, tadpoles were wriggling like black commas, a line of them, side by side, nibbling at a scummy green weed. On the surface water-boatmen beetles skipped, and all the time the water was flecked and ringed, with fish rising, or birds diving, or insects sparkling across its surface.

So he would sit in a daze, not wanting to do anything except gaze at the water, along the water, into the water. Sometimes he would right the boat, because it had been blown awkwardly against the bank: or he would row on and on, towards Earlham. But mostly, he simply kept the boat in midstream, to bask in the sun, enjoying the continual putt-putt-putt of the wind-driven rivulets against its sides, and the boat's gentle rocking movement.

As the sun rose in the sky, and the gleam on the water intensified, he would enter a timeless state, on the little river. He would fall into a rapture, simply leaning over the side of the boat, staring down into the clear water, watching with fascination as a fish, or a piece of stick on the surface, slowly glided past. Sometimes the body of water in the river seemed like a crystal jelly that moved between its banks; sometimes it seemed like the bright atmosphere of another world, which lived in the dark green muddy jungle of the river bottom. Whenever he thought back over the morning, he realised he had done nothing: if anyone had asked him what he had done, he would have said 'Nothing'. Yet in every instant he had been totally absorbed—flowing into the rich wild life around him under the whispering pale grey leaves of the willows, utterly alone, and in an ecstasy of being alone, and alive, among so many living things.

Strangely, even though he lost his faith so rapidly at the age of sixteen, this made no difference to the intense sense of at-oneness he experienced sitting in the grubby rowing boat *Phyllis* in the middle of the little river. Whenever the boat glided slowly on a surface of bright agitated ripples, he entered that timeless state: and knew, as the thoughts flowed through his head, perhaps as he gazed up into the grey bottoms of the moving clouds, that the world could not be meaningless, even as his science lessons seemed to be teaching him that it was. As he watched a shoal of very small fish all lying in the same direction, and then suddenly all turning at once, to face another direction, translucent yellow, with a similar but distinct masking pattern on each back—he knew that he existed in a meaningful world. He could not formulate any meaning in relation to it; nor did he strive to. The great rhubarb-like leaves that curled and swayed in the water on the bottom of the river, with darting creatures hiding in them, perhaps never seen by any human eye except his—these all belonged to a world that went on, under the sun, flowing and leaping and breathing, a slow unfolding and sweeping through the current, which had its own rhythm and purpose. And he belonged to it: whatever 'events' troubled him, and needed his energy to deal with them, there was another realm, where the current flowed, and a strange, languid joy was to be experienced, like the simple joy in existence he felt every morning as he awoke, to find himself breathing and stirring, his heart beating, the bird song in his ears: simply being. It was even far beyond anything he could talk to Moncklet about in the realm of culture and thought.

But when at last he came home, he had to explain where he had been: and even as he tried to pass this off, a deep rebelliousness boiled inside him. It seemed to him that his life was hopelessly compartmentalised. He had to 'pass his exams': schooling and homework went on in their routine ways. Then there was his life at home, and the rejection growing under the surface towards his parents in the little house and its stuffy living-room. There was the new adult life, beckoning from the Maddermarket Theatre, with all its drama and culture. And then, of course, there was sex, where he had no sense of direction at all.

So he wanted to bring Annie into the river world, to try to match the one meaning with the other. Did he love her? Was that love he felt? Was it big enough, universal enough, to merge into that rapturous river world? For years he had dreamed of the woman who could come gliding with him among the fiery dragon-flies of the river world, so that his love for her could hover on those thin glowing rods of red and blue with almost invisible wings. But this shared water-life with a girl whom he dreamed of had never materialised. The girls were too suspicious. At last Annie came out there with him, though she was a town girl and pretended to hate the country. Plump, loose-limbed, with a tendency to clown about everything, she pretended to be totally ignorant of country matters, and her comic mood disturbed his solemn idolisation of nature.

'Is that a *buttercup*?' she exclaimed, making big eyes, with affectation she had learnt from an American comic film. 'Well, what do you know about that?'

Then she pushed her nose in it, and made it covered with yellow pollen powder. So they acted the fool down the long road beside the park. At last they were alone, in the silence of the wild country. Paul had never been alone with a girl in this remote way, beyond the park and the last houses. He became excited and his heart beat noisily. He felt suffocated, and the desire in his body completely distracted him from the river's magic.

Annie bounced along in a wine red corduroy skirt and a freshly laundered white blouse trimmed with *broderie anglaise* and fastened with a white cotton cord at the neck in a fascinating and tempting way. She had a kindly body, with free and full hair, brown and naturally curly. Her mouth was wide and inviting, often smiling broadly, liable to be a little flabby and crushed in disappointment or anger, but mostly wreathed in curves of smiles. Her irises were yellowish brown, large and bright, and her face was always full of liveliness, and alert. She was full of dreads induced by her strict Catholic upbringing, but she was easy-going and seldom anxious, except, she said, when she felt Paul 'looked down on her' sometimes. She found it hard to share his intellectual and cultural interests, though she had been with him to some concerts and plays, which she enjoyed. But there was, they both knew, a growing division between them as Paul became increasingly interested in art and philosophy, and she couldn't follow him. She thought Paul was beginning to be tired of her because of this. This gave her headaches, she said; she often had headaches. But Paul liked the way she smiled broadly with a wry twisting stretch of her lips, rather like a clown's mouth. He didn't look down on her at all, he protested, but rather admired her warm-hearted generous nature. She laughed at the pompous way he put it. Yet she knew he could sometimes withdraw his affection coldly and cruelly.

Annie could be hearty and vulgar at times, but she was warm and serious in her perceptiveness: and this enabled Paul to find out many things he dearly wanted to discover. He was very glad to have Annie because he had no sister. He found it hard to understand 'women'. His mother was ailing and growing old, and was so neurotic that she offered him no sexual potentiality he could identify with. At the simplest, he had no knowledge even of what young women wore, or what they liked for presents, or amusement. The routine of shampooing, washing stockings, sewing up zips and hooks, ironing, and giving oneself a 'face' was bitterly unfamiliar to him until Annie taught him by telling him about these things.

'Don't you *know*?' she would say.

'Do you really wash your stockings every *day*? And your hair every *week*?'

'When do you wash yours?'

'My stockings?'

'Slosh! Slosh!'

'Kyrie Eleison!'

'Tinkle! Tinkle!'

They clung together laughing, like children. Yet they were acting adult life too, and she pushed her breasts into his chest. Paul was fascinated by her woman's world. He pushed his face in her hair.

'Ah!' he mocked, 'Friday night's Amami night!'

'Don't you ever wash *your* hair?' Annie said, shaking her hair out, as he twisted away from her.

41

'I wash it when my mother remembers to tell me, I suppose.'
'Baby!'

Annie had talked to him all the way as they walked up the dull little street of houses and nearly the whole mile down to the bottom of Eaton Park, about the new suit she hoped to get with her clothing coupons for the autumn, what she would wear with it, on what occasions she could wear it, who had a suit like it, and what she could do with it when it got 'old'. Paul wasn't interested at all, and found it tiring to be attentive. He tried to feel it was manly, like a husband, to listen to her dress talk. But he wasn't convinced that anyone could be so absorbed in thinking and talking about clothes for such a long time. Would she talk like this by the river, too? How would he be able to listen to the river's deep flow of life in her presence?

In any case, his attention was absorbed by the pretty white tie-string on Annie's bosom. So had his mother been, as they set off: her brown eyes looked troubled as they waved by the gate. But now Annie went on and on about fashions, and he became less and less hopeful about making Annie the Princess of his River Realm.

Paul could hardly bear his pain of expectation and desire as he dwelt on the white bow corded in the holes of Annie's crisp white blouse. Through the holes of the *broderie anglaise* he could even see the smooth skin of her white breasts as he glanced. As they walked down the road along Eaton Park, his longing for her sparked off every Maytime bud and the fresh green of each tree. Beyond in the valley wound the little river in the darker green of its marsh, where silver willows showed. A few sheeplike clouds wandered along the blue afternoon of late spring.

They made their way through a copse and along a marsh path, where tussocks of reeds grew, and the strawy marsh-grass looked warm and silky in its pink swathes. Grasshoppers buzzed, zilt, zilt. Then they found a high bank among gorse bushes, some of their yellow blossom gone burnt and faded; but the bank was bright with daisies and white umbelliferae. There they spread the mac-intoshes they had brought with them and lay down. Something scuttled away in the dead leaves of the hedge.

'Ware!' shouted Annie, pretending to be alarmed, jumping up.

Paul took her by the sides, just under her breasts, and made her lie down. His restraint on his desire broke, and he lay against her, and kissed her hard. Her sides were slippery and hot under the cotton blouse. A blood pulse beating in his head, he tried to remember what Annie herself had told him about kissing and how one shouldn't try to force one's tongue between a girl's teeth, but wait for her lips to open. He touched her lips now with his tongue: his confined flesh, hard and rising to her, hurt insufferably.

'Paul, *dear*,' Annie drew back to say, 'don't *squash* me.'

In answer Paul untied the string on her blouse. She did not obstruct him, nor when he undid the small hooks of her brassière. They caught behind her back in her blouse as he drew it away.

'Oh, God, I hope no one comes,' said Annie. 'My father'd kill me.'

Paul went tense for a moment.

'He's not down here, is he?'

'No, don't be silly,' Annie laughed. She looked him full in the eyes with amusement and open invitation in her yellow irises. Then her eyes went dazed, and she kissed his mouth with open lips.

How brazen she was! She gasped.

'It's just that I think of him . . . when I let anything like this happen . . . that I know I shouldn't.'

The May afternoon was bright and generous, and Paul felt the colour and force of life opening like flowers to him, like the bushy yellow centres of the buttercups, dusty and hairy. It was the first time he had ever seen a girl's breasts so, hanging uncovered in the shadow of Annie's blouse. Until then he had known them only in the dark. They were delicate and soft, and he was frightened to touch them. Everything was delicate, new and soft. And they took off more of their clothes, daringly, to expose those aspects of their bodies of which they knew darkly, from their embraces in the cinema and the shelter, but now saw, in the light and sun, for the first time. To Paul it was as thrilling as when one first comes upon a rare tree, magnolia or tulip tree, or sees great birds'-wing tulips for the first time. Their body hair amazed them, and the strange differences of their bodies in the full sunlight. They kissed, and rolled off their coats onto the grass, where the small insects busily buzzed or walked the stems. A rich red butterfly with blue peacock eyes in its wings settled on Annie's skirt and they kept

43

still as it stirred its wings, until it fluttered away. Then as they
sank into the rich shimmering heat of the dim afternoon in the
long grass all was heat and pain, until they brought themselves to
an uneasy relief. Paul dare not enter her: his fears were still too
strong. But his head swam with a new knowledge, and with the
beauty of this discovery, now to be remembered for ever from
that May afternoon among the landmarks of his rapturous river
days.

They dressed and lay together, calmer and no longer driven,
still a little in pain. Annie fumbled in her white patent handbag
and exclaimed about her face.

'God, look at me!'

She spat on a pancake of pale brown make-up and rubbed some
on her face. Then she powdered, and made up her mouth. As she
wiped the old lipstick off Paul noticed her lips were reddish with
his kissing and biting, while round her lips was pale, crushed
looking. Flesh! He had wondered at the life of flesh out there, in
their bodies, living its life of blood and nerves. He 'liked' Annie:
in his mind he knew her well. Yet the flesh life they toyed with
seemed separate, a separate pain and beauty, with its own rap-
tures and sorrows, its own rhythms, akin to the creatures teeming
in the gorse and grass around their hidden place: part of the flow
of being, as at the bottom of the river.

He wanted to possess Annie wholly now. But his head swam
with what this might lead to. Did he love her? He didn't know.
How did one? He invoked literary sources. *Ma sœur* he found
himself inevitably calling her, and the thought of possession,
venin. Yet one couldn't pretend Annie was out of Baudelaire. She
wasn't *un tigré dompté*: she was, Paul sometimes thought, too
domptée altogether. She wasn't *onduleuse comme un cygne*, but
rather floppily intimate, like a duck. One couldn't talk about
making a wound in her flesh—yet he was beginning to know what
the French poet meant.

It was late when they rose and dusted the fragments from their
clothes, as the light waned in the evening air. They had forgotten
time, and had fallen asleep together on the strawy grass. But now
they could feel the damp striking through their coats, and the air
was cooling. Sleepy and stumbling, speechless and in great sweetness together they slowly walked, hip to hip, rapt in one another,

44

each with an arm over the other's shoulders, up out of the river valley to home. The only stir in the settling quiet was an occasional May-bug looming low and flying clumsily in the dusk, startling them from their reverie.

4

Outings with Annie had to be rationed, and so too did his commitments to work at the theatre, because of the pressures of homework for the Higher School Certificate Examination. Paul was studying English and History at 'Advanced' level and Latin and French as subsidiary subjects. So, he spent most of his evenings in his small bedroom upstairs in the little suburban house. He was seated in that room all evening nearly every weekday in school term time. If anything momentous happened, like an air raid, or the end of the world, he thought, I am fated to be in this spot, upstairs in the one room, at 25 Lowland Avenue, between 6 and 10 pm every evening, exactly in that latitude and longitude—almost as inevitably as if I were in a prison cell. The window looked out on allotments, established on a field running down a slope with a few elm-trees. Beyond rose Earlham Road, with the local public library and beyond still the city cemetery. The sun would set over these dull places as he watched it wearily on summer evenings, bent over his books, working for those landmark examinations that loom so darkly in every young life.

The little room was sparsely furnished, and the whiteness was his. There was a hard single bed, a chest of drawers, his desk and an upright chair. On the walls were his rather crumpled reproductions, framed somewhat inexpertly by himself.

Before him on the windowsill was a new bright blue edition of *T. S. Eliot's Poems, 1910–1935,* and a copy of *The Oxford Book Of English Prose,* its gilt lettering still shiny on the dark blue cloth. There were also some library books—Woodward on European history, and a book about the Chartists, *But We Shall Rise Again.* On his desk were sheets of lined foolscap paper, on which he made notes with a fountain pen about the clauses of ancient treaties, signed long ago in faraway lands, on rafts on foreign rivers, to suit the policies of statesmen like Palmerston and Disraeli, often in discreditable wars and disreputable international manipulations. What he glimpsed, for example, of the Chinese opium wars appalled him, and the Crimea more so.

As the afterlight from the sunset faded, the space in front of him contracted and the inwardness of the room closed on him. His table lamp reflected itself in the dark window, and he became aware of the glowing red bar of his metal electric fire, scorching his shins. He rose to draw the curtains, cotton curtains with black and white diamonds printed on them, and as he did so he was aware of the bulge of the air raid shelter mound below in the garden, with pale flowers sprinkled over it.

It came to his mind at one such moment the same May, as a fresh reality, that Palmerston was dead: that all those people were dead—the soldiers, the officers, the Members of Parliament, the foreign statesmen—all were dead. The Chartists were dead, too, and so were the issues they struggled with. Of course, these were truisms: but when such realisations come for the first time to a youth they come with a fresh force. Even the Chartists, who interested him most, had been dead over a hundred years. Why should he care? Whatever interest had this old stuff for him? He had never questioned his work like that, before. A wave of rebelliousness came over him again. History *was* bunk: except for exams. He would like to talk to old Monck about that. The old man lived so much in the past—Veronese, Holbein—as though it was here, now—but what had it all to do with him in Lowland Avenue?

In the silence of his little study bedroom, he was always aware that the light and fire were costing his parents money they could ill afford. Whatever would be the outcome? He already had a notion of himself ending in mud, like the corpses in the trenches in Robert Graves's *Goodbye To All That*. Perhaps he would finish up like the stiff in the trench, with its arm stuck out, and men seizing the dead hand, calling: 'Put it there, old sport!' Downstairs, he knew, his mother and father were working still, as they listened to Tommy Handley. His mother was knitting a pullover for him, and his father was trying to invent a device for punching holes in five hundred invoices at once, and binding them into a folder in one operation. It was constructed of Meccano strips, perforated metal brackets and a large piece of wood: whatever it did to the invoices, it was doing a great deal of damage to Frank's

47

fingers. His large hands were all bloodblisters and scarred by his work. His father was always inventing. He had patented a system of using two typewriter ribbons, to do away with carbon papers, only to have his idea stolen by a big typewriter firm. He had invented a tin for a gas mask, whose lid sprang up when you pressed a button, presenting the mask ready to wear, as soon as you heard the warning rattle. He called it the Grimmer-can. Some of these inventions made him a little money. But Frank was always dreaming of making a fortune. He once dreamed of a marvellous new heating device, to be hung in the middle of a room, from the ceiling, burning artichokes and methylated spirit: the only trouble was, it didn't work. And so he turned to newspaper competitions: at the moment he was compiling slogans known as 'Bullitts' for *John Bull*.

'Come on, boy, you've got an intelligent mind—help me win this competition: "CIVIL WAR—AN OLD SPANISH CUSTOM"—how about that?'

'I don't see the point,' said Paul, rather sourly. His father's competition sentences never seemed to him neat or witty. But Paul had no capacity for that kind of thing himself. It always embarrassed him, and he defended himself against becoming involved by refusing to take any part in his father's crosswords or quizzes. Then he felt guilty about it.

But Frank Grimmer never cared whether his son joined in or not. He was a boyish man, even at thirty-nine, with a long bony face and a long big nose. His eyes were green and flecked with orange and brown: rather weak; when he laughed a lot they easily filled with tears. He had short brown hair, big ears and big teeth. His teeth had a groove all along the line, where they had failed to grow properly during a serious childhood illness. He had grown up in a small ugly house in a row of industrial workers' dwellings at Melton Constable. One of the six children had died from tuberculosis in adolescence; one was mentally defective, none were strong. They had lived on a sovereign a week. Each of Frank's teeth looked like a cribbage peg carved in ivory, with this groove in each, like a decorative piece of ribbing marking some terrible plague of infancy. He had a big mouth and slightly hollow cheeks in a long face. In truth, he had been the fittest of his family, and thrived best, in his big-framed, bony way.

His father was always full of energy, quite different from his mother who moved much more slowly. He worked with great vigour at his job—the despatch department of a bicycle whole-salers. When Paul went to see him at work, the little office, full of thin paper invoices, typewriters, staplers and filing cabinets, smelled of stale sweat as the men bustled about, shooting the invoices upstairs to the stores along a humming wire by a catapult. Of course, the schoolboy Paul was allowed to shoot the carriage along the wire, to cheers from the staff, and to receive it back, crashing into the basket. He still liked to do that.

At home, Frank made bed-ends and shelves, kept a few scruffy brown hens, grew vegetables, drew churches, invented and acted the fool in a plough-boyish way with cards and practical jokes. Paul loved him: but there was an area of his father's make-up, of his inner self, to which he could never get through. They were never intimate, in any area of the emotions. Frank even joined a group of evangelical men at a nonconformist chapel; he wrote and gave a sermon. He went up to the bathroom to practise aloud, while Paul and his mother teased him. But Paul and his father never talked with serious feeling about religion, or 'life', or love—or, indeed, anything universal or profound. It was secretly a great disappointment to the tall, thin boy, the awkwardness with which his father flinched from any area of grave importance, and re-treated from conversing in an open and direct way, or, indeed, in any way at all, except for jokes and everyday routine.

5

Paul had been working all one fine evening, on a historical essay, and was glad to get to bed. I couldn't have done more, he thought to himself. Just before going to bed he had gone downstairs to have a biscuit and a cup of cocoa with his mother and father. His father seemed tired too, rather grey. His mother had been trying to persuade Frank to take a holiday at the Jones's farm at Reepham, where he really enjoyed himself, walking the fields with his farmer friend and shooting rabbits.

'Don't you worry about me, Frank. I'd be all right here with Paul. He's gotta work: but you could go off on your own!'

Instead of gratefully accepting the idea, his father said: 'That sound as if you're trying to get rid of me, Nellie!'

What an awkward man he is, thought the son. But in truth Frank didn't like the idea of leaving his wife and son, in case there was an air raid. He would go out for the day: but he wouldn't stay away at night. Besides, he had his commitments as an air raid warden, at the little command post round the corner. Their desultory talk settled round a dull recognition that there was no rest, little relief from routine. Would they be able to get a new tyre for their little Austin Ten? Frank kept saying 'Ah!' and winking: through his work he kept in with garages all over Norfolk and Suffolk, and because of this was able to keep a car going when others couldn't. He and Nellie drove out to the farms, and often came back with a piece of pork or bacon hidden under the seat, given them by a farmer friend who had been allowed to kill one of his own animals. Pieces of meat that size, two or three pounds, were simply unknown under rationing.

There was something to look forward to—roast pork for Sunday lunch.

'I'll show it to you, Paul,' said his mother. They went down to the safe, on the floor of the little pantry by the back door. In a yellow and white earthenware bowl was a piece of pork, pale grey dead flesh, with the silvery hairs glistening on its thick pink skin.

Dropping off to sleep quickly in his weariness, Paul dreamed of crackling. And this turned to a howling of pigs: the pink, maddened animals were chasing him, snapping at him with their jaws. The noise changed to the sound of the air raid sirens, crying out all over the city, up and down the scale of their horrible minor thirds: the alert. At first the noise seemed rather beautiful, musical and strong; but the downward decline of the notes sickened his ears, and the alarm ended with a groaning, long-drawn-out buzz, lapsing at last into a menacing silence. In that silence entered a low, throbbing growl. It was different from usual: it was not the sound of a solitary plane, as it often was. It grew with a definite multiple quality, as if of a determined attack. And now the guns began to go, with distant, heavy thumps, the heavy calibre anti-aircraft guns between Norwich and the coast.

'Bum!' they would go, followed by a silence in which sometimes the coarse whisper of the rising shell could be heard: then a sharp 'crump!' high in the sky.

Paul cursed and eased himself out of bed. It was a damp, dark, cold May night, cold and uncomfortable. He sat on the edge of the bed wondering what to do. Every inclination was against going into the garden shelter; but his father had warned them of the dangers of heavy rocket tubes falling, which seemed as dangerous as anything, apart from the shrapnel and bombs. He heard his father now, dressing in his navy blue siren suit, zipped on up the front, and the clatter of his helmet. His mother pulled a pullover over her nightdress, and put on her tweed overcoat. Grumbling, Paul put on his old felt dressing-gown, and pulled a pillow and two blankets off his bed. His head already ached with weariness and resentment.

His father marched off with his long swinging gait, to the ARP post in the next street, a brick hut, really, with a heavy concrete roof next to a grocer's shop and off-licence in a small corner of an allotment patch. Paul and his mother climbed into the dank, dark space of the garden air raid shelter with a torch, the biscuit tin, a bottle of milk, two mugs, matches, and a china chamber pot. They padded with these across the damp and greasy little lawn, the night wind catching at their bare ankles, and eased themselves uncomfortably into the metal shelter that smelt of stale earth.

Paul and his father had dug the hole for the shelter while listening to the Prime Minister's announcement of the declaration of war. That had been on a Sunday last September when he was still fifteen.

For a long time the curved metal pieces of the shelter, heavy galvanised steel sheets with wide wavy corrugations, had lain on the gravel path waiting to be put up. Once war was declared, they thought they should do something. So, by the end of that September, it was bolted together into something like a steel workman's hut with a curved roof and flat steel ends that sloped at each side, and lowered into a deep hole. Then the spoil dug out of the pit was piled on top.

The shelter had waited, unused mostly, for six months, except for one or two false alarms. Inside, Frank had erected wire bunks on metal supports and they had laid some old mats on the floor and fixed a rough curtain over the opening. Sometimes cats got into the bunker and made it stink; in really wet weather it would have six inches of water over its earth floor. Paul's mother made the top of the mound into a kind of rockery garden, and even now, as they made their way to it, pale clumps of white alyssum glowed in the darkness and made a dim, sweet honey scent. But nothing could really disguise the dull, squat brutality of the thing: it was an eyesore, and a horror to get into, as they scraped their shins on the cold sharp edges of the steel plates, and slipped clumsily into the hole in the ground. However tired they were, they never seemed to be able to sleep in the shelter, except fitfully. Often, they had spent two hours in the clammy darkness, to hear nothing; so, often, they became sceptical and ignored the sirens, turning over to go to sleep. The shelter was so damp, it gave them pains in the joints for days after an hour or so down in its pit.

But this night, as Paul lay on his uncomfortable wire bunk looking up at the corrugated, curved roof metal, slimy with condensation, he was glad of the shelter. Sometimes, he had felt, it was cowardly to crawl into this dark hole: when nothing happened, it seemed absurd to grovel in a pit in the garden. When firing began, he was glad all the digging and banging in of bolts had had a purpose.

'Do you lie down and get some sleep, boy,' said his mother. 'You must be tired after workin' the whoole noight!'

They had lit a candle to get settled, and it made the damp chamber smell vilely of tallow. He blew it out; but before he climbed back into his bunk he pulled aside the old bit of curtain and looked out.

The balloons were up. All around, and especially over the city towards the north of them, the silvery barrage balloons, shaped like tapered elephants with bulgy fins, were aloft on their wires, shining palely in the light of a sliver of moon. Of course the wires couldn't be seen: the great silver shapes simply hung in the sky, as if there were some festival. And beyond them, to the east, huge beams of light swung round in the dark: two of them were fixed, criss-cross, on the aluminium fuselage of a distant plane, a small fish in the sky. The beams lost it, every now and then, but then fixed back on it. It seemed as if the plane was doomed, now it was seen, a vulnerable little inhabited splint. But often, he knew, the lights would be on an enemy plane for minutes, and nothing happened: eventually, it would dive and lose the beams. Looking across the city, he was fearful for Annie. Would she lie in bed? He thought tenderly of her, perhaps in 'their' air raid shelter. He sighed.

'Come you on inside,' said his mother. 'Whass the use of comin' in the shelter,' she grumbled, 'if you're a-goin' to stick your silly head out like a fule?'

He climbed back into his bunk and continued to stare up at the metal roof, which he could not see. A few guns were thumping, more loudly now: the cracks in the sky as the shells burst near the plane were dry and loud. The night began to ring with exploding shells and charges, and high in the air, from time to time, there was the sound of rattling machine-guns or louder cannon fire. Then, suddenly, two anti-aircraft devices opened up near them: some heavy field-guns firing with a tremendous blast; and at last a battery of rockets. These latter went off with a harrowing, snarling roar filling the night with waves of extreme soughing noise, crackling in his ears. Suddenly the night was filled with almost continuous, roaring sound. Then, after soaring up in this scouring storm of sound, the rockets burst, with a ferocious series of shocks in the sky. Hissing and humming, large pieces of shrapnel and heavy tubes fell from the air, some of them crashing on roofs and in the street, loud and near.

'Never heard nothin' like this before,' said his mother, rather faintly, her brown eyes staring into the dark.

Paul said nothing. He was frightened, and his mouth became dry. He found himself trembling, suddenly feeling cold, and panicking a little at the sound. So often air raids had never come to anything, the distant noises had passed, the firing died down, the engine noises had faded, and it had all felt rather a fraud, or just a nuisance to disturb one's sleep.

But now the engine noises throbbed louder and louder, and one suddenly gave a menacing growl, as if a plane had been hit. The attacking force seemed overhead, and the guns and rockets threw themselves into a frenzy, shaking the ground and filling the night with unbelievable crashes and explosions. Suddenly the rough curtain over the entrance was thrust aside and a gasping mass plunged in: it was Frank, hurling himself in. His steel helmet scraped loudly on the top of the entrance hole, and he dropped his feet with a thump to the floor, gulping rather than breathing. He swayed for a moment in the dark, then sat on a wire bunk.

'Blast, thass hot stuff out there, boy!' he gasped. 'Bugger it, I say.'

He was pale and frightened, and licked his lips.

Paul's heart beat loudly, and for a time they listened aghast. He couldn't believe there was any real danger: he couldn't believe anything would destroy their home. The whole thing always seemed like a nightmare or a fantasy, yet the crashing bursts all around them were real enough. The actual smashing of metal into walls, or into flesh, seemed impossible. 'There'll always be an England': a strange jingoistic euphoria protected them from the dreadful reality. His anxiety fixed itself in a tense feeling that the anti-aircraft fire was not working properly. Why hadn't they hit the planes and destroyed them? The drones of the planes continued unchecked. He wasn't to know that thousands of tons of high explosive and metal can be hurled about in war without any damage being done, without any accurate, determined result: all wasted shot. Knowing so little, they simply listened with a vague dread of what might come.

But at a deeper level, he couldn't yet admit to himself the outburst of hate even as it cracked and roared over his head. In a way, although he had dismissed them as dead and irrelevant, the Chartists were more real to him: their conventions and marches, their clashes with troops and police. He had also read with a shock the description of the Peterloo Massacre by the *Courier* reporter, in a book called *Writing And Action*. 'A minute more, the cavalry were around me, trampling down and cutting at all who could not get out of their way.' He had been outraged: what monstrous inhumanity of man to man! Yet thousands of feet above him, men in flying suits with helmets and masks were carrying tons of bombs, intended to blow him and his family to pieces—and this didn't seem half as real to him as the incident in St Peter's Field. So, which *was* bunk—'history'; or England now, being invaded?

He couldn't admit to himself the awful power of organised hate raining down on Norwich in the night. He was painfully afraid for Annie. He didn't think about meaning, or the loss of it; everything now was too real, and there was a meaning even in hoping you would be alive for breakfast. The bombs began to fall, shaking the ground. Each plane seemed to carry four bombs, and the three figures in the shelter listened and counted. Paul could smell his father's fear sweat. If there were any unexploded bombs or fires, Frank would have to go out into the night and locate them. Every now and then he would look out, in case fire bombs were falling. He would have been able to tell, by the flares of thermite cores shining into the night. But the night was strangely dark, except for the long pencils of searchlight beams and the flashes of explosions as the sets of bombs fell with huge crashes on the other side of the city. They could hear them whistle down, horribly. The aircraft groaned, a deep buzzing change of note, as they released their bombs. Then came the long thin scream and the appalling crashes, one, two, three, four as the bombs hit the ground.

Suddenly, as he and his father were peeping out of the curtain, there was a prodigious explosion in the sky. One of the bombers had been hit, and exploded. They saw the burst of flame, with its huge corona of black smoke, searing sparks and glowing cascades of burning oil: then the huge brutal wave of the explosion, deafening. To his horror and disgust, Paul felt a thrill of delight, a coarse satisfaction, and his father gave a cheer.

'Thass one bugger less, any rood!' he said, licking his lips.

Then, as suddenly, lightning began, and thunder. A great blue streak of wriggling lightning streaked down from the clouds, and heavy rain began to fall. It was like an incredible nightmare. The noise was now pandemonium: the guns and rockets became frenzied, and wave after wave of missiles was flung into the dark storm, while pink and blue lightning streaked about the sky. The clouds and rain obscured the planes, and searchlights were useless. Their bombs gone, the German aircraft were now flying back towards the coast. But fragments and cases still rained down: in between claps of thunder, Paul heard a huge piece of spent steel fall with a metallic clatter in their street, the other side of their house. Surely there could be nothing more now?

They sat glumly, back from the entrance now, weary of it all: they hoped, inwardly, the raid was over, but they dared not let it enter their minds for a while, until the all clear sounded. They saw a glow on the edge of the galvanised metal structure: all at once, the night was lit up by some huge fire.

'Whatever's that?'

'If thass a fire, I'd better get along to the post,' said his father. 'Bloody hell! Thass a gossage!' It was one of the barrage balloons, set on fire by the lightning, and falling. The storm was passing too, now, and the rain was easing off. Only in the distance was there a flicker of pale lightning and the hoarse grumble of thunder. But high in the sky burned the barrage balloon, like a huge torch, sinking slowly in the sky. The guns had been silent now for a while, too. The balloon burned with a fierce bluish white flame, and began to swing, collapsed, to and fro, down and down. At last, all its gas burned, it became a rag of a thing, streaming sparks, and fell with a rush among the houses.

As they looked out, he heard his mother using her chamber-pot in the darkness.

'Can't wait for the all clear,' she said, chuckling. They laughed. To laugh! He felt a strange gratitude at surviving. One could laugh!

Paul's father went off to his post. He and his mother clambered out of the shelter, and stood in the rain on the lawn. There was no damage to their house, or to any in the street. They might as well have stayed in bed. Everywhere there was a murmur of voices, as people came out of their shelters. But down in the city there was a crackling noise, and tall flames, as buildings burned. Ought one to do anything ? Paul was too utterly exhausted to decide. He helped his mother into the house and, making sure the blackout was still up properly, switched on the light. The electricity was still on: it was three o'clock. He drew a cup of water from the tap and drank it. His body felt damp, uncomfortable with cold sweat and cramped, full of awkward pains. At long last, back in his bed, still untidy and only pulled together, he fell asleep.

He was wakened at five o'clock by his father. It was still dark and they could not put the light on because his blind was up.

'I'm sorry, boy,' the man said, his drawn face looming through the dark, 'that was bloody bad down the city. We've got about a hundred people up at the emergency centre and I wondered if you'd come and help. We've got to get breakfast for about a hundred and fifty.'

About a hundred people had been killed, his father told him. They were digging a big mass grave up at the cemetery with a bulldozer. The raid and the storm were already like a dream he had had in the night. He had sunk to sleep just as the all clear had sounded, with its triumphant resolution of the diminished anguish of the alarm. He had recomposed himself, ready for another attack on his history books next day.

But now, as he sleepily put his clothes on, Paul realised the raid was more than a noisy interruption of his life of study and schooling. The destructive menace was cutting more deeply into their lives. His father had made a cup of tea and stood in the kitchen supping it, his face grey with lack of sleep and his eyes watery. His black steel helmet lay upside down on the draining board and his hair was matted with sweat. Outside the mass of the lopped elm at the bottom of their garden took shape against the grey morning light.

'I've been down at Ber Street diggin' some of 'em out,' he said. 'Thass terrible down there. The hospitals are full o' casu'lties. And there's a whoole chapel full o' bits, and bodies, boy.'

The casualty centre was the hall of Paul's old primary school, opposite the gates of Eaton Park on the outskirts of the city, half a mile from his home. His father was driving a civil defence lorry, and they went up in that: it was covered with a coating of brick dust from rescue work, and full of strange bundles of blankets and personal belongings, odd shoes, sacks, a clock and a metal stretcher. He looked at it with a ghoulish unwillingness, in case there were ripped-off limbs or bodies. Inside the school hall, where Paul remembered once seeing a small boy publicly beaten in front of the whole school for stealing, were huddles of people, grey and dusty from the blasts, with plaster and brick dust in their hair, wrapped in blankets. None of them was wounded, but all had the blank, dull faces of people who had been in a disaster. It was appalling, the awful sense of shock, of having been close to death and destruction, of having only just escaped the monstrous blasts, of having been flung about by them. The victims had simply been brought out to rest, while rescue workers dug into the smashed wrecks of their homes as the streets were cleared and repaired. Paul went round them with a bucket of strong tea and poured the tea into mugs with an enamel dipper. A WVS woman went with him carrying a basket of mugs.

The huddled groups of people squatted and sat on the polished wood floor of the hall in the pale yellow light of the electric lamps, with the grey light coming back into the sky outside. Some sobbed quietly to themselves, or sighed; but most were in a blank state of bewilderment, old men and women in blankets dazed and oblivious of their surroundings; children, pale and wide-eyed, clinging to their mothers or to one another; women looking like grey ghosts, dirty with bedraggled hair. There was a smell of fear, of sweat and vomit, and the acrid stink of shattered buildings. Everything looked crumpled, and impregnated with the flung dust of burst houses.

It was no more than one little touch of the immense suffering of the war; and there was not one shattered limb or corpse. There was one blood-spattered blanket, which a woman Red Cross worker spotted and removed, giving the woman a clean grey blanket from the civil defence stores. But it was enough to link the pyrotechnic display of the raid with the awful human reality behind it. Later, some semblance of human warmth came back, as Paul helped his father to make toast and carry it round, with a hot serving tray full of grilled sausages. The gas was still on, surprisingly. Some of the refugees put on a brave face and chatted, even joked; but they gave off even so a feeling of being suspended in this strange limbo of emergency care, later that day to be plunged back into the most terrible nightmares, identifying the bodies of their loved ones and sorting through the miserable wreckage of their homes. They were nearly all poor people, from crowded homes in Ber Street, and their wretched clothes and pathetic scraps of belongings made them all the more pitiful.

Later that day he found that Annie and Moncklet had slept through the raid in bed. Annie simply asked, in her zany way: 'Oh, was it bad then ?', while Monck declared: 'I am sixty years old—if I die, what does it matter ?' It annoyed Paul that everyone simply kept on working, as if nothing had happened. But the next night but one, after a good rest, he was back at his study desk, back at his 'history'. There was no further air raid for that month, or the next. But as he went on reading Cobbett and Disraeli and accounts of British foreign policy, those sad grey people in the assembly centre would force their way between him and the pages. He yearned for 'civilisation': to take hold of it, of the paintings, the literature, the music, to possess his own civilisation. But then, as he sweated to reach the university, where (he supposed) he would richly come into that inheritance, the noise of the guns would open up and the fires break out; and civilisation would dissolve into those shocked and blasted bundles of refugees from the city, brought out by lorries from their broken slums and fed with tea and toast as they sat, trembling and weeping, their faces white and drawn with dread and sorrow.

6

'I'm not askin' fifty bob, twenny-five bob, nor rhubob!' the Cockney voice enunciated. 'A quid! One lousy quid, fer an 'ole beautiful Stoke china teaset, covered wiv blahdy rowses!'

No one in the little crowd at the top of Norwich market place spoke.

'Nineteen an' six?'

Not a word.

'Right! It don't make it worf my wile ter sell 'em.'

The vendor, in a cloth cap with a gay spotted red handkerchief tucked in his corduroy waistcoat, picked each piece of china from the teaset he was holding up on a tin tray, and threw it down onto the cobbles at his feet. After throwing three cups to smash at his feet, he suddenly dropped the whole set at once, which broke into smithereens.

The crowd responded with 'Ohs' of outrage and disapproval. 'Smashin' good stuff like that!' they cried, outraged country women who kept their china for years.

The huckster had a ruddy face with strong bones like a horse, and a big nose. He was a youngish man, but his hair was tinged with grey. His eyes were dark brown and quick, with genial crow's-feet at the corners. He had a large mouth and was clean-shaven. Paul was fascinated by the power of his delivery, which rang across the market, and the whole theatrical quality of his act, which was beautifully timed. He would begin by picking up a plate, flicking back the unbuttoned cuffs of his shirt, fingering the china piece with his other hand, and shouting: ''Ere y'are! 'Ere y'are, then! You'll never find bargains like this, where-hever you go, ladies and gen'elmen, hespecially the ladies who carry all before 'em.'

A small crowd would gather, and then he would offer a few cheap items, flinging them on the ground as the crowd remained stonily unmoved and unresponsive. Many were country people, up from their cottages and farms for the day, wearing the protective clothes of rural folk, leggings for the men and tweeds: headscarves and raincoats for the women, clutching their baskets. They were full of tanned vitality under the blue June sky.

The smashing of china brought little screams from the women, and disbelieving gasps of laughter from the men, who shook their heads in a disapproving way, removing their pipes to make wise comments to their companions. Behind, the coloured canvases of the stalls flapped in the wind, as the clouds sailed along over St Peter Mancroft and the wide market place.

'Blast, he won't smash that 'ere teaset, whatever he say,' said a leathery-faced farmer with a crushed pork-pie hat.

Crash, went the teaset.

'Bugger, bor', thass a rum go!' said the farmer with a whistle, grinning with his yellow teeth, wide-gapped. 'Heh! heh!'

He shook his head.

A shiver went through the crowd, and more people scuttled up the alleys between the stalls to see what was going on. They evidently associated the crashing of crockery with domestic fights or serious household disasters. The faces of plump country women were apprehensive and dismayed at the sound. They watched with bated breath as the next tea-service, a blue willow-pattern set, was held up under their noses.

'Hime prepared to stand 'ere!' shouted the salesman, with a tremendous voice, 'Hime prepared to stand 'ere and destroy the 'ole of my stock o' china, rahver'n let it go fer prices wot would disgrice the nime of my family bizniz. Nah then, wot ho!'

He let the teaset wobble, while the wives drew their breath in sharply with apprehension.

'Wot ham I bid fer this genuine Willer Patten tea service . . . Twenny-five pieces . . . who'll start us off at fifty bob? Florin a piece . . .'

He sold five sets in three minutes. The women bought them desperately, to save them from the stones. The broad farmer with the crushed hat put his thorn stick under his arm and fumbled in his pocket to buy one. The huckster scrabbled among his boxes and shavings.

'Nar fer sumfin' special . . . sumfin' fer the parlour . . . not to

61

'ide hunder the bed, though it could come in useful in the middle of the night when the old man is loaded . . . lovely vahses . . . all vilets an' roses . . .'

Two of these objects, grotesquely vulgar and flamboyant, were smashed on the cobbles, to provoke a frenzy of buying—as the crowd virtually grabbed them out of his hands to save them, including the gap-toothed farmer, who now had to look for a box to carry his pile of purchases.

There were several such scenes, all along the top of Norwich market every Saturday. In the mid-thirties beneath the tall new brick City Hall, the City Corporation had built a new square for its market and equipped it with stalls which it rented, with gaily coloured awnings. Paul had come as a school child to see the Queen open it. The schools had been given places on benches along the front of the new long hall. Paul's school had been next to the Girls' County High, behind one of the new bronze lions, rather kitsch as municipal sculpture goes, with its testicles brutally displayed to the mixed school parties. The huge open space, between the ancient black and white Guildhall, the long noble mediaeval church of St Peter Mancroft and the blue and white Marquis of Whitby public house, is the heart of Norwich. There the best produce of the countryside is brought in to be sold, the best fish from the East Anglian ports and the best meat, poultry and eggs from Norfolk farms. Ever since he was a child Paul had loved it: his mother always shopped there and he had learned from her to struggle about from stall to stall, eyeing the greens for their crispness and the apples for their shine; deciding which fish still looked white or displayed rainbows on its scales, which meat glowed red and firm, and whose greens were tightest. The vegetable and fruit stalls glared with bright life colours. And all the time there were the rich voices, crying their wares, as the wind flapped the canvas awnings.

'Purr Roodes,' from the Norfolk seller of day-old chicks. At his feet feeble cheeps came from boxes marked 'Rhode Island Reds'.

'All ripe an' juic-EH!' from the man with a pyramid of bright red and green apples. 'They're LUV-LEH! Cue cum *bahs*! . . . Thrippence a pahnd, thrippence a pahnd, lahvely spring greens! fresh greens! Keep you movin'!'

The white gnarled cauliflowers were fresher and twice as

large and yet cheaper than those in the greengrocers' shops. There were chip stalls, clothing stalls and flower stalls with brilliant displays of lilac, tulips and roses, glowing brightly in the bursts of sunlight as the wind blew the streams of cloud across the sky, releasing that bright light that shines from the clean air near the Norfolk coast.

On dark winter days before the war, the stall-holders used to burn brilliant clear electric bulbs, or naphtha flares that threw a garish flickering light over their piles of carrots and cabbage, their trays of broken rock and toffee, or pet-foods and bird-cages. Now, they were restricted to heavily shuttered lamps after dark. But in the spring the market burst out in bright colours and all the scents of the new season.

Paul Grimmer moved on this Saturday from the china stall, where gesticulating figures stood above little groups of gazing people, and trampled over the earth scattered from the lettuce crates along the row of mountebanks. He passed the medical toffee-maker, where a row of small boys waited patiently, watching the man work a long garland of brown toffee swung on a hook. They knew that when the man began his barking, he would distribute free small white twisted packets of his sweets to the boys and firmly persuade them to 'cut'. He not only drew his crowd by this act of generosity, but also removed quick eyes and cheeky voices that might otherwise rumble his tricks. For instance, sometimes he paid an old man to cough loudly in the crowd, to really gasp and gargle. Calling him forward, he would say: 'That's a nasty 'acking cough you 'ave there, sir. Try this helixir!' Of course, the vicious spasm was arrested as soon as the old man took the first spoonful.

'But you don't have to take it 'orrible neat and in that hun-pal-a-table form. All you do is carry with you a packet of my haromatic lozenges, and hevery time you feel a tickle . . .'

He leaned over to a plump woman who blushed and giggled.

'Hevery time you feel a tickle coming on, madam, pop one of these lozenges in your mouth, and subdue your heructations as if by magic.'

As the man in the white apron rattled on, he was rolling out his cough sweets from a board with grooves, onto a metal tray sprinkled with icing sugar.

Further on, more dramatic cures were offered.

' 'Ere I 'ave the yewer-rine . . . the *yewer-rine* of a man wiv' a serious corrosion of his water-works. 'Ave a look at that, sir. Are you a doctor ?'

'No . . . I'm sorry, I'm an accountant actually.'

Embarrassed, the formally dressed elderly man held the glass phial of coloured liquid rather unwillingly.

' 'Ad you been a doctor,' said the mountebank, a dark sharp-looking individual in a white laboratory coat buttoned over a grubby brown suit, 'I would 'ave hasked you to diagnose that sample. Hobserve 'ow clowdy it is, and the hun'ealthy reddy-brown colour. *Any man wot passes yewer-rine in that condition is very seriously hill . . .*' he shouted, *'very seeriously hill hindeed*! Nah,' he went on, producing another phial of yellow liquid, ' 'ere I take only one of the hingredients of my helixer; only ONE, mark you, and pour it into the sample hov yewer-rine . . .'

The liquids mingled and turned pale straw-colour.

'Hat once hit becomes 'ealthy!' he declared. 'Perhaps you'd pass that round, sir.'

' 'Ere I 'ave hanother specimen: the hunealthy blood of a man sufferin' from himpurities in 'is system.'

'See 'ow funny and dark it is ? Hinsert only a drop or two of my patent helixer, and this 'ere blood becomes as clear and 'ealthy as claret. Clear and 'ealthy has first-class *wine*!'

Cloudiness fell from the phial of 'blood', but the scales did not fall from the eyes of the watching crowd. Paul grinned: he remembered once, at the height of the chemistry set craze among him and his school friends, how they saw at once through these simple tricks, and how they must be done with chromates or phenolphthalein. Callow boys, they had shouted: 'Ger! That ain't urine—thass potassium bichromate!'

The magic was momentarily dispelled as the medical wizard sprang at them, tweaking one boy's ear.

'Now bugger off, will yer, or I'll fetch the p'lice!'

At that time the police lived in an octagonal shed built of wood and corrugated iron and painted green right on the marketplace itself. The mountebank's threat seemed like a real one; though the police might well have taken more notice in the event of the fraudulent claims of the patent medicine dealer. The boys, however, had contented themselves with jeering from a distance. But year after year the man went on turning urine and blood clear with his elixir—and selling gallons to Norfolk people to purify their systems. To get educated boys out of the way, he had learned to distribute little bounties before he barked.

Further along there was 'Alf the Purse King'; a vendor of trusses and surgical stockings; and a man who sold packets containing either cotton wool, five-pound notes, or gold watches for half a crown. This again, Paul had watched for years—yet he had never discovered how the trick was done. The man, in a grubby raincoat and cap, opened a suitcase filled with small sealed packets, and turned them out onto a trestle table. Then he placed a gold watch into an envelope of the same kind, sealed it and thrust it into the heap. Four five-pound notes, the old big crackly white kind with black copperplate lettering, were also sealed into envelopes. These packages were all rolled into the pile, scuffled about, and the envelopes then offered for sale. Paul knew, from his long observation as a child, that the gold watch was always 'won' by the same man—a partner in the business. It had been the same gold watch for four years at least. Sometimes a fiver was won by a stranger. But for the most part, all members of the public obtained was a little bit of cotton wool for half a crown. As Paul watched, one man became obstreperous.

'Ah!' he shouted, flinging his puff of cotton wool down, 'thass a bloodeh swindle! There en't no fivers nor nawthin' among any o' them bloodeh old envelopes!'

'Pick out two or free then, mate!' said the seller, a disagreeable-looking swarthy man, with a blue stubbly face. 'Pick out two or free—no payment, no prize.'

Angrily, the farmer in britches and long leather gaiters, grabbed a handful of envelopes from the top of the pile with his big hard hands. He tore them open as if he were topping turnips: inside one was a five-pound note. The crowd gasped and laughed, and the bulky man flung the scraps of paper on the heap, disgusted.

There was a loud chuckle from a huge round man next to him, who said to Paul in an educated accent: 'I've been watching it for years, but I still can't see how it's done, can you?'

The man had a long head shaped like a rugby football and in his hand was a black clerical hat, a big felt circle with a broad brim. He wore spectacles with thick bull's-eye lenses and sucked a pipe. He fussed at this pipe, which he was trying to light in the breeze. He had on a rather shabby brown coat over a big purple pullover with holes in it. When he smiled, he displayed a gold wire on his eye-teeth. He had a cultured voice, rather smooth and sibilant.

'I've been coming here since I was a small boy,' said Paul, 'and haven't got it yet. The packet with the gold watch must be marked in some way.'

'Yers. Oh, yers,' said the big man. 'Yers. But how is it he doesn't lose three fivers in a day? That would surely take all his profit? I think I've seen you before,' he went on, 'working at the Madder-market?'

'That's right,' said Paul. 'I help Monck as secretary—and do the sweeping up, that sort of thing.'

He blushed, and wondered why. Perhaps he found himself thinking, this is a homosexual pick-up by someone who . . . The man grinned, showing the gold wires in his teeth.

'Terrible old reactionary, Monck, don't you think?'

'I've never thought about it much,' said Paul, but he went on:

'I don't like his thing about the Jews. You know, he's always on about their money-making. Yet one of his best actors is Dr Heilpern, and it's no more than a personal quirk, so I forgive him.'

'But his politics are quite . . . I mean, he has no interest in modern politics . . .'

'He's a pacifist of a kind, like me.'

'Oh, are you a pacifist?'

The older man smiled, and stripey lines appeared along his jaws, rather mocking, though there was also an impish twinkle in his eyes and from his piece of gold tooth-wire.

'I'm a clergyman, you know.' He held out his hand, having got his pipe more or less alight. 'Yes. I'm called Billy. The proper name is William Frost. For my sins, and other people's, profession-ally. I'm rector of Booton near Reepham; it's a splendid Victorian church, very eccentric, with twin towers. But I also run a dis-cussion group at the Music House here, down in King Street, and I wonder if you'd like to join us?'

'What sort of thing do you discuss?' asked Paul warily. Damn silly question, really, he thought to himself. There was a crash of china from the huckster's end of the market. He had broken with the Church definitely two years ago when, immediately after his confirmation, it had failed him. He had taken his sexual problems to a clergyman, who had shown no capacity to understand what his perplexities were; and just as he was trying to make up his mind, in some anguish, about whether or not to register as a conscientious objector, the Bishop of Norwich blessed a battleship, and his God died. He had had nothing to do with the Church since.

'Oh,' said William Frost, 'pacifism, socialism, social credit, Nietzsche, whether life has a meaning, masturbation . . .' He chuckled. 'All young people . . . there's some pretty girls, even. Why don't you come along?'

Paul took the piece of duplicated blue paper the clergyman gave him with some misgivings. But one night, when Annie had gone away to see some relatives at the seaside, he went to see what Frost's thing was all about.

7

The Music House was a strange ramshackle building, part of
which seemed originally to have been a church or a chapter-house,
but then further rooms had been added in Tudor times, with
massive beams and huge timber-framed leaded windows. It was
buried down among the breweries in King Street off Prince of
Wales Road, not far from the castle, below the cattle market,
where the air smelt of malt. It had once been another home of the
Norwich Players. Now it was rented and used by various cultural
societies, including the Music Society which mostly listened to
gramophone records but occasionally held chamber concerts and
talks with lantern slides. The Reverend Frost's discussion group
met there each week, members paying one-and-sixpence for the
rent of the room and a cup of coffee. Paul made his way up the
creaking wooden staircase and entered a large dark-panelled room
with a wide stone fireplace.

In a leather chair by the fireplace sat the clergyman in his big
holey purple pullover and tweed trousers, filling his pipe by
enclosing tobacco in a round piece of thin paper, twisting the top,
and inserting it twist first into the bowl. Seeing Paul come in, he
glinted with his spectacles and the piece of gold wire in his teeth,
and said: 'Oh, good!'

Around him on chairs, on old floppy sofas and mostly on the
druggeted floor, sat a number of young people and adults. Some
of these Paul recognised from encounters at Monck's house, or in
the foyer of the theatre: a woman doctor from Hellesdon Hospital;
a senior surgeon; a plump lawyer who had once played Dogberry.
Paul saw that he had come in for something serious, not a crack-
pot little church thing at all. There was one young man from the
science side of his own sixth form and Roy Short, who was on the
arts side of the sixth, senior to him, a man with a big toothy smile,

who was going to Cambridge and who cracked his fingers by pulling them, in the silence.

'Pacifism,' said Frost, puffing his pipe as if getting up steam. 'Yers! Would you let a German rape your sister?' he grinned.

'It's appalling,' said an earnest young man with spectacles. 'You make that a joke. But when you go to the tribunal they actually still use that ridiculous example, to browbeat serious objectors.'

'Well, I hope we're going to be a little more serious than that,' said the clergyman, looking round with a strange air of nervousness, rather ducking his long head, with its neatly combed close cut hair, as if expecting hostility.

'Let's start from a proposition,' said a girl with bright auburn hair, in a long flowered frock to her calves. 'I believe it is wrong to kill another person, in any circumstances, even when legalised by the state.'

With a series of growling chromatic sounds, a siren not far away burst out into long rising and falling wails. Somewhere a German bomber had been sighted. There was a burst of laughter, but Paul felt a chill run through his bowels.

'Yers! Well there you are,' said Frost huskily. 'Here they are trying to kill *us*. And the gunners will try to kill them. If we don't kill them, they'll kill us. Doesn't it seem a bit academic to assert in these circumstances that it's wrong?' He chuckled and glinted.

There was a thoughtful pause. Paul could hear distant anti-aircraft fire, like remote drums.

'I can't ever conceive of any human world,' said the serious-looking young man with glasses, 'in which all men would renounce the use of force. I mean, you can only have pacifism when *everyone* accepts it.'

'What do you mean "*have*" pacifism?' asked a tall boy of eighteen sitting on the arm of his sofa. 'We're surely discussing how one acts according to one's *own* conscience? It's what *I* do that counts.'

'But it's only worth it, surely, if there's some chance of it spreading?'

'That's a silly let-out!' cried a girl.

'It would never spread so that everyone gave up violence, so what's the use?'

69

There was now a definite throb of a German bomber, growing louder every minute.

'But look here,' said William Frost, 'you're all arguing in a frantically pragmatic way. You're taking a line that if a campaign or an idea isn't going to succeed, then you're not going to endorse it. Where would the early fathers of the Church have got if they'd been like that? Surely such an issue can only be discussed properly on matters of principle, on questions of the sanctity of human life, the right to kill, "Thou shalt not kill", and so on. If we have ideals, let's declare them, not feebly say we'll wait till everyone else thinks the same.'

'No one can assume the right to take another man's life,' declared the auburn girl.

'What about that fellow up there, then?' asked the clergyman, pointing upwards. 'He may not be going to rape your sister, but he could blow us all to pieces in the next half-hour. Is it wrong for us to have a go at him to stop him?'

'If he hits one of our barrage balloons, then that's his fault.'

'Oh!' they all cried.

'But what about the soldiers just about to let off those horrible rockets at him?'

'Basically, they're wrong . . . but they have to do it.'

'You're really very confused, morally, Sammy. Yers!'

'If we knew,' said Paul, his voice trembling a little and his head swimming to find himself speaking, 'if we knew it was true that Hitler was killing people because they were Jews, and had everyone who disagreed with him in prison . . . if we *knew* that, we'd have to fight.'

'So there are circumstances when killing is justified?'

'In the face of tyranny, yes . . . but . . . I don't think I would want to kill, myself . . .'

'You'd leave that to the other fellows? Yers?'

Outside there was a terrible roar of soughing and vibrating anti-aircraft rockets, rising into the sky among the barrage balloons. Then with deafening crumps they exploded, and a little dust puffed out of the ceiling as the old Music House shook. Some of the girls had put their hands over their mouths and gasped, and other men and women bowed their heads under their hands. There was a tense silence, while everyone listened for the huge metal tubes of the rockets to fall. With a horrible whistling, one fell clattering onto a neighbouring roof, smashing it. William Frost turned pale and blinking a little, fingered his pipe, but sat still. The German plane, close now, altered its engine tone and seemed to be speeding up. Paul felt cold sweat on his body; he wished he hadn't come. Blast old Frost for his silly talky-talky in the middle of a war! Norwich was known to be a 'Baedeker' target. But quickly the noise of the aircraft faded; Paul prayed it hadn't dropped a landmine on a parachute, sailing now perhaps towards them. He sat rigid and was bathed in sweat. But gradually his fear subsided. There was a long silence.

'Yers,' said the clergyman faintly.

There was a burst of laughter.

'Perhaps, Billy, we ought to go into the shelter?' asked the boy Frost had called Sammy.

The young people laughed again, nervously.

'Bit late now,' he replied. 'Seems to be running away. Seems to be over.'

In the distance there were four successive explosions, followed by the rattle of machine-gun fire.

'Ah, you see. They've got a fighter on his tail and he's unloaded his bombs to make a getaway. The all clear will go in a minute, I'll wager. Now where were we?'

He struck a match and sucked the flame into his pipe. There was a stir of nervous relief in the large room. The young people murmured and laughed again.

'Paul, you don't want to kill, yourself?'

He replied with an effort. 'Well, it's something of a phoney war—I mean, do Halifax and Vansittart and all those upper class people really want to fight this war?'

'Oh, come on,' said a neat young man in a blazer.

'Then your conscience about killing is somehow connected with class and politics?'

'I believe,' said a hefty blond boy with a Norfolk accent, 'I believe that God has prohibit'd me from killin'.'

'How do you distinguish,' said someone across the room, 'between what God tells you, presumably through a voice in your own head, and what (say) a leader of the Church tells you God said? Or plain cowardice for that matter?'

71

'*They* bless battleships,' said Paul, bitterly.

'Well, if you worked in a battleship,' said the clergyman, 'wouldn't you like it blessed?'

'But that's just man justifying his own destructiveness: the Germans think God is on their side, too. It's ludicrous. The Church shouldn't bless armaments.'

'Yers. But you don't believe in the Church. So what's it got to do with you?'

So it went on, until one o'clock in the morning. The all clear went an hour after the bombs had fallen. As Paul walked home, he saw big fragments of shrapnel lying in the gutter. The silver barrage balloons, raised for the raid, remained high in the sky around the city, shining prettily like silver gondolas in the sky, a half-moon among them. They were fantastically beautiful, like something in a great masque. He had to walk over two miles out to his parents' home at the Colman Road end of Unthank Road. His mother was still up, having made herself some tea during the raid, and only now felt quietened down enough to try to sleep.

'Oh, I'm glad to see you, boy, that I am. I was so worried.'

Paul hugged the anxious little woman in her pink flannelette nightdress and slippers, with her red eyes. Her long dark brown hair, rich and shiny, hung down her back.

'We were having a discussion on pacifism.'

'Huh!' she said. 'That old fool Frost want his head examinin', keepin' a lot of youths jawin' into the small hours all through an air raid.'

'Well, mother,' he said, 'we're all going to be flung into it, and no one seems to know whether they should fight or not, or what reasons they have for anything.'

'Did you lot come to any conclusions?' Her voice rose at the end, in the Norfolk way, and she looked curiously into his face. She didn't want him to go as a soldier. He laughed.

'Old Frost—what he enjoys is knocking everyone's arguments on the head. He really enjoys that. He sits there with his pipe and doesn't leave anyone with a leg to stand on. "Yers!" he says, "Yers! Yers!"'

'Lucky any of you still have your arms and legs and heads on, talkin' all that hot air right in the middle o' the city like that, with all them old rockets whizzin' about. Do you get to bed at once, boy.'

72

But on the whole, his parents never bothered what time he came in or where he had been. He admired them for that. Sometimes the Music House discussions went on until two in the morning, and to him it was a great boon to be able to argue questions of politics, meaning and belief in this open way. At times he found Frost maddening, always disagreeing, with his superior smile and the glint of gold wire in his mouth. But he gradually came to see that the clergyman's position was as full of holes as his purple pullover—indeed he had no position, and simply thrived on being Socratic, as he considered it, teasing the young. He meant to be Shavian, or perhaps somewhere between being a Fabian and a Quaker. But he was really pulling away all their supports in quite a nihilistic way. Maybe that had its value. But then he felt confused: there was absolutely no one whose views he completely shared.

'Frost,' Moncklet said to him one day. 'He's an inexhaustible gas bag: and so fat! No one can be intelligent who is so *fat*!'

While he was in such confusion between these adoptive fathers, Paul had a terrible row with his own father, and this disturbed him deeply. It had been so sudden: and it wasn't an issue over which he might have expected to quarrel with Frank. It was enough to cope with the feelings aroused by the confused reality of his life—exams, raids, the late-night discussions, the theatre. But the rage against his father seemed to come from nowhere, and this troubled him more than the air raids, or the exams, or worrying about how far he should go with Annie, or towards Frost's free thought. It was another moment like that during flu, in which he had felt threatened by a total loss of meaning in his existence, and strangely it turned him towards subversive politics, picking up the nihilisms he encountered, here and there.

Paul Grimmer loved his father, and loved his easy capacity to be childish with him: they would make kites out of newspaper and splints of thin bamboo, or would cook toffee on Sunday afternoons while Nellie had a rest in bed. At such times, Frank would behave just like a naughty boy, giggling and acting the fool. Nellie would come down to find them unable to speak with laughter—Frank whimpering with laughter, holding his big nose, his head ducked sheepishly. Two saucepans would be filled with burnt sugar, blackened and misshapen, while on a baking tray sprawled a blob of brownish mixture, which Paul and Frank would break up and

73

eat when it became cold. It was gritty to eat and hurt their gums, but they declared it quite good.

'We can't never quite get that right, Mother,' Frank would say, 'that "softball" stage, or that "crackin' " stage. We'll have to get a sweet thermometer.'

'Huh!' Mrs Grimmer would say, 'they cost a couple o' quid. You can buy a lot o' sweets for two quid—better'n that old muck.'

She pointed to the glassy, brittle toffee.

'Never mind, we had a good time making that,' he would say defiantly, like a child caught in the act.

Mrs Grimmer would sniff.

'An' I shall have a nice old time, cleaning my saucepans. That un't come off easy.'

'It'll all dissolve in water, given time,' suggested Paul.

'Ah, specially them cindery old bits, I bet. Give them about a year in boiling caustic soda, I dare say they might,' she answered, taking up a brass net pot scraper and her rubber gloves.

The worst conflict came over a rather similar episode. Paul had some chemistry apparatus in his bedroom: he had purchased a burette with a ground glass stopcock and had practised titration with this for his School Certificate chemistry examination. He had practised the analysis of salts and had done very well in his practical chemistry papers, using this instrument. Now, he no longer studied any science, and so his chemistry equipment was redundant. In between reading history books, he sometimes played with his chemistry equipment, but not very seriously.

One night, in between chapters, he mixed some chemicals and put a spirit lamp under the flask of his retort, turning back to his books. He did this almost unconsciously, using some strong nitric acid. Looking up, he saw a browny-orange gas streaming from the delivery pipe. It was a fascinating product, very heavy, rolling out of the tube onto the little chest of drawers, and across its surface, wispily. He couldn't actually think how it had happened. Then, like a small dark waterfall, it cascaded to the floor. He put the top on the lamp to stop the reaction, and turned back to his books, trying to think what he had set off, what the formula might be.

But behind his back, the chemical reaction, once set off, continued vigorously. And the dark gas, with almost the autonomous energy of an animal, rolled down onto the floor, and under the door, and down the stairs, streaming heavily down the precipice of each stair. The little hall grew full of it, and it seeped under the door of the living-room, where his parents were listening to the nine o'clock news.

He suddenly heard coughing and choking, and cries of alarm from downstairs.

Paul's reaction was a strange one—strange to himself. He couldn't pretend he was doing anything useful in his school work: and his parents knew he had given up 'science', at least as far as examinations were concerned. But he hadn't been experimenting, even, in any disciplined way: he had simply seen this heavy brown gas, and liked the look of it. Then he had, as he supposed, switched it off. It might, after all, be poisonous.

But when he saw the dark, strongly coloured gas had made its way downstairs and realised it was now choking his parents, he felt strangely pleased. He felt more alarmed by these feelings than about the possibility of its poisonous effects. But as they began to shout at him, he felt defiant and almost glad. Could he have committed this nuisance, in some way unconsciously desiring it? He began to feel an odd fiendish delight in it.

'Boy! Boy!' his mother shouted, 'what *are* you a-doin'?' She was gagging, seriously; the acid fumes were sickening and burned the tissues in her nose.

'Bloody boy!' cried his father, noisily, flinging open doors. He flung open the garden door and drew Mrs Grimmer out into the garden, choking. Then he rushed in at the front and stormed up the stairs, making the dark stream fly up in puffs. 'What the bloody hell do you think you're doing? I've never known nothing like it!'

With a strange wilful rage come upon him, Paul bolted his bedroom door. His father hammered on it for a moment and tore at it, but then rushed, choking, into the bathroom, and flung his head and shoulders out of the window there, gasping, all the jars and dishes on the windowsill tumbling noisily into the bath. For a moment the big man lay there choking for breath.

'What is it, what is this filthy rotten stuff?' he shouted across the landing.

'I don't know,' said Paul, sullenly, behind his bedroom door. Some half of him pointed inwardly to the easy solution—to show concern, to make a confession, to be deeply apologetic. But as the acrid smell of the gas hurt his nostrils, he retreated into an impossible alternative, of hatred and resentment. His heart began to beat, and his head seemed to fill with angry words and beliefs directed against his father. He pretended to be outraged.

'Don't make such a fuss.'

'Cyor!' his father cried, in a guttural, gassed voice. 'Cyor! This is the reward we get for his education—to be bloody well poisoned as we sit in our own sittin' room. Come out of there, blast, you stupid young bugger!' he added, rushing across the landing and thumping on the door panels.

'Oh, shut up and calm down,' said Paul. 'It's stopped.'

'The house—hough! hough!—the house,' his father gargled, 'is full of it.'

His mother began to call from the dark garden.

'You know your father's chest in't all that strong. Turn that off at once, Paul.'

'He don't even know what that is,' gasped his father. 'So p'raps he don't know how to stop it. Give me that whole thing and I'll put that out in the street. Bloody poisonous old rubbish in wartime,' he concluded without logic.

By way of an answer, Paul opened his bedroom window and flung the whole apparatus, glass flask and all, onto the little strip of concrete along the back of the house. It shattered, and he felt a pang of trembling rage. He remembered saving up lovingly for that big fireproof retort, the pierced rubber stopper, the curved glass tubes, the cooling coil . . .

'Take the bloody lot,' he said, absurdly and with a strange feeling he was acting, acting out some alien hostility in his mind, enraged and violent, his heart beating now.

'He ha' flung that all out in the garden and broke it,' called his mother. 'Oh, Paul, you are a fule, to get into such a paddy about nawthen'.' She lapsed into broad Norfolk in her excitement, 'Oh Frank,' she concluded, bursting into tears.

'Open up! Open up!' shouted his father. 'You *must* open up. I *order* you to open up!'

'I'm rather enjoying this,' said Paul, surprised at the sneer in his voice.

'It'll be the worse for you when you do open up,' said his father menacingly.

'My heart alive, boy,' shouted his mother. 'Whatever do you want to quarrel with your father for like this? Whatever did you make that nasty old gas for?'

'Oh, go to hell both of you,' cried Paul, now rather tearful. 'Just leave me to my books. I've got to pass all these bloody exams for your sake.'

'You don't have to pass them for *my* sake,' yelled his father. 'I'll just keep you while you go on playing with poison gas. I don't pay to keep you for *my* sake, I can tell you!'

'It isn't poisonous,' Paul said, sardonically.

'You don't even know what it was. Bloody vile stuff. Promise me you won't make any more of it! Come on out o' there, boy!'

Frank thumped on the door. It was now a meaningless scene. Or, at least, Paul thought in his beating head, it has a number of meanings, which we can't recognise to ourselves. I'm sick of them, because they are living out their ambitions in me. I've heard him, talking to others, about 'my boy—this' and 'my boy—that!' All right, then, I'll show him! I'm not his boy: if I work, I work in my *own* right. But then he grew ashamed of his boiling thoughts, and thought how much it meant to them, in a really altruistic way, that he became an 'educated' man and did well as a 'scholarship' boy. They had suffered privation: his mother's family had once lived on potatoes for a fortnight; his father's family often lived on rabbits they caught in the fields, and stolen turnips, because Old William used to spend half his sovereign on beer before he got home on Fridays. But all the same, he would do it his own way: he would be himself, not 'theirs'. I'll show them who I am! he thought angrily; but then this impulse seemed ridiculous. Now he was feeling confused, amazed at the violent conflict in himself. Over nothing, really! He hadn't even consciously intended the pollution of his home.

There was a reasonable stream of thought in his head, making allowances for his parents, whom he loved. But there was another, new voice, that spoke powerfully to him—a proud, destructive, rebellious voice. Under its command now, he heaved his chest of drawers across to the door, and pushed it hard against it.

'What are you doing now, boy?' his father called. He seemed now puzzled by his son's behaviour. He felt a new aggressiveness directed against him, urgent and ruthless.

'Putting my chest of drawers against the door.'

'Whatever for?' Frank's voice was scathing, provocative. 'Silly young bugger,' he muttered.

'Stop you getting in,' said Paul, breathlessly.

'Wah!' his father sneered.

They were in a strange deadlock of opposition. His mother came in and up the stairs a little.

'Come down now, Frank. He'll come to his senses in a little while. P'raps thass overwork?'

'I'll overwork *him*,' his father said bitterly. 'Making the house stink like that. I've never known nothing like it.'

Nor had any of them. It was a strange breach: the smashed flask, the acrid stench, the furniture heaved against the door, the rage in the small space, the woman on the verge of tears, the men angry, ill with headaches now, and tight feelings in their chests, knots of fear.

After an hour or so, the father and mother, sitting pale, he with his newspaper and she with her knitting, heard, startled, furniture shift back again upstairs. Then Paul came slowly down and went into the room. He looked drawn and red-eyed, as if he had been crying.

'I'm sorry, mum and dad,' he said, quietly. 'It was all an accident really . . . I shouldn't have got riled. I can't understand it.'

'Ah!' said his father flatly. His face was hollow and rather shrunken. He was unrepentant, and angry still. But he had no energy to recriminate with his son.

'That won't do,' was all his mother could say.

'I'm going to bed,' Paul said, his voice trembling, looking round the room. Where was all the smoke, the anger? He had felt, behind his bedroom door, as though some great fire of rage were burning at him. Now, all he could see were two rather exhausted middle-aged people, sitting embarrassed in their brown rexine armchairs, in the litter of newspapers, knitting and biscuits.

I shall have to leave home, he thought, I can't bear these awful times. He said 'times' to himself, but it was the first time: and yet, somehow, it resembled that dreadful moment when everything had seemed to dissolve. Here was the war, the air raids, the real menace, whereby everything could actually go to pieces. Yet this great rage in him, with its voices—hating his father, contemptuous of his mother for her weakness, her fondness—seemed immensely greater and more terrible than the war. It made the bombs and guns seem nothing at all. That night he lay awake for a long time, wondering why he hated his father so much, and what connection the outburst had with the dreadful moment in his mother's room. Was he mad?

In a moment of lucidity towards dawn, he thought it all came about because he could no longer fit into the child category, and his parents hadn't yet accepted his adult existence. While he was there, he couldn't find out who he was.

Yet that thought was still unformed, and inwardly he was going through a painful struggle to know who he was at all. Was he the young man Annie knew? Or the people at the Maddermarket Theatre? Or at school? There was a time from the age of twelve to sixteen when, in his prayers, he was the boy whom God knew, if no one else did—knew him to the core, his anxieties about having teeth out, his worries about having a fatal disease, trying to stop himself masturbating, or being hostile to his parents. Then he had lost his faith only a month after receiving his confirmation certificate, with its picture of a bearded Jesus pointing the way over the gunwale of a boat. God, who had answered his prayers so immediately, graciously granting him two 'A's and four 'B's in the School Certificate, and releasing a stream of fervent thanks, had completely withdrawn from his life. He stopped praying. For a while he felt uncomfortable. But then he had felt nothing at all. He thought he would feel a dark and deep catastrophe: but he did not. He just felt empty and bored, until the crisis in his illness. And now with these rages against his family, he felt simply lost. All this was far more important to him than the news that Hitler had invaded Russia.

What he needed was something to happen, some sequence of events through which he could find out who he was in the eyes of others. Who would stand by him? Who would be true to him? Who would be Peter, or Judas or John? Would he then know who he was?

79

8

He kept going to the Music House discussions all that autumn, and to recitals of music on gramophone records or on instruments at the Music Club in the same building, to which his parents had been persuaded to pay his subscription, as well as his work at the theatre. He used to put out the chairs for the Discussion Group and had been given a key, so he could get in to do this, by the secretary. It was of great importance to Paul Grimmer to take on responsibilities like that, in the adult world.

School was beginning to irk now, as his work there began to come to an end. In June he sat his Higher School Certificate Examination. A little later he sat scholarship examinations for Oxford and Cambridge, writing on big strange sheets of lined paper with punch-holes in the sides, on baize-covered tables in the combination rooms, where heavy clocks ticked and college masters of the past looked sternly down from their oil-paintings. After that he ran away from school, and this brought a definite end to his childhood.

His headmaster, Reggie Earlham, was a sympathetic, short, easy-going man, with grey hair and rather puckered eyes with genial crow's-feet. Paul could never quite make him out. He had a disquieting habit of suddenly opening up a conversation with a boy in the grounds of the school or in a corridor. He would suddenly give an odd sidelong look, pull at his small grey moustache, and move quickly up to the boy.

'Oh, yesh, Grimmer,' he said, with his rather slushy way of talking: 'I shaw a very nyesh painting of yours in the art room.'

'Yessir,' said Paul, blushing and messing about with his feet, not knowing how to stand. He was afraid he would say 'yesh' in reply, instead of 'yes'.

The grey-haired man smiled and intensified the crow's-feet at his eyes, putting his hand on Paul's shoulder, looking round at the gravel path and the lawn covered with spent leaves. Reggie always wore rather neat tweed suits and striped shirts with big points to the collars. He must have had them made. His head was small and sleek like a seal's, and he had a gold crown on one of his side teeth.

'You really have a pershonal *shtyle*,' he said.

'Yessir,' agreed Paul. 'I like to leave a painting a bit dauby,' he said, lamely.

'Oh no, itsh better than that. You're too modesht.' He tugged at his face, because he was a nervous man, and didn't find it easy to be father to three hundred boys. 'I'm jusht finishing an oil-painting, and I shomehow can't quite finish it off. I'd like your advishe. Can you shpare a moment?'

My advice, thought Paul? At sixteen? His head seemed to go all full of echoes, and his heart beat in his ears with embarrassment. But he went gladly along with Reggie as the headmaster strode across to his house in his neat tweed suit, pale grey, with an orange fleck in it. They entered the drawing-room by a french window —it was a handsome Regency house, painted white, across a lawn from the school—and there Paul felt he wanted to melt and sink into the ground with shame and awkwardness. For he was faced with a canvas five feet high, displaying a plump nude lady with prominent breasts, brown nipples and pubic hair, seated re-vealingly on a wooden stool.

'Shee?' spluttered the headmaster, with a benign, happy look. 'I've graduated the shadowsh, but the figure shtill ishn't bal-anshed in the canvash. What can I do to reshtore *balansh* and form?'

What can I do to restore balance, thought Paul, reeling and wanting to run. He liked the picture, which was rather like a Modigliani, and fortunately he was able to say so, which de-lighted Reggie and made him twitch his moustache happily. He was glad to find a boy in his school who not only knew Modigliani, but could also pronounce him, with a Norfolk accent, too. But such a huge nude! And such prominent nipples and pubic hair! These were still only things to giggle about in the library, as they pored over the watercolour 'September Morn' in the Royal Academy *Illustrated Guide*. Paul really didn't know where to put himself. But then he said: 'Couldn't you put something else in the space to the left?'

'Yesh, I thought of that: but you shee, I don't want to dishtract the eye from the figure.'

Paul thought of a pot plant but then suppressed the idea, as this would have brought out the vegetable quality of the lady, whom he suspected was the headmaster's wife.

'Then all you can do is to keep working on your *pointilliste* shadows . . .'

'Oh yesh! I'd never thought that my shadowsh were *pointillishte*: how clever you are.'

At that moment Reggie's wife Troth came in, booming in her deep voice, which put Paul back into deep embarrassment, because it was evident that it was she, stripped, in the picture. Paul was glad to escape.

'Troosh,' called Reggie after her, 'I musht fly! Shanks, Grimmer, mosht usheful!'

Reggie filled the school with reproductions, from Giotto to Braque. The sixth form room collared six of the best, all modern works by Paul Nash, Ivon Hitchens, Pissaro and Monet.

But now came a catastrophe. That year, there had been a row in the City Council over the number of boys from Paul's school who had registered as conscientious objectors. One Councillor denounced the headmaster for teaching pacifism. It was painfully untrue. In fact, the record of the school for sending out boys who distinguished themselves in the fighting services was better than that of many others. But Reggie Earlham, who had been seriously wounded in the First World War and was still full of pieces of shrapnel twenty-two years later, did not spare his pupils an awareness of the horrors of the battlefield. They had read Wilfrid Owen, Graves and Siegfried Sassoon, and had been to *All Quiet On The Western Front* in the cinema. In the sixth form they discussed religion, politics and ethical views continuously, with passion, and some became pacifists with the same devotion that others became paratroopers. They also loved their headmaster, even though they called him 'Slush', not least because of his evident sorrow that they were growing up to suffer in war, as he had done as a young man.

But Reggie was forced to resign. The first thing his successor, a man called Rickson, did was to remove all the pictures from the hall. The whole school environment went blank and boring. The man was an economist with business associations, a Rotarian, a respectable academic nonentity, appointed because he was a nonentity, with a face like a boar, covered with white bristles. His attitudes to life were wholly commercial, disciplinarian and materialistic, and he talked in dreary abstractions, in a North Country voice. His duty, he said, was to 'tehm the unruly pupils in the school'—especially, he said, the sixth form, looking at them menacingly from the platform. He was especially concerned to tame Paul Grimmer, and said as much to the older boys. One of the staff, the only one to welcome this new screw of a head, had warned him of the least conventional sixth formers. Things were going to be very different from that September.

Paul was surprised to hear it stated publicly that he needed 'tehming'. He had considered that his political views and his tastes were not eccentric. But he was developing a certain kind of joky irony, and this infuriated the Bradford mediocrity, as he found when he began to write essays for the man. To the latter, it was outrageous to challenge the values of a commercial, materialistic world, the existence of God, or the need for obedience and duty. He was a Gradgrind, only his utilitarianism was repulsively combined with patriotic Rotarianism. Reggie had frequently read them Pericles's Funeral Oration. Rickson's mentors were Bentham and Malthus, in so far as he had any intellectual interests at all. He was really simply a brutal and stupid Philistine, and what he was chiefly concerned to put down were ideas of any kind, any glimpse of human potentialities beyond the horizons of low commerce. His Mecca was that of the Rotarian Convention, men dressed in dark suits wearing pathetic club ties, sporting perhaps ribbons or even hats, and going through absurd ceremonies, singing the National Anthem out of tune after a boring dinner.

'Ah don't like those pictures on the wall,' he said one day, as he paid one of his surprise visits to the sixth form room. The sixth formers had already been told to stand up when Rickson came in. They never had for Reggie and it had never entered his mind that they should. In protest, they lifted themselves laboriously from their armchairs, with affected slowness. The man turned dark red with rage. He attributed all such demonstrations to Paul's influence.

For the next month the paintings lay on the floor against the wall. When he came next, he demanded crossly: 'Why are those pain-tin's lyin' on the floor like that!'

'You said, sir,' said Len Daunt, who was head boy, 'that you didn't like *those pictures on the wall*.'

'Are you being insoolting, son?'

'Me, sir?'

Daunt put on a haughty, sneering face.

'Who did this?'

'We all did, sir,' said another boy between his teeth.

'Is this soom of friend Grimmer's antics?'

There was silence.

'We're not fourth formers, to be asked to "own up",' said Daunt loftily. 'What we do is unanimous, something for which we *all* take responsibility.'

The man went dark in the face again.

'Well, my lad,' he said between clenched teeth. 'I s'll have to break your spirits soomhow or oother.'

He licked his cruel-looking lips and glinted behind his horn-rimmed spectacles.

'You shall all stop in fer half an hour.'

The sixth formers stood, after he left, in stunned silence. 'Keeping in' the sixth form! The whole upper and lower sixth—treating them like little kids! They could hardly believe it possible. Some of them, like Paul, had been prefects for three years and were leaving for the university that year.

'The bastard,' said one with cold contempt.

Recklessly, Paul threw open the long balcony windows and did one of his Hitler imitations to the boys roaming about below, and the kitchen staff. He no longer cared who heard him, so angry was he at the injustice.

'*Dieses Insulten*,' he declared in pidgin German, '*gegen den Übersixt und der Untersixt Battalionen von diese Schüle must nicht mit kein Vergeltungsblitz gepassen . . .*'

He muttered, screamed and choked, catching Hitler's accents and mimicking his frantic gestures. The dictator could be heard on the radio every few months, and everyone knew what Paul was at. It was insanity within insanity. There was some mad under-current in Reggie's removal: some Masonic conspiracy, perhaps?

All the good things seemed to be breaking down under the threat of air raids. So Paul was insulting the humourless new headmaster but in such a way as to make it impossible, he hoped, for the man to pin him down and punish him. He strode up and down like Charlie Chaplin's imitation of the Dictator. He muttered low, gutturally, then let his voice grow to a scream: '*Diese englisher Schweine* ... *diese Nordern Reich capitalistischen economischen* ... *Schweine-hunden! ... diese überofficieren ... Stunk! Stunk! die übergauleiten stunk ... Rickson stunk! ... Sieg heil!*'

There were cheers from below and Paul stuck out his arm in the Nazi salute. He screamed dementedly: '*Wir müssen diese über prisonier-gubernachisten Typen ... diesen Prison-screwen ... smashen und piss-off-er-en! Sieg heil!*'

He was really enjoying his act and the other sixth formers were shouting: '*Sieg heil!*' and roaring with laughter. Suddenly silence fell behind him. He paused and looked round. There was Rickson, looking bull faced and self-satisfied, his spectacles glinting in the doorway, his white whiskers bristling.

'*Ja wohl!*' said Paul, saluting and clicking his heels, trying to laugh it off.

'Grimmer,' said the disciplinarian, his thick lips pouting with rage, 'I could pass [he said 'pus'] this off as a display of 'igh spirits. But today, and knowing you, Ah'm not disporsed to.' His Northern accent thickened as he grew more angry. 'You can coom to my stoody at the end of the day.'

The sixth formers began to wonder whether, as well as keeping them in, Rickson was going to cane Paul Grimmer. Was he to get a wigging? At seventeen?

'If he does,' said Daunt, who was an Earlham man, 'we shall go on strike.'

'Don't worry,' said Paul. 'I hate that bastard, and I'm going.'

The man would say he was mad. But he was not mad. Why had the fool gone out of his way to attack their dearest interests, their life-style, demanding conformity, demanding their submission so cruelly? That was what was mad, that sadistic demand for conformity. One couldn't stay and suffer it.

'Going where?'

'I don't know. Anywhere but here.'

The long weeks of exchange between the new headmaster and

Paul had disturbed him deeply. The acid remarks in red ink at the foot of his work had gone beyond the bound of fair comment. At one point the bull-faced economist had written: 'You and I seem to share so little by way of values that I shall say no more.' But he had the power and he was determined to crush Paul Grimmer as the focus of all that he had been appointed to crush. For the older boys it was intolerable, as they had liked Reggie and understood his humanity. Rickson they recognised as a barbarian, not only because he was stupid and unfair, but because they knew and hated him for what he was, for sound intellectual reasons. From Reggie's teaching of *Hard Times*, they knew he was an enemy of the human spirit. He had no right to be a headmaster: they were sure of that from what Reggie had conveyed to them of Greek thought. They saw through Rickson as the limited pragmatic utilitarian type that had threatened civilisation throughout the ages, and did so never more than in the present moment, when there was a war against barbarism itself. Of course there was no answer, no possible answer, while he had the power.

Paul Grimmer never went near the headmaster's study. Next day, he set off early in his thin brown tweed overcoat. It was November now, and cold weather. Instead of going to school, he stood on the Newmarket Road and waved his thumb at motorists. He had never done it before, and it felt brazen and offensive. It hurt his pride at first, as if he were begging. But then a man stopped and was laughingly interested in Paul's request for a lift. It was going to work! Two hours later he was in Cambridge, and an hour after that, Bedford. He had seven shillings and sixpence in his pocket, and had formed only a dim idea of where he was going. Reggie had taken a teaching post at A. S. Neill's experimental school, Summerhill, evacuated from Leiston in Suffolk to Llan Ffestiniog, somewhere in the mountains near Snowdon in North Wales. He had had a pleasant letter from his old head, the kind words of which contrasted astonishingly with the calculated animosity of the new man: so he would go to Wales, and talk to Reggie about it all. After that, what? He didn't care. It was the break that was important. By lunchtime he was in Wolverhampton, and looking around him with astonishment and fear.

There had been a number of severe air raids on Wolverhampton and the Midlands that autumn. Of course, Paul had experienced a few raids in Norwich. But now he rode in the cab of a lorry through street after street in which all the roofs had been torn off and the windows smashed. Here and there, there were ruins of demolished houses, direct hits, flat sprawls of broken brick. But what struck him most was the widespread effect of what must have been huge landmines coming down on parachutes, which had ripped the fabric of houses for hundreds of yards around. Black tarpaulins fluttered in the cold wind, and here and there building-workers up ladders were trying to mend roofs and walls. But the devastation was vast, and people were walking about the blasted streets in shocked and miserable despair among houses which showed their naked and broken roof-timbers for mile after mile. Over it all the barrage balloons hung in silvery menace, and in parks and open spaces here and there huge anti-aircraft cannon pointed to the sky half-covered with camouflage nets.

He became frightened and lonely as dark fell, and by evening he had only one and sixpence in his pocket. Cars and lorries on the road were few and far between now, and some drivers obviously regarded a lone hiker after dark with suspicion. The headlights of vehicles were covered and drivers were only allowed a thin slit of light.

At last he found himself in a Black Country village called Shifnal, in Staffordshire, where the public houses were beginning to close for the night. He came to one pub, an old timbered building, the Bull, and went in.

'I'm joost shuttin',' said the woman at the bar.

'I'm ever so sorry,' said Paul, determined to put his cards on the table. 'I'm hitch-hiking to Wales.'

'What, in this weather? In November? By God, you want your head examined, lad.'

Paul stuttered his requests desperately.

'I wonder if you can help me? I've only got one and six left, and I can't go on tonight. I wonder if you could tell me where I might find somewhere to sleep?'

He looked hopefully at the bar benches.

The strong, well-built woman looked hard at him. He was pale and tired and obviously frightened; only a child really.

'Ar'ye lookin' for work?'

'No . . . I've run away from school. I'm going to see a friend, an old headmaster, in North Wales.'

'Ah, I see,' she said, looking closely into his face. 'One of them awkward yoong boogers. Just hold on a minute. Yer nobbut seventeen, aren't you, lad?'

He nodded. She went into the back of the bar, and murmured to her husband. Paul looked around at the dark wooden walls, the dying fire, the hard seats of the benches of the public bar. He heard her say 'young fellow . . . doesn't look too bad . . . only a kid really . . . can't turn him out on a night like this, war or no war. Look, Harry, I'll stake me savin's on him.'

The man came in, a stocky man with grey hair and broad shoulders, wearing a grey pullover and slippers.

'Got stoock, eh?' he said. 'Ye're right booggered on this road for the night. Look—Ah tell ye' what I'll do. I can lock you in this bar 'ere. You kin have this roog as belongs rahtly to t' tomcat, and thee can sleep on't bench there.'

'An' here's piece o' bread and soom 'ard cheese left after makin' sandwiches tonight.'

'It's very kind of you,' said Paul almost in a whisper. 'Here's my one and six!'

The man laughed, a kind, rather bitter laugh.

'We doan't want ye' bloody eighteenpence, lad. Anyone kin do a kindness, once in a road. Our boy's out there soomwhere, only a kid like you, and props he's in't some bloody ditch terneet, like yow, for all we bloodiwell knaws!'

He gave something between a laugh and a groan.

So Paul slept a deep sleep, on a hard pub bench, tasting the full aroma of the tom cat from his one blanket. Next day, the landlord's wife gave him a boiled egg and toast, and he was on the road as the first wave of lorries came along. These people had been so good to him. Why? He could think of no reason for it

As he reached mountainous country, his heart became light. He had never seen a mountain before: he was amazed when the great blue forms of earth rose, sticking right up into the moist Welsh clouds. His fear and anxiety turned to a sense of adventure. As the forests and moors went on for mile after mile everything seemed remarkable and dramatic. It poured with rain and there were clouds drifting across the road which seemed at times to be hung on the side of a precipice. The lorries he rode in thundered through forests and broke out over huge plains and valleys that stretched before him in bright intervals, like magic countries.

There were strange coincidences, too. Somewhere near Penmaenmawr a man gave him a lift who had a child at Neill's school. This neat, rather smooth and sophisticated man, a doctor, insisted on giving him a cold chicken lunch. He poured Paul out a gin and lime beforehand, which made the boy sneeze when he drank it. The doctor had a limewashed stone house on a mountainside, with a huge open fireplace burning logs. It was hard to tear himself away. At Conway, he took a bus to Blaenau Festiniog, and under its dim blue blackout lights he realised all the people in it, mostly older women coming back from shopping, were all talking Welsh—and mostly talking about him, with the passion and curiosity of a coven of witches. His tired head swam with the strangeness: he had never realised that it was possible, in his own country, to get into a bus in which everyone talked in a foreign language. And the steep hills and rocks left him stunned with excitement—what a triumph of his soul over that conformist rogue, to be here in a foreign land!

At last, high in the mountains, with the rain beating down in the night on the slate walls along the roadside, he reached Reggie's cottage.

'Hallo!' he said cheerfully to his astonished old headmaster. 'I've come to see you.' And fainted.

9

'I have asked my colleague Mr Softfoot to attend,' said Rickson, with a bullish thrust of his thick lips, 'because this affair is so serious.'

Paul licked his lips. He was still afraid of the man. But he held a trump card, he knew, and it burned in his pocket like David's pebble. Behind the bull-headed headmaster sat another master who had come to the school with the new man, a teacher who was always excessively deferential to Rickson, naturally nicknamed Creepy Softfoot by the rebellious sixth form. He was sickeningly small and neat in his hands and feet. Others called him 'the Worm'. He looked as if he had worms, so slight was his build. He had curly hair, neatly brushed, and wore a neat dark blazer and a navy old school tie. He nodded, and looked grave. He had a soft, puppyish face, and was so thoroughly groomed from his clean-shaven cheeks to his little fingernails that he exuded conformity. But his eyes were oddly expressionless, and only flickered with an anxiety to follow the wishes of his headmaster. Softfoot always looked at Rickson with a flicker of his eyes before he spoke, and licked his lips. Paul loathed meeting Rickson in head-on collision. But he was even more afraid of this neat servant who often seemed to him like an executioner in a play, in the same obsequious and evil role.

'Your parents wish to talk to me, and these interviews moost be condoocted as I believe in the presence of a witness. Have you any objections, Grimmer?'

'No,' said Paul, making a small dry noise. He knew he was finished with the school now. But he also knew the man had the power to wreck his career, and would not hesitate to do so. So he wanted 'witnesses': what malicious forethought!

'Would you mind asking your parents in?'

Paul rose and opened the door. His mother and father were

sitting in the little passage between the front door of the school and the hall. On the wall were long rectangular photographs of the three hundred pupils of each year, sitting on forms rank above rank, six hundred eyes fixed on the spectator. His father wore a tweed overcoat and carried a grey trilby hat. His mother wore her old musquash fur coat and looked bewildered, with her perplexed big brown eyes. Paul felt a pang at giving them such trouble. They walked in, rather uneasily, shook hands with the two schoolmasters and sat down. Rickson was actually quite charming to his parents and Paul's heart sank: would they be disarmed? Would the man get them to agree to a caning or something?

'Now, let me say,' said Rickson, in his pedagogic manner, with a kind of public relations smile, screwing up his nose like a large white pig and rubbing his short fat fingers together, 'I was appointed to tighten oop discipline in this school, and woon of the tassks I set myself was to tehm Paul Grimmer . . .'

He smiled nastily, thrusting out his lower lip. But it was no joke.

There was no response from Frank and Eleanor, although his mother, Paul could see, was inwardly making comparisons with Whackford Squeers.

'In that,' the man went on, 'I have had little or no soock-cess. And now he has defahyed me and the school, by roonin' away, instead of facing his joost punishment, for a personal insoolt to myself. He has coom back, and we moost now decide what peth to take. I cannot go on suppoortin' this young man, if he is to be sooch a rebel.'

There was a pause. Frank was obviously struggling with his dislike of the man. He began by clearing his throat, and putting down his hat on the rexine seat of a brown wooden chair. He was calm and rather magnificent: Paul had never seen him so good and grave.

'Naturally,' he said, 'I take my boy's part. I don't think you've been fair to him, Mr Rickson.'

'My colleague here will confirm that I have been extremely wooried by this pupil.'

Softfoot nodded vigorously, patting his little hands.

'Of course, I haven't been here to see it, and I've mostly his accounts to go on. But I've also talked to other boys in the sixth form, and I don't feel from these accounts that you've been fair to Paul,' Frank went on. 'You've taken the view that the whole of the old regime under Mr Earlham is represented in him.'

'Ah, but it is. He is oondisciplined. His political views are extreme. His sense of right and wrong is not . . . is not my sense: indeed, it could not be more remote . . .'

'Is his work bad, though?' put in his mother. 'Were you complainin' that he's lazy?'

Frank put himself forward forcibly. 'You've come to dislike him because he doesn't like wearing his cap, and he finds it difficult to adapt to a system which he has not been brought up to, not by me and my wife nor the school, up to now. You want a strict rule here and none of us have asked for it before. Then you don't like his political ideas. I've looked at his essays and I think you let this personal dislike get the better of your judgement, Mr Rickson. You singled him out because he's a pacifist,' said his father, who had evidently rehearsed his speech quite carefully.

'Coom, coom,' said the man with one of his cruel-looking smiles, 'can you really believe that?'

'Yes we can,' said his mother. 'These boys—you know—they aren't little children no more. Maybe you want to treat them different. But Mr Earlham, he treated them more like grown-ups.'

'Do you call Paul's behaviour recently grown up? My dear Mrs Grimmer . . .'

'No!' said his mother fiercely. 'They were all forced to go back and behave like children. That would have been better to have left them alone, till they'd left, them older ones.'

'You felt you had to make an impression,' said Paul's father, 'and you started on the ones you disliked. You wanted to make an example of them. Well, my boy, he've worked ever so hard this last three year. He's had his problems. But for him to run away, hundreds of miles, in wintertime like that—he wouldn't ha' done that unless he'd bin very unhappy. And that wasn't altogether his fault.'

'That weren't *us* that made him unhappy. We've had little old rows at home. But thass a *happy* home. You made him a scapegoot,' his mother added, with a conclusive Norfolk nod.

'I hear he's been living in the city and not at home.'

Paul pricked his ears up. How did Rickson know that? He was watched, was he?

His mother looked at both men with some disdain.

'He's been working down at the theatre and for Mr Monck. You can't keep a big growing boy like that cooped up in a cage. Anyway, I don't see thass anything to do with you.'

'If I may say something,' said Paul. 'I very much appreciate the way in which my parents have let me be free to live where I like.'

Rickson looked quite startled by the Grimmers' self-possession: people usually quailed before his scarcely concealed aggression. He looked pale and hostile.

'I think it would be better if we heard what your parents have to say first, Grimmer. We have been watching Paul Grimmer's behaviour for some time,' he added menacingly.

Softfoot nodded, and Paul realised what this meant.

'We're not happy about the coompany he keeps, or the life he leads.'

His father responded marvellously.

'I'm sorry,' he said. 'I don't think what my boy does out of school is anything whatever to do with you, unless that interferes with his work. And as for his company or whatever, I trust him: he's been brought up in a good home and I trust him to make proper judgements on his own. As far as I know his friends in the city are respectable and respected people.'

'That's roight,' said his mother. 'Anyway, whatever he does in his leisure time is nothin' to do with noosey parker schoolmasters.'

'Our view is different,' said Rickson.

'Well, thass what I mean,' said Frank. 'You've got no right at all to use any information you sneaked up out of school, to make my son an example. The only complaint I'll take from you is about his work, and you can't fault that.'

'His views are extreme, and, as you know, New College Oxford found them too much for them.'

'I always thought teachers and educated people,' said his mother, also rising well to the occasion, 'were *glad* when boys had strong opinions.'

'Ah,' said Rickson craftily, 'properly *based* opinions.'

'*Properly* based opinions,' echoed Softfoot.

'You mean opinions you agree with,' said Frank, smiling. 'I've seen some of your comments on my son's essays, Mr Rickson, and that strike me you're less concerned with how well the essay is written than with rejecting the boy's opinions because you don't agree with them. You seem to take that as a personal insult if he don't take your line on economics, for example. If my son has views of his own, and can support them with arguments, that's what I'd expect from an educated boy. Of course, he's young, maybe extreme. But you shouldn't squash boys' opinions . . .'

'Come, come, Mr Grimmer, don't try to teach me my job.'

'Any old how,' said Paul's father, lapsing into Norfolk emphasis, 'we've got somethin' to tell you. Out with it, boy!'

Paul drew a letter out of his pocket and put it triumphantly on Rickson's desk. The man glinted at it through his spectacles and pursed his lips. Softfoot looked nervously over his shoulder, licking his. Their faces went stern and rather blank, behind small forced smiles. The letter offered Paul an Open Exhibition at Pemning College, Cambridge.

There was a long pause, during which Rickson licked his ugly lips, rather baffled. That was the end of him. Paul nearly got up and gave a Hitler salute to mock him.

'This is a superb achievement,' said Rickson, holding out his hand to Paul. The boy noticed it was trembling. He has a bit of generosity in him, then, thought Paul, taking it. It was unpleasantly damp. 'All you have to do now is pass Littlego. I must congratulate you,' he added to Mr and Mrs Grimmer, shaking hands with them in turn.

It was all a farce, really: a bloody awful farce, Paul thought. He felt deeply shaken, by the adults' conflict over him.

'I wish you had mentioned this earlier. It might have saved a little . . . unpleasantness.'

'All very well,' said Frank. 'I didn't want Paul to leave under a cloud of unjust disapproval.'

'Leave?' said Rickson. 'He isn't officially done with school until the end of this year, you know. And if he requires testimonials, he will still need to refer to his headmaster.'

'I think, under the circumstances,' said Frank, 'it would be better for all concerned if you could turn a blind eye to his existence—or, rather, to his absence, for the rest of this year.'

'I can't authorise this, or promise anything. But,' said Rickson suddenly seeing the advantages for himself and his new regime, 'if I find Grimmer missing from my school I shan't exactly go looking for him or sending out the attendance officer.'

Outside, Paul heaved a deep sigh of relief.

So that was the end of school. Strangely, he felt he would miss it.

Until the New Man, the school had been at least in some respects one pathway to civilised interests—old 'Daddy' Watling encouraging one to paint, letting 'God's hand', as he put it, take over the brush; Lance Harris with his spotty bow tie reading extracts from *The Mookse And The Gripes*; Reggie encouraging them to write and perform their own weird plays. But now the school had ceased to be that kind of place, difficult though it was to believe it. It became a place where absurd outward forms were inflicted, but where the cultural heart had gone dead. School now was nothing any more, and he took no interest in it, he never visited it again, contributed nothing. Later, he heard, his was the last name to be inscribed on the panelled walls in the hall: Rickson even stopped that tradition. But the new headmaster, though defeated for the moment, nursed his frustration. He had not crushed Paul Grimmer but hoped in some way to get his revenge for that later.

'So, it's to be Cambridge?' exclaimed Monck, as he let Paul into the Crypt when he called one teatime.

'I shall get a year there, at any rate.'

'You're not going to get killed, I hope?'

'I shall have to go into the Army after a year.'

'And then come back.'

'*If* I come back.'

'People do: *did* at any rate, after the last war. And you'll get a very good grant. So, congratulations. Of *course* you'll come back.'

'Let Moncklet read your palm,' said a plump young man in a smart brown tweed suit, sitting by the fire, and showing his big white teeth in a smile. It was Roy Short, his head boy last year, who was already up at the university.

'I only do that with people I know *very* well,' said the little man, in mock modesty. 'And in any case, it's a dangerous thing to do with people who are going into the forces.'

'Is that why you wouldn't read mine?' asked the fair-haired young man.

'Roy,' said Moncklet, 'is already at Cambridge and will tell you how to behave there.'

'We must initiate him into the Socialist Club,' said Short, Paul thought to annoy Monck.

'You were lucky to leave school when you did,' said Paul, 'just as the new reactionary régime came in.'

'That dreadful man!'

Paul had always been a little jealous of the plump Short, who was a step ahead of him in everything, and felt a pang now because the undergraduate seemed so self-possessed in Monck's presence. Actually, as he came to see gradually, Short was not very much at ease in the producer's presence, but acted for Moncklet in an artificial way that was a bit vain and self-regarding. Indeed, after a while he detected a strong undercurrent of hostility between them.

'I remember you as the champion underwater diver.'

'Oh yes,' said Short, looking pleased and rather vain. 'I made myself good at holding my breath.'

'He is *fat*,' said Moncklet. 'So that is why he is good at swimming sports.'

'What can I tell you about Cambridge?' said Short, ignoring this. 'Where are you going?'

'Pemning.'

'Oh!' he said, with a face. 'That's rather a dull college.'

Paul had noticed before this odd mixture of geniality and destructiveness in Roy Short. He had seen him occasionally among the discussion group crowd, arguing in a strong, polite voice. He was short-sighted and peered at his opponents with frowning intensity. But then, in quite another mood, once he had established rapport with somebody, he would relax and lean back and laugh a great deal, even immoderately, sometimes holding his stomach as if he were afraid he would burst if he laughed too much. But after an outburst of laughter, he would reveal his underlying tension by pulling his fingers and making them crack like floorboards.

'A dull college? That's rather a bitchy thing to say, isn't it?' Monck protested.

'Well, I suppose colleges change year by year,' said Short, making it worse, 'it could be quite an interesting college *next* year.'

'I've no doubt you judge from a very dialecti . . . I can never pronounce the word . . .' the little man spat dreadfully, 'dialectical materialist point of view.'

'It's true we sell very few copies of the *Daily Worker* in Pemning. You can be literature secretary of the Socialist Club,' he went on to Paul. 'I must introduce you at once to Euan Cooper-Willis.'

'I . . . I'm not sure I'm a socialist,' said Paul.

'Why ever should he be a socialist?' cried Monck. '*I'm* not a socialist. The socialists would take my theatre from me and put on dreary plays about railwaymen and factory-workers . . . I should say,' he went on with a wave of his arm at Paul, 'I was the first theatre in England to put on *Distant Point* and *Squaring The Circle* . . . But I am not willing to be *dictated* to by the state. So I am certainly *not* a socialist.'

97

'Anybody who is anybody nowadays at Cambridge is in the Socialist Club, except for the Catholics and the Fascists.'

Roy Short spoke the last word with contemptuous disdain.

'Where do you put people who don't know what they are?' asked Paul, genuinely puzzled.

'You don't have to be put where he tells you,' urged the older man. 'I see you're going to get a very biased view of Cambridge if you take *his*.'

'Cambridge is itself something of a bourgeois epiphenomenon,' said Roy Short.

'We are not going to ask what an epiphenomenon is,' said Monck, 'because we don't want a half-hour's lecture. In any case, I am *hungry*. Stay here while I fetch a cake from the baker in Davey Place, and talk. When I get back we will have tea.'

He trotted out and Paul could study his sometime head boy more attentively. Short put his feet up on the sofa, a posture Paul knew Monck hated and which he suspected was why Roy did it.

'Silly old ass. Let me warn you,' Short went on. 'Monck is a very *reactionary* old man, and you must take care not to be influenced by him.'

'Perhaps we shouldn't eat his cake then?' suggested Paul.

'I don't think eating people's cake corrupts one,' said Short. 'You can always reject their views *as* you eat it.'

'But,' said Paul, 'I meant that if you despise them, you should refuse their cake for your *own* sake.'

Roy cracked his fingers. 'It sounds to me as if you have some very bourgeois idea of conscience. We rather escape from that kind of nonsense at Cambridge. You must be more expedient. The essential criterion is what serves the inevitable goal of *history*.' He dug Paul in the ribs, quite painfully.

Paul stared amazed at his broad-shouldered, plump companion, smiling at him from his squarish, tubby face with its big lips and teeth. His mouth was handsomely formed, with a touch of cruelty in it, a touch of the Steerforth disdain. He had big, short-sighted eyes, and thin fair hair. When he laughed, stripes formed along his jaw and his face turned pink and ruddy, and he drew his head in backwards as if it pained him somewhere to laugh. His finger-cracking disturbed and annoyed people, and then he did it all the more. If any of his mannerisms were evidently annoying people he exaggerated them at once. He wore beautifully made Wigby and Digby suits and Norwich silk ties. You might say that outwardly Short was everything bourgeois: inwardly, everything *sans culottes*.

So in Paul's close and persistent observation, Roy was a double-sided character. When in company with adults he was neat and respectable, pulling at his cuffs and his tie, but glancing sideways at them to see if he was being appreciated. He would smile and bow his head a little ingratiatingly, really working on people at times, to exert some kind of power over them.

But along with young companions he would giggle and act the fool, expressing contempt for adults with a puff of his breath, and clown in the most preposterous way, even tearing his clothes or abandoning them altogether. Paul knew this from sixth form swimming outings.

In the general social life of the sixth, he recalled, he had admired Short enormously from afar, looking up from the bottom of the lower sixth to the university freshman-to-be. It was his idiotic sense of fun that attracted Paul most to Roy Short. He used to do crazy things that filled the sixteen-year-olds with admiration.

Once the Remove played the sixth at cricket and the match was ended by a fierce hailstorm: the dark sky was exploding with blue lightning. Roy Short threw open the window of their sixth form room where they were changing after the match, and thrust his bare chest into the hissing hail. Large ice pellets bounced in the window against his flesh and into the room, and a pinkish explosion ripped into the earth outside, blinding them. Roy only laughed, squinting his eyes at Paul, who was pale with fear and alarm, and struggling to shut the window.

'Ha! Ha!' exclaimed Roy, 'wouldn't it be awful if God shot it straight in there, into one's belly button! Ough! Bang!'

He held his finger in his umbilical knot and held his other hand in the teeming ice, as the thunder bludgeoned the roofs, hurting their ears.

One day that summer Paul and Roy had been swimming in the Yare at Cringleford. There was a pool among some willows by a wooden railway bridge, and there they could dive, because of the deep gravel bottom without weeds or wire. Roy was an amazing swimmer, winning most of the school competitions, especially that for the longest plunge—a dive without raising one's face to breathe. He could hold his breath under water longer than anyone in the school, causing cries of amazement and concern in the swimming sports, as he quietly drifted forward on the surface of the water. Two others were with them.

'Let's swim downstream as far as we can go without stopping. No costumes!'

Roy flung his suit away, and Paul dragged his off. The river was beautifully clear: the weeds had not grown yet, and although the water was cold the sun was shining and the boys did not feel cold swimming along. Paul became lost in his naked free movement in the water, twisting and turning with pleasure as the river stroked his body. One slipped through the water so much faster naked: it gave him a thrilling feeling of freedom, as if sailing through the air. He could only do a breast-stroke and an odd kind of side-stroke, which sometimes involved turning over and over like a fish. On and on he swam, winding his way through banks of weeds, in the clear channel.

He saw only the water, the young green reeds and the king-cups, shining golden on the bank. Suddenly he became aware that there was no sound of Roy or the others, and at the same time he was almost under the road bridge, where several people were staring at him, laughing and pointing. For a moment he grinned back, but then realised he was naked: he also realised that the river went very shallow under the bridge, he would not be able to conceal his body under the water. He splashed and struggled, and made off with a flurry back towards the pool, and then heard a roar of laughter from behind a thicket of reeds and rushes.

'Ho! Ho!' roared Roy. 'Entertaining Cringleford with an underwater display, were you!'

'You bugger, Short,' cried Paul. 'You might have shouted!'

'I was watching those old women on the bridge, trying not to look and then having a good eyeful. They'll be ringing up the police I'll be bound. Oh, you'll be for it! Ha! Ha!'

He threw himself in and swam strongly back to the place where they had left their clothes.

'Ha! Ha!' he roared, bubbling and blowing in the water, his big teeth shining.

'How stupid,' said Paul, spluttering. He swam laboriously,

feeling he was slinking back to the pool in shame. He was angry, because swimming alone and naked he had felt that rapturous at-one-ness with the leaves of the grey willows shaking in the light, and the long reeds streaming with the current below him, sometimes caressing his thighs with their papery swords. He didn't want his nakedness to be furtive. But Roy had made it all into a silly practical joke, and now he stood, dressed and clicking his fingers, flushed with exertion, saying: 'Hurry up! They're after you!'

He was always like this, strangely cruel, strangely triumphant in his dominance. The others only laughed. When they were dressed Paul insisted on going back by another way, along a river path, so that they wouldn't meet the people on the bridge at Cringleford. Roy simply laughed, calling out: 'Over here for the dangerous sex maniac! This way for the exhibitionist!'

And with an odd malevolence he began beating Paul with a bit of thin stick, quite hard and painful.

It was strange, how, after hating him for such things, Paul still found him fascinating. Short had obviously forgotten all those school episodes, and how he had exercised such influence over the younger sixth formers. He had a strange power of making himself attractive by his charm, even when he was being dominating. Paul recalled how, drawing himself up and flushing, Roy had called their English teacher, in his blue spotted bow-tie, a 'beastly man'— but 'Twit' Harris had only smiled urbanely, and said: 'When you are installed at Cambridge, Short, I look forward to being asked to tea, all the same.'

Everyone had roared, and Roy, turning theatrically on his heel in his well-cut suit, had stalked out, slamming the door.

'Beastly, horrible pig of a man!' He had become even more of a hero to the boys of the school for this.

And now—his unruliness had become undergraduate subversiveness. He told Paul about the meetings they held—banned by the proctors and refused permission by the Guildhall managers. All the dons, or most of them, were fools and fuddy-duddies: the Socialist Club put it over everyone, especially when their meetings were banned.

'So D. N. Pritt spoke out of the windows of Gibbs Building, and the audience stood on the lawn—a thousand of them. And those of us who were in the middle kicked great holes in the turf.'

'Whatever for?'

'Because they were beastly. All college dons are beastly. The university is the class enemy, part of a corrupt system, and *very beastly*.'

He prodded Paul again in the ribs.

'I see.'

'I'm sure you don't really see . . . yet,' said Short, pulling his fingers into an ecstasy of cracks and clicks.

'You didn't say much of this kind of thing at the discussion group.'

'No, well, you see . . .' said Roy Short, looking at him sideways with an odd expression. 'I'm a front man there. I have to establish confidence. It is hoped that the effects of this will be seen later.'

'You mean someone, some group, sends you there, to gain people's confidence?'

'That's right,' Short's eyebrows went up into an expression of sophisticated innocence. 'The CP.'

'The Communist Party?'

'Right! Ha! Ha!' cried Short, his nose high in the air.

'I'm sorry, I think that's bad.'

'Bad? Why?'

'Well, everyone is there . . . on trust, of some kind.'

'Old Frost's trust! Ha! Ha! He's a silly old fool, a milk and water ILP pacifist,' he went on before Paul could say anything.

'I like him.' Paul was getting annoyed. Yet he found himself always polite to Roy, and deferential, because the man had been his head boy. And there was something that appealed to him at a very deep level—in Short's subversiveness, his ironic hate, even his nihilistic destructiveness. But how could it be true that these people like Monck and Frost belonged to a culture and values that had to be overthrown? What would be left? Roy peered sharply into his face.

'Have you been to those discussions for a long while?'

'Only since the summer. Old Frost picked me up one day in the marketplace.'

'In his holey purple pullover! He's one of those maddening people who say they like the company of young people, but who really like picking holes in their arguments to put them down and triumph over them. But even his kind of political goody-goody religion is still the opium of the people.'

He arched his back on the sofa, stifling a yawn. 'It boosts his weedy sense of superiority to chip at people's arguments.'

'Do you really think so?'

'Oh, he's a *gauleiter*.'

'*He* thinks he's the soul of democracy.'

'But I liked some of the people there. Have you noticed a nice lanky girl with long auburn hair? I found her fascinating. Ha! Ha!'

'But why do you really go?'

'Secret!'

Roy had always liked to be secretive. Paul had already discovered this side to his character—clowning, mischievous, dangerously reckless, even delinquent, not least in his closest friendships. Yet he could be so charming and amusing that even those he had led into serious trouble forgave him. He peered closely again into Paul's face, lifting the lid of Monck's octavino virginals and letting it fall with a slam.

'Who is that girl, do you know?'

Roy gave him a sidelong glint through his spectacles. He projected the air of an experienced man-of-the-world to Paul, and Paul was profoundly convinced by it.

'Can you get me introduced to her?'

'I've no idea. I don't know anyone really except Frost himself.'

'Well, let's cultivate Frost, and then perhaps we can find out who she is.'

Paul was most disturbed by this calculating streak in Roy Short's nature. The man seemed always to need an ulterior motive for doing anything. If he took part in a play it was in order to get to know the leading lady or some girl in the cast. If he joined a club, it was a way of getting sports clothes or equipment at a reduced price. He was in the discussion group to put over some 'front' line, from ulterior motives decided by the Communist Party. But this duplicity also fascinated Paul in some strange way; he wanted very much to identify with Short, to grow into his sophistication; but he was troubled by the man's powerful egoism. He admitted it wasn't a brutal and insensitive egoism: indeed, it was often charming and amusing. It was like having a very selfish and yet lovable brother. But then, beyond the selfish motive, there was the continual suggestion in Roy's attitude to the world that there was an ultimate goal to which one must submit; there was a 'scientific' socialism which had established by evidence that there was a communistic society which was eventually to come into being. Everything might be sacrificed to this future: every relationship, every value. So between his own egoism and this unquestionable 'other' future to be brought into being by political action, Roy Short pursued a relentless nihilism. Paul could find no answer to this philosophy of life; yet he felt it was seriously wrong. But at the same time it touched a hidden chord in his nature: an impulse to give himself up to hate and to renounce every value and get what satisfaction he could out of a strange destructiveness, and even a kind of impulse to revenge. But whom was he taking revenge on?

At this moment, just as Paul Grimmer strove to formulate some objections to Short's nihilistic views, the little man returned. They heard the clack of the gate latch.

'Let's get him to give us parts in his next show,' whispered Roy.

Paul felt dismayed. In all his turmoil in recent months there had been one untroubled trusting relationship in his life—that with Moncklet. From his point of view, there could never be any question of exploiting the little producer: he was too innocent. Monck was sterling in his integrity as an artist. Paul almost laughed at his thoughts as the little elderly man came in clutching his paper bag of cakes. Innocent! He wondered what Monck would say if he knew what thoughts were in his mind? He meant, he protested to himself, Monck was disingenuous: he was good-hearted. He would never suppose that Roy Short was capable of being charming to him merely to get a part in a play. Or would he? The little man stumped rather angrily across to the kitchen.

'I think you might have made the tea.'

'Sorry, Moncklet,' said Paul. He felt guilty, having fallen under Short's spell so much as to forget the proper Crypt 'drill'. He jumped up and followed the little man, collecting cups and plates, knives and spoons, bustling, while Monck slipped the cakes onto plates out of the paper bag. The plate was a white one with china moulded into the shape of basketwork all round the edge, fragile and delicate. Paul loved these plates, which Monck had bought at a junk shop. 'Sixpence,' he would say jubilantly, as he produced them. 'Sixpence in Elm Hill. I think they're French.'

Monck was in the remotest scullery making the tea, the blue gas flames flickering on his sad clown's face. Paul carried in the two plates, one with a chocolate cake, one with round flaky Eccles cakes. Roy Short sat by the fire making himself a piece of toast with a long extending toasting fork.

'What silly plates,' he said.

'Why do you say that?' asked Paul, genuinely puzzled, but angry, too.

'All the crumbs will fall through the holes. And it is bad design to have one thing imitating another. They aren't basketwork: they're china.'

'Moncklet says they're French.'

'Ha! Ha! I expect they were made in Wigan.'

'That's scientific, too, I suppose,' said Paul.

'Roy would have everything modern,' said Moncklet, coming in with the teapot held high as he negotiated the step down through the door onto the living-room bricks. Despite his often protested deafness, he had heard more of the conversation than Paul or Roy had supposed. 'In my house, it would be ridiculous. I am modern enough to have gas, electricity, a fridge and a Hoover. But in everything else I am old-fashioned by choice. I do not have a radiogram or wireless, because people will have it on. Then I have to say: "Would you mind putting it off?" "Oh," they say, "don't you like music?" "I am sorry," I reply, "but I am a musician. I am musically trained, and I must listen, even though I don't choose to. So would you mind turning it off?" ' And he smiled with exaggerated sweetness, making dramatic gestures with his face and arms to act out the scene between himself and some portable radio hog.

Roy Short laughed. But Paul felt annoyed: it seemed to him that Short was laughing at the little man, even as he tried to impress him.

'What's your next show, Moncklet?' he asked.

'The Passion Play and then *Twelfth Night*.'

'Oh!' said Roy Short, clutching his foot, meaning that he had always wanted to act in that play.

Monck ignored the gesture, studying a piece of cake he was raising to his lips. Paul lifted the lid off the teapot, and stirred the tea, before pouring it out into the blue and white willow-patterned cups.

'I'm sorry . . . It's already cast,' said the little man. 'Barbara Gough will be a little weak as Viola, a little cold. But Benny will make a hilarious Malvolio and Bobbie is coming to play Olivia: she has such a lovely husky voice. I can't give you a part because they are all cast.'

'All rather in the family,' said Roy, cracking his fingers.

'You mean, all the old Norwich Players again?'

'I didn't say that,' said Roy. He was looking sulky. How insolent the man was. 'You haven't even a part for Paul here.'

He's trying to make trouble between us now, Paul thought.

'Sebastian was the only part—you've played it at school I think?' Paul nodded.

'We *might* give you half the week. But I have promised to give the part to an airman on leave—Richard Drake. He's a professional actor.'

'I don't mind in the least.'

'An old . . . friend?' asked Roy Short, looking coy.

Monck ignored him. Paul hated this cynical knowingness of Short's. He knew that, outside the house, Short would mock Monck for his homosexuality. Yet he pretended so demonstratively to be 'in the know'.

'Poor boy. He's incorrigibly one of "those", and his life is hell, he tells me, out at a dreary aerodrome at Coltishall. He's good: I *hope* he doesn't make Sebastian camp. He can just get leave to do it, and I shall have to keep him under control.'

'There's a great deal of ambivalence about gender in *Twelfth Night*,' said Paul and quoted:

> 'So comes it, lady, you have been mistook:
> But nature to her bias drew in that . . .
> You are betrothed both to a maid and man . . .'

' "Or what you will," ' said Monck, and began to sing, in his very bad cracked voice:

> 'When that I was and a little tiny boy
> With hey, ho, the wind and the rain,
> A foolish thing was but a toy . . .'

'Charles has written some lovely settings to the harpsichord. I shall need a great deal of help backstage, Paul, so I hope you'll forgive me for not giving you a part.'

'I tell you what I *would* like.'

'What's that, ducky? By the way, I must buy you some china before you go up to Cambridge,' he added, emptying the cups for a second pouring.

'No, no. That's very kind of you. No, I mean, I'd like to come and stay here, while I work with you on *Twelfth Night*. It's just ... well ...'

'Life at home has become intolerable? Well, of *course*: I'd be delighted. You're capable of working *quite* hard!', he chuckled crumbily.

'What a compliment!'

There was a bit of a sneer in Roy's voice. Short was jealous, and Paul found he was pleased. He watched him cracking his fingers with some glee, putting his willow-pattern plate down to do it, and fussing with his turn-ups. He realised he was asserting his loyalty to the little man, his full endorsement of the man's life and art, never mind his homosexuality; and Short could go to hell, with his politics and his advice on how to undress in front of a woman.

And his scrounging around for parts. Paul scoffed at him inwardly, from the deep sense of having begun by sweeping up the bus tickets, graduating to a minor apostle in the Mystery Play, and now to the full role (he mocked himself inwardly) of harpsichord shifter.

When Short was gone, Monck said: 'He'll never marry.'

'He's not a "once always" is he?' Paul asked with surprise.

'No, just selfish. He's a confirmed bachelor at twenty. And I don't like his politics.'

'He certainly doesn't like yours,' said Paul, carrying out the dirty china to the sink.

11

They did cultivate Frost, but instead of finding out about the red-haired girl for Roy Short, they were invited to read the lessons at a nine-carol and lesson service out at the radical clergyman's church at Booton.

They had to bicycle there because there were no buses on Sundays. It had snowed a little and the roads were icy. Paul called at Roy's house in good time, but the man was still lingering over his breakfast, munching toast and drinking coffee, while his stocky little red-faced mother waited on him. Paul was braced for the fifteen-mile cycle ride and clad in overcoat and knitted scarf; invited in, he sat on the edge of the sofa, restless and anxious to be gone. Roy peered at his Sunday newspaper and cracked his fingers, eating his marmalade and toast delicately, and munching it even more slowly, the more agitated Paul grew.

'The roads might be bad out towards Aylsham,' he urged. 'I think they had more snow in the north.'

'Don't fuss,' said Roy, wiping his lips with a white napkin, and holding out his cup for more coffee.

How his mother stands there and waits on him, thought Paul. What a firstborn lord he is! Paul was an only child, and was often teased for it. But Roy, who had a younger brother, was a Grand Cham at home compared with me, Paul thought. At last, Roy got up from the table and he searched for his things, his mother fussing like a valet.

'Why can't that old parson come and fetch you boys?' she asked in her Norfolk voice. 'If he want his lessons read, he orter put himself out a bit more. Are you goin' to wear thoose today, Roy?'

Roy was going through a row of eight pairs of shoes and boots in a cupboard in a corner of the hall. Paul looked over his shoulder astonished: he never had more than one pair. But Roy had shelves of hats and belts, two overcoats, three raincoats and an umbrella.

At last, when Paul felt he must be ready, Roy 'must go upstairs again' to find some waterproof leggings to put over his trouser legs: these took ages to fit on.

'Woon't they get in your bike chain?' his mother kept asking, her voice rising in the Norfolk way.

'Oh, stop fussing!' said Roy, and Paul was surprised by the intense anger in his voice. They seemed to be locked in a strange struggle, the mother exerting her power over the boy like an over-attentive maid, while the son both relished her interference, basking in being a served lord, and yet resented it bitterly. So it took nearly an hour to get Roy out on his cycle, ready to ride out to the village fifteen miles away. The last struggle was over a packet of sandwiches for lunch. Paul heard her say, in a fierce whisper: 'Don't give *him* any!' And yet she was always very generous to Paul, who had had several enormous teas at her house. It was simply that she must, in some way, control her son.

They set off along the Newmarket Road under the great trees lining its wide thoroughfare of houses belonging to surgeons and lawyers, to the new roundabout where the Ring Road began. This road took them past Paul's home again, past the city cemetery, and down the hill to the Wensum past Harry Pointer's yard where lorries and trucks were parked in rows behind fences. At Mile Cross they turned left and took the Aylesham Road, forking left at Hellesdon, taking the Reepham Road through Attlebridge.

As they climbed the hill at Mile Cross, Paul felt exhausted already. The long roads of ribbon development, of ugly little semi-detached houses with their shabby comic faces and no proportion or form, seemed to extend for ever. It was ten o'clock already, and they were late. Roy was a strong cyclist, but he still seemed to be hanging back, as if the time didn't matter.

'Silly old Frost,' he said. 'He'll have to wait.'

'But it's an eleven o'clock *service*,' said Paul. 'He can't wait: there's all the people turning up and waiting for the thing to begin.'

Fortunately, after that hill the roads were level, and the flat open country flew past flecked with patches of snow. Towards Felthorpe there were woods which looked beautiful with snow on the branches, and with the white trunks of the birches. The sun came out, and the scene looked very Christmassy. Paul's mood thawed, though his legs felt tired and his bottom felt sore. The snow was gilded by the pale morning sun, and blue in the shadows. The fir trees were dark and mysterious, like trees in a European forest.

Roy, sensing that Paul was angry with him, and enjoying it, began to sing carols loudly, riding his bicycle no hands.

'I wonder what carols silly old Frost will have ? I bet he has all the most commonplace rubbish like "Good King Wenceslas" and so on.'

'Parsons have to. They have to have what their congregation like.'

'But him with all his culture nonsense—he could do something out of the ordinary, but I bet he doesn't.'

Paul was wondering, in the clear frosty air as he rode through the lovely woods, why he went about with this man. There was some strange attraction: Roy seemed to be able to attract people to him, even when he despised them. He seemed to be always so critical of others, so contemptuous of adults, and talked of them as if his sole reason for entering their world was to expose them as shams, or to make them uncomfortable.

They talked a bit about Moncklet. Roy was now openly jealous of Paul's connections with Monck and the theatre. Roy rather fancied himself as an actor, but he was too plump and middle-aged in stature for the young heroic parts which he fancied. He was handsome in his full-faced way and his big teeth; but his manner, and the way he pulled at his big hands, suited better for a part as an elder statesman—Warwick or York or Montague, rather than Mercutio or Hamlet. Because this was how Monck cast him, he had never forgiven him for being a mirror to his own tendency to plumpness and pomposity. So Paul was amazed at the man's awkwardness in the little director's presence.

Moreover, he had detected in Roy a strange fear of being homosexual, or of being thought homosexual because of his rather histrionic manner. Yet Roy's mannerisms, like the way he pulled at his fingers, were often very feminine, as was his continual obsession with his clothes and his desire to appear well-mannered and polite, even though he was seething with disdain. Paul noticed that he always dressed smartly when he called at Monck's, and tried to impress him, whereas he himself was happiest there, and at the theatre, in old pullovers and paint-stained corduroys.

'Do you think Frost is a homosexual ?' Roy asked him.

'He's got five kids,' said Paul, laughing, 'and adopted another half-dozen.'

'No, he took them over from a brother, who was killed. The wife was killed, too, in a car smash I think.'

'Well, I'm sure he's normal.'

'Monck is a homosexual.'

'Of course. He tells everyone. But he doesn't "practise".'

'That's what he *says*. I bet he does if he gets the chance.' Short gave a strange prudish pout.

'I believe him,' said Paul.

'You're so naïve. I can't think how you can stay there.'

'At Ninham's Court? Why ever not?'

'Well, people will *talk* about you,' said Short darkly.

'You're worse than my parents. They don't fuss. My mum said something once about "funny men", but that's all. I like working with Monck and being in his house, meeting all those people, and I like his gossip, so "Mer!" to everyone!'

'I bet he's spiteful about a lot of people.'

'He's caustic rather than spiteful—people amuse him, like characters in plays.'

'I bet he says beastly things about me.'

'I can't remember—oh, yes. We were discussing various people and marriage after we'd had cake with him last week. We talked about you, and he said: "Oh, he'll *never* marry!" '

'Blast him then,' said Roy, really very angry, his bicycle all over the road, wobbling.

'Well,' said Paul, without thinking, 'I think he thought you would become a comfortable bachelor.'

'Damn and blast him, then,' said Roy. 'You see what I mean. That's the most spiteful thing you can say about anyone.'

'I suppose he meant you were selfish,' said Paul, thinking of the fuss over Roy's breakfast.

'Oh, go to hell!' said Roy, riding ahead with majestic disdain.

Two twin Victorian Gothic towers of Booton church now appeared above the trees, and Paul was relieved. It was only half past ten, and they would be in good time. They were pretty, slender towers with fine carved stone decoration and the snow-flecked landscape enhanced them. St Michael's church was built at the end of the nineteenth century by the Reverend Whitwell Elvin,

Frost had told him, an editor of the *Quarterly Review* and rector at Booton for fifty years.

As the church appeared, Paul looped round it the thread of his lifeline, which he often latched around such signposts, despite his lack of belief. He felt muddled and confused by his jangled relationship with Roy that morning. The man had been so maddening; and now he had made it worse by giving away his conversation with Moncklet about Short, and had perhaps set Roy against the little man and even done harm to the theatre. So he detached himself and curled his attention round the two pretty stone towers, rather fretwork in their effect against the winter sky heavy with snow.

The unreliability of people seemed to him the worst thing of all. Some things belonged to the endurable, the reliable: music, books, the theatre; the spinets, the seascapes in the museum, the mediaeval church towers, the lovely woods in snow. Around all these he wove a web, a structure, on which he could rely. There was himself, and the world to which he responded—the world of meaning and beauty. He often wished, as on this trip, that he was alone in untroubled relationship with the world of the Reepham Woods, the cold winter sunlight and the frozen road covered with glassy, compressed snow.

People, by contrast, betrayed you: or you betrayed them. He didn't think Moncklet would ever let him down, but he now grew suspicious of everyone, and Roy's warning about people talking had worried him. He wanted to be himself. When he heard a symphony or went to a play, he felt he was coming more to know himself reflected in it. He felt now he knew himself, at least, in relation to the tall slender towers created by the editor of a great nineteenth-century review: and he attached himself to them.

But as he and Roy bicycled down the lane towards the handsome church, he couldn't feel right being with Roy, or coming to read the lessons for the eccentric Frost. Yet, as he rested his bicycle behind the wall of the churchyard in the wan winter sunlight, his boyish impulse to enjoy every possibility that offered itself took over, and he and Roy were in the best of spirits as old Frost, in a huge black surplice, its hem touching the snow, warmly greeted them.

'Ah—you got here! Well done!'

He gave a big man's chuckle, the stripey creases along his face giving off benignity. And whereas in Norwich, in his discussion group, Frost gave off an air of superiority, knocking the ground from beneath the feet of the young and laughing at them in his teasing way, here he was nervous. He behaved as if he was being inspected and dreaded criticism, explaining everything to the young men.

'Well, as you see, it was built by an eccentric,' he said, apologetically, glinting his spectacles and shifting about in his robe. 'But it's quite nice really.'

'The towers are beautiful,' said Paul. 'You can see them miles away, sticking up over the trees.'

'Of course,' Frost muttered confidentially. 'Yes. Our flock are mostly peasants, and deaf old ladies. A few Conservative county people. Never mind!'

He looked crafty and grinned.

'You must speak up. Slow and clear. I'll put you in the front pew on each side and then it will be Box and Cox, through the nine lessons. I've written a list for you on the lectern. And then I can give all my attention to the choir and organist. No sermon!' he grinned. 'Think of that! Blessed relief for everybody.'

'We have a bit of smoke now and then,' he whispered. 'I like it a bit High.'

All their criticisms of the clergyman, the church, the arrangements for the service and the quality of the music faded, now that the boys were confronted by the people of Booton in their church in the snow. The nave was simple and spacious, and its stone-work was beautiful in the winter sunlight, which emphasised the depth of the shadows. The choir was small, made up of children and young people, but sang well to the organ, which was in tune. So the Reverend Frost did attend to his professional affairs! It was clear from the way the people greeted him that they liked him. At last everyone was in place, and the clergyman was in his white robe.

Roy and Paul read the lessons alternately. The choir sang first 'All Christian Men Rejoice', and then 'In The Bleak Midwinter'. and then Paul was half-way through the lesson about Caesar Augustus decreeing that everyone should be taxed, when something appalling began to happen immediately before his eyes: just as the ritual began to move towards the transcendant, it broke down into a disgusting scene, and the hand of what seemed like death intruded dramatically, deeply disturbing his feelings.

In the front pew sat a family of country people, a rough-looking boy and girl in cheap overcoats whose lapels had curled with the damp; a sad-looking middle-aged woman with sandy hair, and an older man in a dark cloth cap, with a badly-shaven face. A little way apart from them sat a very fat woman, probably, Paul thought, the grandmother, with a thin brown tweed overcoat spread round her, and dark brown hair, very fuzzy and spread out. She was a very striking old lady, and she had already caught Paul's eye as he looked over the congregation before he read each lesson.

But as he read now, he could see this massive matriarchal figure move, in strange rhythmical movements, and heard groans.

'Ah! Oo-oo-er!' she said, and huge convulsions heaved through her body as if she were suffering prodigious riftings.

Paul couldn't decide whether to go on reading, or to stop. He paused, and suddenly the old woman turned her eyes right up into her head, so that only the white could be seen, except for a tiny sliver of the pupil under the top lid. And then her face, instead of turning white or black, turned a dark brown colour, and she slid horribly down onto the pew.

The clergyman, Roy and Paul rushed to her aid. The family stood back, the children bursting into tears, and the middle-aged woman calling out: 'Oh my God! She've had one o' them tarns o' hers. She had one before week afore last, oh my God what a trouble!'—keeping this up as an incessant mumble while the dark-jowled man comforted her.

But the strangest thing was the involuntary convulsions of the huge, bulging body of the old woman on the pew. Though her eyes were closed, she seemed to be conscious, and she called out and grunted: 'Oh I am. Ugh! Oh I am! Oh I have! Ugh! Ooer! Oh I am!'—and as she did so, she humped herself along the bench, heaving herself along with her fat hams and her great thighs, until she reached the end of the pew ten feet away, whereupon she pushed herself backwards by the same method, to the other end, while the great black priest and the two boys pushed and shoved, to keep her from falling on the floor, while the rest of the congregation murmured and gave little gasps of anxiety, calling out: 'Pore old thing!'

'Oh I am! Ugh! Oo-er! Oh I am!'

At last, the travelling body reached one end of the pew and the white-robed clergyman lifted her top half by an enormous effort into an upright posture, against the solid oak back.

'We ought to try to get you outside in the fresh air, you know, mother,' he said kindly.

Surprisingly, the huge old woman rose swaying to her feet, whereupon the boys, waved in by the clergyman, pushed themselves in under her arms. So, ponderously, they heaved her along, as the clergyman ran out to telephone for a doctor and an ambulance from his home. Every now and then, the big figure paused, leaning heavily on the boys' shoulders.

'Oh I am! Oh I did!'

They couldn't make out whether she was convulsed with pain, or had simply lost control of her limbs. The great body had simply become a horrible mass of limbs and guts, afflicted in some dreadful way, no longer aware of appearance or forms or indeed any reality outside the physical catastrophe.

'Ugh!' she cried, as they reached the porch, which seemed to take an age. The boys didn't know what to do with her. But then two men produced a big canvas stretcher from an air raid post, and they were carrying it through the gate into the churchyard. Suddenly the body was seized by a most awful earthquake within, and horrible sounds rose from her throat. A stream of hot, dark red blood suddenly shot out of her brown face, splashing over the dark green laurels, the gravestones, and the snowy grass. It was terrible, to be almost beneath this smoking fountain of vomited blood, and the boys nearly fainted. Then the great body, collapsing, was eased by many hands onto the stretcher, and the bloodstained figure was covered with a blanket. Apart from one or two tiny spots on their shoes, the young men were not splashed, and they went back with relief into the church.

Frost rose well to the occasion. It was clear from his white face that he was frightened and upset, but he put on a fatherly smile and displayed the lines round his jaws, glinting at the congregation, and called: 'Let us pray!' He used prayers for the sick, and so gave his flock a chance to compose themselves, and helped push the event into the universal plane. At the end of the prayers he said, quietly: 'It always seems worse than it really is.' He made a signal to Paul, who began again the lesson he had left off. Outside they heard the noise of an ambulance driving off, and the clank of a bucket as the sexton cleaned up.

But the rest of the service went on in a chastened atmosphere, everyone having been thoroughly frightened and alarmed. The choir was a little flat with nerves, and the congregation were not even reassured by the final magnificent passage about the light of the world. Old Mrs Potterton wouldn't die for another ten years. But the convulsed impulse of her body to burst, all among the village gathered there, had brought the shadow of death into everyone's Sunday: certainly, it undercut the great meaning of Christmas.

Nancy Frost, a jovial but harassed woman, served up the Sunday dinner, a huge Irish stew and rather gritty baked potatoes, to Roy and Paul, her husband and the ten children.

Frost reverted to his political self and threw out barbed and provocative remarks over the restless mass of little Frosts scooping their gravy and potatoes into their mouths with spoons and inverted forks. It was a big, untidy room with a characteristic vicarage mess of tennis rackets, pamphlets, an old brown wooden radio and frayed armchairs in dull colours, the *New Statesman* evident everywhere, in various stages of yellow decay.

'I bet she doesn't have much of a life,' said Roy, sceptically, as they rode home through the slush and gathering dark.

'It must be difficult for her to be a free-thinking radical, with two broods to bring up. He was nice to his congregation, though,' Paul added, reflectively. 'Especially when that old woman had a seizure. Surely she'll die?'

The shock of it hit them in the dark road. So they began to act clownishly. Paul skidded and fell, gasping as he picked himself out of the wet ridges of snow.

'Ow!' he cried.

'Oh I am!' cried Roy. 'Don't *you* start. Oh I am! Oh I have!'

He roared with laughter, helping Paul pull his bicycle up and straighten it. His own slithered about.

'It's freezing!' he said. 'We'll never get home. Oh, I am! Oh, I have! Ugh-arggh!'

He rode ha-ha-ha-ing off as Paul followed him, wet snow sliding down his neck and his feet as cold as stones, with a strange dread in his heart. Short took his sandwiches home.

That experience alone did much to make him feel that, after all, the world was meaningless. Roy Short, who was an aggressive materialist, rubbed it in, urging him to believe that everything, not least he himself, came into being by chance. Paul could not argue against this view, for he felt that he learned this from chemistry and physics. Short seized the opportunity to persuade him towards nihilism. A new orthodoxy took over now his belief had failed—the metaphysics of chemical and physical laws, and the Final Cause of Ultimate Entropy, of everything seeking equilibrium in death. Everything was no more than little particles and forces bumping into other particles and forces, a temporary flow of energy. He forgot himself, a complex autonomous creature seeking the meaning of his existence. He forgot that all living creatures strive, and succeed or fail; by contrast with physical phenomena even thunderstorms, which do not strive, do not try to use their world, and cannot be said to succeed or fail. And he forgot man's moral dimension, even the dimension of being. At the theatre, it was the moral and imaginative dimensions that seemed most real; but he couldn't sustain his faith in these meanings against physics, mortality, and Roy Short.

At times, since the awful nightmare he had experienced in flu, he felt overwhelmed with meaninglessness, the ugliness and formlessness of his home, the drudgery of examination work, the astonishing perplexities of sex. What was real in the world? He wrote one or two poems, but he could feel no conviction in his own creativity: it was like making sandcastles as a child—the stormy waves of matter in motion would sweep them all away.

Yet in Monck's house and at the Maddermarket he met individuals to whom the search for meaning was not mere sandcastle play, to be swept away by some inescapable recognition of the brutal nature of the universe. Meaning was the major preoccupation of their lives. It was this that sustained them, night after night, even through the air raids, the darkness, the shortages; a recognition that man could not live without meaning, and that human beings could create meaning by the exercise of their own powers. He learned there that meaning can be very real indeed—and is so because it is a creation of persons, of persons in relation, and they, in turn, are the creation of the same processes which made the stars, the stones, the trees and air. Meaning, such as men and women strove for by their consciousness in the little theatre, was itself a product of matter, and so—how could matter be meaningless? There was no one with whom he could argue these inward perplexities.

Yet there was no attempt in the theatre ever to pretend that the art was 'real', in the cinematic way. They were content to live with the striving imagination. In *A Midsummer Night's Dream* the fairies wore Elizabethan costume, as they would have done in the wooden 'O' in 1596, while the fixed nature of the 'Elizabethan' stage prevented the scenes from ever being fully realistic. Rather, the dimension of the moment was transformed by poetry. The audience would file in and seat itself in the rows of tip-up seats before a drawn curtain. The little man would be fussing, and behind the scenes there would be a pungent smell of spirit gum and Leichner, mingled with the fumes of coffee. Then, at last, Moncklet would beat a gong. The gong was an important focus of the ritual. He would beat it wildly for half a minute. Then there would be three transforming, magical strokes.

One would extinguish the house lights.

The second would switch on the coloured floods.

The third would spring off the actors, who would pull aside the curtains and begin speaking at once.

> 'Behold it is naught, all that we do!
> In all our matters we profit naught . . .'

So spoke Annas, at the opening of the *Norwich Passion Play*, in which Paul Grimmer had his first speaking part. It was Moncklet's own version of the Passion Play from the *Ludus Coventriae*. At that time it was most revolutionary to present a live actor as Jesus Christ on the stage: indeed, it was illegal. Monck had been arrested earlier in the century for putting on a mediaeval mystery play with Christ on the stage. To get round the law he had to form a club to which everyone in the audiences had to belong before they could see the play.

Christ was played by the local headmaster, Benny, very bony and tall. He had a presence that was compelling and somehow terribly sad. For Benny it was a transforming experience in his life to play Christ. And yet rehearsals were sometimes almost blasphemous.

'CHRIST *moves apart and kneels*,' called Monck at the first rehearsal. 'THE DISCIPLES *sleep*. No, please, don't arrange yourselves so symmetrically like a boy scout group photograph. Remember, I am trying to present every scene like a Renaissance painting. Disciples! Look through Michelangelo and Italian paintings in those Phaidon books, and study the ways in which the disciples stand, sit and lie. Now Benny, come right to front of the stage.'

The actor's legs were bare: he wore a rough cloak.

> 'O Father! O Father! for my sake
> This great passion thou take from me,
> Which is ordained . . .'

'Oh, Christ, Moncklet, Barbara has left some bloody great nails on this stage!'

He nursed his knee, which was bleeding.

'Barbara!' Monck called in a high and greatly admonitory voice.

'Hallo!' called a voice from the recesses of a huge canvas and batten 'rock'.

'We must have the stage swept carefully every night. It's an occupational hazard, with so many bare feet and so much kneeling.'

'No old iron in the Garden of Gethsemane,' said the designer, disappearing again into her rock. 'OK, Moncklet.'

But even at rehearsals, the simple directness of the language and the poetic concentration of meaning caught them all up though they were in their day clothes (for the costumes for the Apostles were not yet ready). The episode which moved Paul most was Mary Magdalen's presentation to Christ of a box of ointment:

> 'I worship thee on knees bare.
> Blessed be the time that I thee sought,
> And this ointment that I hither brought,
> For now my heart is cleansed from thought
> That just was cumbered with care.'

The woman had a high, rather trembling voice, and was dressed in a fine woollen cloak with bare arms. She broke the box at Christ's feet. Judas stepped forward.

'Lord, me thinks thou dost right ill
To let this ointment so spill,
To sell it were more skill,
And buy meat to poor men . . .'

In a deep voice, Christ replied to him:

'Poor men shall abide
And I pass forth in a tide . . .'

At this moment, Paul noticed, Monck's eyes filled with tears. And then Christ went on to speak of treachery.

'One of you here sitting my treason shall trace . . .'

Paul, who was Matthew, knew this as a distance signal for his own two lines:

'Alas! My dear Lord, what man is so wood
For gold or for silver himself so to spill?'

As he said them for the first time, he was surprised by the tautness in his throat, the blood pounding in his head, his feeling of being throttled. But then, as the rehearsals went on and they came to wear costumes, he became less and less preoccupied with himself, and more and more absorbed into the play itself: indeed, one might say, with the events themselves. The bright light began to feel like the sun in Israel, and the performances of the leading players began to convince him as much as they would the audience. The woman who was Mary had a deep, passionate voice, as she exclaimed:

'On all mankind now have thou pity,
And think on thy mother that heavy woman.'

The scene in which Christ washes his Apostles' feet took on the ritualistic feeling it must have had for the mediaeval peasant, while the crucifixion itself was always appalling, especially when Christ called:

'Heloi, Heloi, lama sabacthana !
My Father in Heaven on high
Why dost thou me forsake?
The frailty of my mankind
Dear Father, have me in mind
And let death sorrow slake . . .'

How could God not be mindful at that moment? From entering into the happenings on Golgotha and Gethsemane, Paul arrived at many perplexing theological questions which the simple mediaeval text did not solve. But just as he pondered gravely on such matters, Benny would call, angrily, interrupting the little man.

'Moncklet, do you think you can fuss about the position of the centurions when I'm off the cross? I've only got this little bicycle saddle to sit on, and I'm really suspended on an optical illusion.'

'I'm sorry, Benny—yes, let's run quickly through the crucifixion, for Benny's sake.'

'It *is* crucifixion, I can tell you!' said the good-natured Benny.

So it was continually in and out of fantasy, until the first night, with the thrilling noise of the gong. Waiting in the little space between the Green Room and the stage, as the opening scene began, Paul watched Moncklet prowling round to see everything was in order: often he came ambling along on his short legs with an anxious frown—'I can smell gas!'—he had a dread of the new gas heaters blowing up. But tonight everything had gone with a particularly solemn efficiency. People rose above their mere roles.

Paul forgot his second line: the lights and the sea of faces made such a roaring in his head that he could only remember:

'Alas! My dear Lord, what man is so wood?'

—and there was a long pause until Bartholomy said:

'He that thee doth sell for gold and for other good
With his great covetousness himself he doth kill.'

What would the press think? Monck had abolished the interval for this religious play, because it seemed outrageous to have coffee and biscuits in the middle of the Gospel story. 'And where,' he said comically, 'would one have refreshments? After the veil of the temple was rent in twain?'

'But,' he went on, 'sometimes I make as much out of the coffee as I do from the tickets . . . I do hope it's *packed*, this play. I'm staking everything on this thriller!'

The testing moment was the death of Christ.

> 'In manas tuas Domine
> Holy Father in Heavenly see
> I commend my spirit unto thee
> Nunc consummatum est.'
> [*Thunder: all kneel except* CENTURION]

Monck himself shook the thunder-sheet: the auditorium was plunged into darkness for a few seconds. When Mary spoke, there were sobs, and many in the audience were weeping as Paul could see through the crack in the door of the little music room where he stood.

> 'Ah Lord God, I thee pray
> When my child rise at the third day . . .'

Then the centurion declared:

> '*Quod vere filius Dei erat iste* . . .
> The very child of God I suppose that to be . . .'

Blasphemy! thought Paul, deeply stirred within himself. If only it were true! Trying to control himself, he thought: It's the word 'child' that is so moving, and the simple, childish faith of the mediaeval playwright. Monck's translation, he thought, wasn't very good: its English was too archaic. Paul had read a bit of mediaeval drama already, and knew what liberties the little man had taken with the text. But the production had caught the spirit of the direct, poetic enactment of the mystery; and the mystery of it was taken by the hundred or so people in Monck's converted baking-powder factory.

And what did it matter, after being stirred by such drama, that he was irritated with his mother for urging him to wear his pullover, or with his father for refusing to change from the *Daily Express* to *The Times*? What did it matter that Annie was going away to Lowestoft with her family for three weeks, or that he couldn't keep up with his quota of four pages of Virgil that week?

He had actually felt for one moment, as if it might have been possible for Christ to outwit Pontius Pilate and the Romans, as he outwitted Satan. And then, he thought: What would have happened to Europe over the last two thousand years, if Christ had not died as he did?

'I'm really an atheist—or, rather, I suppose, an agnostic. To me, Christ was a man,' said Monck.

'If only it was all true,' said Paul.

'If only it *were*! But how can anyone today believe in the resurrection of the body?'

' "Quick and breathing of flesh and fell",' Paul quoted from the play.

'All I hope,' said Moncklet, as he bent down to get the key from under the mat and turned it in the door of the Crypt, 'if mine is resurrected, I hope my rheumatism won't be resurrected with it.'

13

His increasing enjoyment of Moncklet's world modified Paul Grimmer's more nihilistic tendencies. The Crypt was the one place where he felt transported into a sphere in which meaning was primary. Of course it began to fade after the show, after the party on the stage at the end of the show, when everyone had washed off their greasepaint and gone home, and he and the little man were left eating their stew and bread by the dying fire. Now the precariousness of meaning would be disturbingly evident. At such times the little old man's face would look sunken and lined, and his facial gestures would seem tired and strained. Sometimes he would even snap at Paul, almost always apologising afterwards, saying he was weary. At such moments he would say: 'When I die . . .' or 'when I am gone . . .' and relate his art to these premonitions, recognising with a sad sweep of an ugly hand extended at the shadows that he would leave little or nothing behind him. They always carried away this feeling, after switching off the lights in the theatre, when everyone had gone home.

'But somewhere one can always find a gesture towards meaning,' he said. 'Outside, the bombs fall and the politicians talk, and in that public world everything destroys meaning.'

'I often feel that, during a raid,' said Paul. 'Our little home seems likely to be swept away, and us with it, and I wonder what would be left.'

'Of course, one's home and one's parents are important.'

There had been no breach with his parents because Paul had gone to live at the Crypt. His parents understood that he was fascinated by that literary world of the theatre: they themselves often attended the plays. They were glad for him, and his mother even brought him eggs and odd jars of her marmalade, which Moncklet, receiving with a gracious smile, pronounced the best he had ever tasted.

'And your parents are so *kind*. But then one grasps out, at your age . . . towards . . . towards something that is larger than life . . .'

'What a pity,' he went on, fetching a book on Canaletto and his school, 'that you can't get to Venice . . . Ah, Venice! I hope it won't be destroyed.'

'It looks magnificent,' said Paul, unable to believe, on this war-time night in a Norwich February, that such a place could still exist.

'And *very* theatrical. It's a complete façade, and little or nothing behind it, behind the splendid fronts of the palaces. The Ca' d'Oro! But it's always been like that: a place for masked balls. And yet you can feel there all the searching, searching for God, for love, for the riches of the East, for meaning . . .'

'I wonder if I will ever go there,' Paul sighed.

'I can tell you where you *can* go . . . Let us go sometime,' said the little man. 'There are still buses. Audley End House, in Essex, not far from Cambridge. There is this huge palace—it was once a palace of kings, as huge as anything in Europe. It has been drasti-cally reduced. But it's still a big, rather vulgar palace, rather a demonstration of power and riches . . .'

'Conspicuous waste,' prompted Paul, fresh from Veblen.

'And there's an Adam Room, with an alcove in which there's a couch, all ready for stylised seductions. But the decoration: so much decoration, so many patterns; it's really too much. And as for seduction—nowhere could be more public! How could anyone be seduced in an alcove in an Adam Room? They'd be *too* much on their formal behaviour.'

'I can never understand how Vronsky could seduce Anna Karenina on that couch. Love will find a way, I suppose.'

'But . . .' The little man had obviously lost his point.

'Meaning,' said Paul.

'Oh, yes . . . the most *meaningful* moment in the whole place at Audley End is Vanbrugh's stone façade in the Great Hall. The playwright and architect; there's this great hall, all carved caryatids and figures. But at one end there's a grand staircase—and a façade like the theatre, in stone. Somehow, it draws the whole thing together and suggests all one's life is entrances and exits. "All the men and women merely players . . ." Mind you, Venice does that too, only your exits and entrances are made there by water . . . You can go to La Fenice Theatre by gondola!'

There were tears in Moncklet's eyes again, as he wondered if he would ever see Venice, or for that matter Audley End House, again.

The world he unfolded so feelingly to Paul was far more influential on the young man's attitudes than Roy Short's politics. Moreover, it went with a way of life: Monck taught Paul Grimmer some of the pleasures of civilised middle-class life—the pleasures of bathing every morning, for example. Paul learned to say: 'Have you had your bath?' He experienced the delight of sitting around at breakfast in a dressing-gown, in front of a gas fire if it was chilly—the pleasures of food prepared with a real interest, and served with its own setting and drama. Monck lived with great intensity, and drew this out in those who stayed in his house.

Whether it was true or not, the little man declared he had grown up in the slums; his mother was strict and aristocratic; his lineage (he said) going back to General Monck, who went to Ireland with Cromwell. His father was the Reverend George Gustavus Monck and his mother Hester Isabella Nugent, an Irish woman of wit and strong character. He spent his early life in the slums of Liverpool. He had begun life as a poor actor and became stage manager for William Poel. He even hinted at having been a male prostitute. Allowing for all this to have been embroidered on the basis of the hundreds of plays he had read and produced, and filtered through a vivid and self-dramatising imagination, there seemed a great deal of truth in it: certainly, it was clear that Moncklet had suffered. And this suffering gave him sympathetic insights into the torments of adolescence. His house was always full of young people, men and women, and he played a special part in their breaking away from home, helping the process to be a benign one rather than a conflict. And, of course, he was always looking for talent for his plays, as well as sweepers.

Strangely, what young people liked him for most was his old-fashioned standards: Yeats and Synge had both visited his theatre, and Monck himself was half-Irish. (When W. B. Yeats and the critic of the *Morning Post* visited Monck in 1911 they found themselves persuaded into tying the ticket numbers on the seats.) But he aspired to be 'well-bred' too, in his tastes and manner of life—though he had been and always was a pauper. Recently, he sold some of his silver to pay for the repairs of his roof; and when he came to die, he said, he would leave nothing. 'There's nothing to leave!' His life was given over entirely to his art, which vanished into air as soon as the lights went out at the end of the week's performance. The silver pen-tray on his desk, his shelves of editions of Shakespeare by distinguished presses, the virginals and spinets, the copies of drama journals—all these, Paul came to see, were both a stage set, and not a stage set. They all belonged to the theatre. The very furniture would, from time to time, disappear on a barrow, be trundled down St Giles's, and be put on the stage for a play: the musical instruments were always 'down at the theatre', or on loan to the Castle Museum for concerts. Similarly with the people: they were always coming and going in some drama —and this too was a mode of existence dear to Moncklet's heart.

He tended not to become involved himself: he only produced, and he applied this to life. The most negative element in his production of life-situations was his envy of women, which manifested itself sometimes in a bitchy hatred. But even then he could be kind, not least to the most unstable women—those who were both profligate and suffering. His ideal woman was Mary Magdalene, and the woman he most admired, Bobbie, was the illegitimate daughter of a great and promiscuous painter, who herself seemed to have spent her life seeking love, finding however nothing but an endless series of searingly broken affairs. She was an actress; and a mocking, ironic, self-protectiveness seemed to bind them together. Paul met her later that month one day at Ninham's Court, at breakfast. She had come to play Olivia. People often came down from the professional theatre to work for Monck free, for the experience. Monck waved his hands, introducing them.

'I've told Paul he's safe with me,' said the little man, his mouth full of toast.

'It's true you've never tried to seduce *me*, Moncklet,' she said, in a deep, husky voice, laughing.

He fluttered his eye-lashes like a woman, for Bobbie's benefit. What struck Paul was that they were so astonishingly alike, even to the expressive eyebrows. The three were sitting having breakfast in the small timbered room to the left of the scrubbed wooden staircase as you entered the house facing the courtyard garden. In the breakfast-room was a big old gas fire that popped and banged when it was lit, but gave out a fierce heat from its pink and cream-coloured honeycombs of fire-clay. Monck was still in his blue and white Marks and Spencer pyjamas and a black and white rayon dressing-down. Bobbie wore an old threadbare, red flannel dressing-gown over a pink nightdress. Paul had on his brown tweed overcoat over his pyjamas: he didn't have a dressing-gown. On the small oak gate-leg table was a big butler's tray containing green and white porcelain cups, a brown jug of coffee, toast in a white china rack, some of his mother's marmalade and butter in a white china dish shaped like an oyster shell.

'International Stores sell the cheapest butter,' declared Monck, 'and I shall have to look for some cheaper bacon, the way this boy scoffs it! Have some more coffee: I can always make some more. It's only half a crown a pound at Dakin's.'

'I'll put the kettle on.' Already, Paul was now so house trained that he made all the beds with Monck and did the shopping; Paul had been out to buy the coffee beans the day before at Dakin's shop in Davey Place off Gentleman's Walk where the wheels of a coffee-roasting machine spun in the window and blue fragrant smoke filled the air.

'At home, they leave everything to mother. And they become so *lazy*.'

He spat out the word: the worst offence in Ninham's Court was to be lazy.

'*I* am lazy,' he declared, 'and so I have to discipline myself. I will not *allow* myself to be lazy. So no one in my house is allowed to be lazy. Except Maudie—and she is beyond hope.'

'Maudie' was his cousin, an eccentric old lady of seventy, who visited him from time to time. She had lived in a little house in Fiesole with a 'maid' of sixty-eight, before the war, but was now camping out in Ireland.

But in reward for being trained not to be lazy, the adolescent in Monck's house was treated as an equal. Those at breakfast were joined at that moment by Elsa, a distinguished older woman, a musician who was arranging some Elizabethan songs for the theatre. She was staying too, and the women occupied the beds in the attic room.

Monck rose to his feet and Paul followed suit. This, too, was new to him, to rise to his feet when a woman came in.

'Do come and join us. I think we're decent.'

128

They rearranged themselves on the chairs and stools. The older woman was given the best chair by the fire. Her hair was grey, and her neck scrawny. Lace frothed at her neck and her dressing-gown was an embroidered scarlet silk one, with needlework flowers.

'What a marvellous dressing-gown, Elsa: I must borrow it for a show sometime.'

'I got it at a market stall in Paris. I think it must have come from Greece or Turkey.'

'This is Paul Grimmer. Did you meet him last night? He's helping me a bit as a secretary . . .'

'General labourer and housemaid,' said Paul with a grimace.

'That's always the price of being a friend of Moncklet's,' said Bobbie in her deep voice. 'I'm simply experiencing hotel luxury.'

The new guest was provided with toast and coffee. By now, the sunlight was thrusting its way into the little court, and there were a few rather timid snowdrops in the small scruffy beds outside the window among the cobbles. Paul felt a deep glow of satisfaction.

It was, he reflected, satisfaction of a kind he never felt at home. He knew he was experiencing sophisticated pleasures, impossible at home. He was deeply anxious about becoming a snob: but how could it be snobbish to join Moncklet's poor and simple household —working for his share as hard as he did? They didn't have 'conversation' at home, and everything was a muddle: moreover, one always fell into childish habits and family insouciance. That is, people didn't think of one another's welfare: life had sunk to a level at which members of the family didn't impinge on one another, that was all. They really just existed together. As he came to realise this Paul felt guilty: was he getting 'superior'? He found himself hating his home; and then hating himself for doing so. But if this was bourgeois life (as Short might put it), then he liked it better than whatever his home was. He liked it because of the middle-class civilities and rules that Monck taught him, simply because they all made life easier and more agreeable.

What appealed to him most about Ninham's Court was the ritual—the ritual that was, he realised, derived from a way of life celebrated in some of the plays and novels. Moncklet liked talking to his young men while in the bath, very largely because he needed help to get out now his joints were getting stiff, though no doubt there was some distant homosexual pleasure in it for the little old man, who looked so plain and pot-bellied naked. Either before or after the bath, they took breakfast and read the papers in the breakfast-room. And whereas at home one would hog a paper and lie about in everyone's way reading it, in Monck's house one did not read the newspaper while there was company to entertain and amuse—rather, one selected items *from* one's newspaper to discuss, in *conversation*.

Moncklet was continually drilling his young helpers in manners, like a governess. While Paul resented the 'rules' of civilised behaviour at first, he soon found how beneficial they were to everyone: they made it possible for instance for a callow boy like him to be treated like an adult. And this was the greatest joy, knowing how gormless he was within, how uncertain of himself, he could act a part at the Crypt and have his contribution received as an adult part. He had never before sat with a girl of nineteen and a woman of fifty, in their dressing-gowns. This simple experience itself was enough to give him a thrill. It thrilled him more when Elsa asked: 'Are you thinking of writing for the theatre?'

Paul was so startled he couldn't think of a reply at all. Monck came to the rescue. 'He can't even write a literate *postcard* yet. And he's got to do his university entrance Latin still. He has, however, I'm pleased to say, a distinction in English in Higher School Certificate, and an Exhibition to Pemning of forty pounds a year.'

'Oh, congratulations,' said the older woman, looking at him with generous curiosity.

'I don't think they teach you to write at school, at all,' said Bobbie.

'The only way to learn to *write*, I am sure,' said the little man, 'is by having to earn your bread and butter by it. Shakespeare simply had to produce a play by the end of the month. So he *had* to write a good one.'

'But Moncklet,' said Bobbie, 'not everyone who has a dateline turns out to be a Shakespeare.'

'No, it's hardly pressure that makes a writer!'

'Don't I know it,' said Monck sadly, with a melancholy gesture of the hand and forearm. 'I simply cannot write—I can't write at all,' he wailed. 'I can *talk* . . .'

'Your pageant play was a great success,' protested Paul.

'*That* I improvised, and Benny acted as an amanuensis and took it down. I can invent *ad . . . ad libitum . . .*' he had difficulty with the phrase and spat some toast crumbs onto the carpet. 'I can *ad lib*. But writing comes very hard to me. And now I'm getting vague— like Mrs Malaprop, too many allegories on the banks of the Nile . . .'

'I don't know what I'm going to do,' said Paul. 'But I love the theatre.'

'Don't let Moncklet disillusion you,' said Bobbie.

'*Work* never disillusioned anyone,' said Monck with emphasis. '*I* make people work: they must defer to the art. When people say they "love" the theatre—they don't mean what Paul means. I believe he has a genuine love. They want to be *artistique*: they want to posture and fool around and exhibit themselves. Especially the *women* . . .'

'You're going to get onto your hobby-horse, I can see, Moncklet,' said Bobbie huskily. 'But you can't indulge in a woman-hating session with two *artistique* women sitting at your fireside.'

'But you know what . . . I almost said *who* . . . I mean?'

'Oh, God, I hate 'em, too; don't tell *me*,' said Bobbie.

'Who does he mean?' Elsa was a bit doubtful. Did the little man think her only *artistique*?

'Do you remember *that woman*?' Monck asked Bobbie, 'About four shows back—what was it called?'

'*The Constant Wife*.'

'*The Constant Wife* . . . She wanted to "arct". Nothing I said, *nothing* . . .' He really bared his teeth. 'She would do *nothing* I asked her to do. It was only a minor part—but she would have ruined the show out of pure vanity wanting to draw attention to herself. A real *bitch*.'

Specks of spit sailed across a sun-beam.

'So what did you do?'

'I said that anyone, *anyone*, coming to my theatre to act must be prepared to submerge their own beastly egos into the part. Famous people—Ruth Draper for example—have been *delighted* to come and perform here, for the *experience*. My first show in Norwich at St Andrew's Hall, had in the programme a foreword by Rider Haggard and a two-colour cover by Munnings. W. B. Yeats has spoken of my work on the stage here. And I am not going to have vain little people *of whatever sex*, seeking provincial publicity, spoiling *my* productions.'

He raised his head majestically.

'You didn't say that to her?' Paul was appalled.

'She wept . . .' Monck put his head on one side, and knuckled his eyes. 'And *then* . . . she did what I told her.' He dramatised the phrase with a pause, and a wave.

He raised his eyebrows and hand in triumph, with a crafty expression in his grey eyes, his arched eyebrows bristling.

'Because I'm a *homosexual*', Monck went on, 'I am *jealous* of women—and so I *understand* them.'

'Sometimes!' Bobbie couldn't help thrusting in.

'And I don't idealise them, as most men do. Some women have exceptional gifts—like yours, Elsa.'

Elsa knew from their work together that he respected her, but she was grateful to have it confirmed. She had the rather girlish vulnerability of the older, sensitive woman. She smiled wryly at Paul.

Moncklet was on another of his hobby-horses.

'But many women *do* let themselves go. They don't *wash*, for example. The young men who work for me: their girlfriends' necks are always *dirty*.'

On this tack, Monck made Paul uncomfortable. He recognised that under the surface the little man was afraid of women—afraid of their bodies. So he expressed a strangely energetic hostility, and it was difficult to tolerate it, especially when, as with Paul now, it was difficult enough to develop one's sexual powers.

'The boys always bring me their girlfriends, because they think they're so beautiful, and the girlfriends always want to "arct" because they think they're beautiful, too. I always say, "what lovely hair!" and lift it up at the back. Their necks are always *grey*!' Monck exclaimed triumphantly.

> 'Above the waist they're centaurs . . .
> Below, there's the sulphurous pit,
> Burning, scalding, stench, corruption . . .'

Paul came out with the apt quotation: rather too apt, for it revealed Monck's horror at what lay beneath a woman's hair. He was afraid Moncklet might be angry.

'Yes, Moncklet, remember King Lear.'

'I do. And I remember Goneril and Regan, dearie!'

132

He really looked devilish as he laughed that riposte, toothily: but he was only sharpened by Paul's reference.

'Yet the women in your productions are often the best of all your actors,' said Elsa.

'Once the relationship is right, and they're prepared to co-operate . . .'

'You mean to *obey* you?' said Bobbie. 'To be completely submissive?'

'Oh no . . . prepared to work with me, in understanding the way in which I am interpreting the play . . . once that is seen, they can have their own freedom. And some can use it—Cicely, for instance: she is superb!' He glinted at his beloved Bobbie. 'You don't call my Beatrice submissive do you?'

Paul had been silent: Monck's reference to girl-friends had set him thinking about Annie, and as he looked up out of the window now, he saw her coming up the path. A major problem was that she couldn't be fitted into the new Ninham's Court set-up. Intelligent and sophisticated as he was, Moncklet had no understanding at all of an adolescent's groping sexuality.

Monck smiled charmingly and bowed as he opened the door to her.

'Good morning, Mr Monck,' said Annie smiling cheerfully. Paul could see that she'd made a mess of her make-up and Monck-let was inwardly noting the smudges on her nose. But she looked like the spring, gay and blowsy in a bright floral blouse, and the old man gave Paul the morning off to take her out.

'If you can't be good, be careful.' he said, smiling and bowing at them rather cynically.

14

He had to admit it: Annie wasn't that intelligent. It hurt him to admit it, and his back went cold if he allowed the thought to form in his mind.

But all the same he had much to learn from her. She was superior to him in something: in relating to a woman he was her pupil. She wasn't beautiful: she had this plump nose, and her face was too round. But her smile was pretty, and her eyes were full of amusement: she could be vivacious. And she was generous and kindly. So she was attractive, and he loved her.

It was in the sensual realm that she was his tutor. He could be at his ease among adults, talking about Wilde or O'Casey. She couldn't, and so she sat silent and rather bored. Looking round at her at the height of an argument, a shadow would fall over his quick words, and he would move out warmly from his body to hers, seeking instruction, seeking the truths she could teach, as none of the talkative people round him could.

He was torn between two excitements.

The city, to him, was the narrow back streets, where you walked under the archway down to the little alleyway which led to the theatre courtyard. You turned in onto the paved yard and the door would be open. Within, there might be the sound of a harpsichord, or a man's voice speaking a passage from *Romeo And Juliet*, or a woman's voice singing a Schubert song. In the little building the school books came to life, so that Padua was embodied in doublet and hose with a sword and hanger and a lute—a lute that was really being played, with its wooden belly.

Or further down the alleyway and across the marketplace, there was the old Central Library, its doorway flanked by two plain pillars. There he would walk through to the 'Recent Additions' shelves, seeking the pretty bright cloth bindings of the new books published by Faber and Faber, or the latest James Joyce, Herbert

Read on modern art, or some new Phaidon picture book of paintings.

These excitements the city gave him, and gradually he associated this Norwich in his mind with the cities of the Italian Renaissance, and with London, Paris and Zürich. Or, if one climbed up to the Castle Museum, there were the Cotmans and Cromes, and the Dutch sea paintings that could transform one's perception of the East Anglian scene with its great dramatic skies and its low alluvial landscape with soft muted colours.

But it was impossible to get this expanding awareness of European culture into harmony with his emotional life and his body-life. Here the excitements were still the furtive ones he enjoyed with Annie in her air raid shelter. They longed for comfort and privacy, but they couldn't love as they wanted to, either in her home or his. The cinema they came to dislike, because they felt so overlooked.

They would hug and kiss in the cinema at night: but really to let themselves go they had to go elsewhere. Walking swiftly up St Stephens afterwards, they would make their way warily into an air raid shelter at the end of Annie's road. This should have been closed by a wooden grille, but after a spate of recent air raids the catch had been torn off. So they could slip into the damp, dark interior of this brick structure, constructed above ground on the pavement. At first, their spirits would sink a little in the chill, damp, interior of the raw brick box. But they were lucky, for there was a wooden seat along the wall. At first Annie would be nervous.

'Whassat?' she would exclaim at a noise, and then Paul had to show her that it was only the wind moving the grille, whose hinge was squeaking.

But then they would feel relaxed in the silence of the dismal shelter. At first Paul would stroke her breasts outside her clothes, but soon he would undo her clothes, while she would help him undo her hooks and zips. She had big soft breasts, with strong firm nipples, and Paul loved holding them and palping them. It gave him a thrilling delight, as it did as she stroked him. He didn't enjoy touching her so much, except for her warm soft thighs. He was still afraid of her hot, moist secret life, and disturbed by its strangeness. As Annie panted her legs opened wider and wider and she pushed at his hand: but he became fearful, and didn't know what to do. He would have his shivering orgasm, and he would leave her to recompose himself. It was strangely one-sided, but Paul didn't know what to do, becoming confused when Annie panted loudly and gasped into his ears. She never asked him to do more for her.

At last they spent a night together in the theatre, or, at least, until the small hours. Paul was on the fire-watching roster at the theatre, sleeping in the office on Tuesdays each week. There was a camp-bed and blankets, and a gas fire. Paul persuaded Annie to come in to be with him, and then go home after midnight. She daren't stay out all night: she was too much afraid of her father. He didn't seem to mind how late she was, but he wouldn't stomach her being away until morning. She could creep in at the back door and not wake her family.

They bought themselves some oranges and a half-bottle of red wine. It was real winter now and the little office felt very homely as the gas-fire burned away. Paul's bed was made up under the ticket counter, and they sat on it eating oranges and kissing. Everyone had gone home early after rehearsal, about nine-thirty, and it was now half past ten. The little man had gone early too, after testing the stirrup pump. The fire-watcher, after raising the alarm, was supposed to spray water over incendiary bombs with this hand pump operated from a bucket. There were also three sand-bags and a whistle.

The coast was clear, and Annie removed her brassière entirely, letting her breasts swing free in her blouse, open at the neck, as she sipped her wine.

'It's lovely in here,' she said. 'It's just what we need, a bit of comfort to love in.'

Paul's heart was banging loudly.

'I'm sick of that air raid shelter,' he said. 'It gives me the creeps.'

'Oh, it's a lovely air raid shelter: think of all the sweet things we've done in there.'

He laughed, biting a segment of orange in half, and holding it out to her. Her hair swung freely over his hand and brushed it. Her mouth looked full and generous and her eyes were dark brown, full of excitement and invitation. He put out his hand towards her neck opening.

At that moment there was a rattle of the door-knob, and a figure leaned above them.

'Oh!' said a mincing voice, lofty and thin, 'I'm sorry to disturb!'

It was Peter, the seamstress. His face was hard and hostile, with a homosexual's hatred of the sexuality between a boy and a girl.

Paul's mouth was dry, and he didn't know what to say. He just blushed scarlet.

'Just having a bit of company,' he explained lamely, 'for the first part of the night at least.'

'So I see,' Peter went on sternly, bitterly. 'The little man is very keen on people not sleeping together on fire-watching, you know.' Paul wondered whether he would order them out. 'Gets the theatre a bad name.'

'We're not sleeping: we're drinking and talking,' said Annie pleasantly, with some defiance.

'Oh!' exclaimed Peter, in a squeak, with as much hostility as he could concentrate in the vowel, giving a sharp little wriggle of the hips. 'Well,' he added wearily, 'I wish you joy.'

And with a theatrical gesture, like the Commendatore in *Don Giovanni*, he went, taking with him the stapler, which was what he had come for.

The apparition chilled them a little, because thay had assumed they were alone and unlikely to be disturbed. The office was blacked out of course, so no one could see in. And now Paul released the Yale latch and snecked it up. For half-an-hour they sat cheek to cheek, waiting for the shock of being interrupted to pass.

'Now!' he said, suddenly.

It was strange how they flew at one another, fumbling, in the warm rays of the murmuring fire. But they had no experience. They could only do their old thing. This time, however, Paul looked at her body-hair and caressed her boldly there, so that she breathed raucously and writhed. He held her breasts and sucked them with his winey mouth, while she worked at his straining body softly until the room seemed to burst with flame-pink light, and he felt his throbbing release flow out against her thigh. He laid his head gently into her hair, and snuggled down against her. They lay so for a long time.

'Oh, Annie, Annie, how I love you, Annie,' he murmured.

137

She was wondering, with her big loose mouth, her face gentle and happy, flushed: 'Isn't it funny with us? It's never *fulfilled*, somehow.'

He was anxious, and puzzled. 'Did you want to go further?'

'No. I'd be too scared. I love doing this with you. But it isn't the complete thing, and I want it to be: it's so beautiful with you.'

But she never complained about her rather unequal share of the bargain. She was content to sit with him, cheek to cheek, in the glow of their physical contact.

The little man was furious when Taylor-Smith told him.

'My theatre is *not* to be used as a brothel!' he spat at Paul.

'Well . . . I'm sorry, Moncklet.'

'You're not sorry at all.'

'We didn't have sexual intercourse,' said Paul. 'Anyway, in a brothel you have to pay.'

But he didn't want to explain anything, and sulked instead.

He was so comically put out that Moncklet grew less angry and jealous, but became moralistic instead.

'Whether in fact you had sexual intercourse with your girl in my theatre or not is beside the point. You may spare me the details, but a boy does not lock himself in an office—in *my* office—with a girl with a bottle of wine and a bag of oranges, in order to discuss logical positivism. And I have some responsibility to your parents.'

'Parents!' exclaimed Paul. 'Oh dear. I'm sorry: I never thought about them. It was all in the spirit of your "If you can't be good be careful" line.'

Some of Monck's annoyance dissolved into comedy, and Paul felt relieved. The little producer was not, however, to be diverted.

'But when my theatre is being fire-watched, I want it fire-watched. I don't want it burned down as lovers are gazing into one another's eyes, or gazing at other things.'

'Oh, Moncklet, don't be so unromantic. You know I love this girl: I've shown you the poems I wrote about her!'

'And what a fuss about a little copulation! Oh! The young! "There's nothing between fourteen and twenty but wronging the ancientry and getting wenches with child." . . . but I suppose I'm jealous, really,' he added, with a strange, lonely expression on his plain, transparent face.

138

15

Yet, while it seemed impossible to import Annie satisfactorily into the Maddermarket world, a certain kind of cultured sexuality leapt out from the place itself, and left him even more perplexed. There was a party at the Music House, organised by the Players, at Easter and both Elsa and Bobbie were there. There were about thirty people in the room, and there was a big bowl of wine-cup on a table by the open fire. It was almost a private party with printed invitation cards, so Paul had no way of inviting Annie, who was furious. Moncklet was cutting *The Constant Wife* for his summer production, which he preferred to do alone at night by the fire. All the people at the party were adults while Roy Short, Bobbie and Paul were the only ones under twenty-five.

There was a gramophone playing fox trots, and a few couples danced. Paul had never learned to dance, and so stood talking by the punch bowl, a glass in his hand, to various Maddermarket people: the dark-faced Dr Heilpern and Mark and Cicely, about the production of *Much Ado*. Paul watched Roy Short enviously, dancing with Bobbie: the man had obviously been to dancing lessons and was doing it extremely well, rather showing off, peering into Bobbie's face and showing his big teeth, laughing and moving his legs with active grace. Paul felt awkward and left out. Roy seemed so confident sexually, with his talk about how to seduce women. Would he seduce Bobbie? He still found the idea of two people wanting to have sexual relations disturbing, really.

Bobbie already had a woman-of-the-world manner, a world-weariness. She had been working in the professional theatre for two years already, and she knew in any case about the turmoil of adult sexuality from her father's endless affairs. When such topics came up for conversation she gave a deep, mannish, ironic laugh. Paul couldn't help wondering, as he watched her expressive, definite eyebrows go up in derision and her handsome full mouth pout in sophisticated amusement, what it would be like to make love to Bobbie as he did to Annie. But then he felt foolish and inept, because he felt sure his ways of making love to Annie would make anyone as sophisticated as Bobbie laugh.

Suddenly, he found Elsa coming up to him. She wore a long, embroidered frock and had put her hair up. With her silver rings and earrings she looked attractive, and he liked her intelligence.

'Would you like to dance?' she said.

Paul stammered. 'I . . . I'm afraid I don't know how to . . . I never learned.' He blushed as he realised it was impolite if not insulting to refuse a woman. In any case, he liked Elsa, and wouldn't want to hurt her feelings.

But she was undeterred.

'If you never begin, you'll never learn. Just come out on the floor and follow me. Come on!'

She took hold of him, and made him hold her. Again, he had that thrilling feeling, of being close to the body of a woman of culture and experience. He moved his feet as he thought he saw the other men moving theirs.

'Don't look down,' she said. 'Just move your legs from the hip, and feel yourself into the rhythm. Try to follow my movements.'

He was stiff and embarrassed, and for a moment felt he must say, please let me go, I can't do this. But then he suddenly felt he could enjoy it, and relaxed. He gave himself to allowing his thighs to touch her slightly and go with her body. She swung him skilfully, and apart from a few moments when his feet seemed to catch a crab, he was dancing.

'Am I hurting you?' he asked.

'Not at all. You're doing very well,' she murmured. 'In fact, I'm enjoying it very much. Only go on talking.'

'Moncklet,' he said, 'has stayed at home cutting his next play.'

'He works so hard. And he makes us all work hard. He treats me with a mixture of respect and disdain—as he does Barbara over her marvellous sets.'

'The *Much Ado* one was splendid, I thought.'

Oh, did you, he thought to himself: quite the Count Smalltork, a voice within him said. And he felt embarrassed, suddenly, a boy dancing with a woman so much older than himself. But he

140

struggled with this feeling as she went on. Whenever he looked at her neck or cheeks, he found them wrinkly and off-putting.

'Monck can't bear to recognise that women can be so good at creative things. He is fiercely possessive of his old stringed instruments, for example.'

'Yes, he always says to everyone: "If you finger it too hard, you'll break it." '

'Well, of course, I know infinitely more about harpsichords, spinets and virginals than he does. But I have to be discreet—even over the expense of having them tuned.'

'I thought he was strict about that?'

'Yes, but so *mean*. They have to be tuned every performance. And in the end I had to pay for it myself, except where I could tune them myself, as I can the little virginals.'

'They seem to have a special significance for him.'

'*He* plays them in such a clumsy way he nearly always breaks something.'

They both laughed.

'Well, my dear boy, I ought not to corrupt you by such talk, but they're symbolic of course.'

'How do you mean?'

'These old instruments are symbols of women's sexuality, upon which he wishes to play, but dare not. They're surrogate female genitals: but, of course, not on a real woman's body. So, he won't let anyone else play them.'

'And he busts them!'

'You must have noticed how many harpsichordists are abnormal?'

'And what about women who play such instruments?'

She blushed and laughed.

'Well I'm not a queer woman, if that's what you mean. Just a lonely normal woman.'

It was his turn to blush. They had now danced through a number of records, a quick fox trot, a slow fox trot, and then a waltz, which Paul found easier. He felt quite triumphant, and had laughed in a pleased way as they had passed Roy and Bobbie, when Roy had said: 'Good heavens!' But he noticed that the older woman clung to him with a strange, strong clinging, as the hour of dancing passed.

It had never entered his head to think that older women had sexual feelings: his mother had denied such emotions so strongly within herself. But the woman's enjoyment of their closeness alarmed him. Supposing they went beyond the amateur theatre camaraderie, and found themselves in private, in bed, or undressing? He actually shuddered a little, and then felt unkind. But he couldn't imagine making love to someone so physically like his mother, however cultivated she was.

'You don't have . . . a young lady here?'

'No, I have a girlfriend . . . but I didn't see how she could be invited.'

'What a pity. Would she have enjoyed it?'

'We don't dance, oddly enough.'

'You're dancing well. You should teach her.'

'I must.'

She gave a sigh. Paul sensed a desperation in her, a recklessness, in the old Elizabethan room with its huge fireplace and its oak timbers. It was the same room in which Frost held his discussion group, but with the drugget matting taken up and the floor polished, shining in the firelight. Paul could sense that if he wanted it, he could have Elsa that evening—that she would enjoy him, with all kinds of experienced and sophisticated tendernesses, and that it would count between them only as an adventure, like something in a play. He looked in her intelligent yellowish eyes as she talked, and saw a beseeching yearning in them as they circulated, holding one another close, round the floor. But he couldn't get her motherliness out of his mind: deep down, the idea of physical contact with her repelled him.

'I'm very grateful to you for teaching me.'

'It's one of the privileges of age, that one has something to teach.'

A pulse beat in his breast: he knew she meant she would teach him how to make love fully. She knew, with that feminine way of knowing, he was still a virgin, and wanted him for that, but as soon as the moment came in which she offered herself to him, he retracted and withdrew again coldly into himself, from fear, and out of loyalty to Annie.

He was relieved when Roy came up, smiling, in his neat worsted suit, and asked Elsa for the favour of a dance. Roy liked older women very much, and was always very polite and courteous to them. Bobbie stood abandoned for a moment, and Paul said to her: 'I've been learning to dance for one hour only. Would you like to risk it with me?'

Bobbie gave her rather raucous laugh. She was a slightly plump short girl, with full breasts, and a bold, handsome face with big lashes and highly curved plucked eyebrows. She gave off a puppyish vitality combined with a subtle sadness, with her rather contemptuous mouth. She was wearing a cream wild silk frock with a frilly neck, very low cut, showing a pretty cleavage between her breasts. She had her fair hair up, and wore some big pearl earrings. In a bold kind of way, she was beautiful and fine.

'Don't kick my pore feet,' she said, imitating a stage cockney voice. 'They're wore out doing chores for Peter T-S at Scutcheons.'

'The amount of work people put in at Monck's theatre is enough to win the war!'

'I'm going to take a day off,' she said. 'Roy and I are going with some friends of his to the seaside tomorrow. Will you come?'

'Would you like me to?'

'I think it would be good for you.'

For a young girl, Bobbie always had this motherly air. Here's another mother, he thought. Why do women always want to mother you?

'Everyone seems to have my welfare at heart.'

'What do you mean by that? Ow!' she exclaimed as he tripped over her feet.

'Sorry.' He blushed. 'You're not quite as good as Elsa when it comes to leading me on.'

'She's lovely, isn't she? I hope I'm as attractive as that when I'm fifty-odd.'

'Is she?'

'She was drawing you along well, we thought.'

He was silent, out of loyalty to the older woman and her loneliness. He sighed. He had the idealistic young man's horror of anything except absolute love. He thought perhaps both Elsa and Bobbie wanted to seduce him in a passing sexual encounter, just out of friendly warmth, no more. Anything like that appalled him. Yet only a year ago, before he began with Annie, he had actually knocked on the door of a local good time girl, and boldly asked her to sleep with him, because he wanted that. When she went to unbutton him, he fled. The first steps seemed to torment him, his ideas always clashing hopelessly with the feelings of his body.

He blushed violently and Bobbie noticed as they gyrated to a quickstep.

'You're having some entertaining thoughts to yourself, Paul, by the colour of your ears.'

'Did you like dancing with Roy Short?' he said, trying to divert her.

'He dances very well. Dear Roy. He's such an *egoist*.'

She said it like Moncklet.

'Am *I*?'

She gave a great laugh, all down the scale, grinning at him with her sophisticated eyebrows high. Suddenly, she looked brazen to him.

'You're such a . . . such a *boy*. Oh, you're bruising my feet! But you're so naïve, and it's so nice to find that, Paul.'

'Oh dear.'

'But will you come tomorrow?'

Next day they bicycled out to Bacton, a seaside place only some twenty miles away, with sandwiches. It was April only, but a warm day with some drifting cloud. There was Bobbie, Paul, Roy, and a slight boy called Hindry who wanted to be a painter. Bobbie obviously wanted to throw off her wartime London repertory theatre sophistication and be childish again. They raced one another down hills, and sat and drank fizzy drinks from bottles in the birchwoods. At last they reached the dunes by the sea and chained their bicycles together.

All day they raced about on the beach, with a chilly east wind spinning across it, drifting little wisps of sand. Although it was a warm spring day the North Sea was grey and cold, but the bright Norfolk sun dazzled them at mid-day when it came in patches over the beach and the dunes, where thick blue spikes of grass thrust out of the soft powdery sand. Some troops were erecting barbed wire "Double Dannett" beach defences. But most of the beach was free of obstacles. They played ducks and drakes with stones on the small waves' backs, and ran barefoot along the surf for miles, exclaiming over starfish, little dead crabs, and shoals of almost invisible shrimps darting in the crystal water, little brownish sandy-coloured scraps of life.

The boys couldn't keep their hands off Bobbie's body. They played leap-frog: they splashed her and chased her in the surf; they played tig for the pleasure of touching her warm smooth shoulders; then, finding a piece of flotsam rope, all bleached and sandy, they tied her up, carrying her, rolling her in the dunes, and coating her with dusty sand that got into her hair and eyes. She gasped, laughed, and revelled in it, wickedly, the boys heaving her up by her thighs, and clasping her round her plump breasts.

In the end, they were almost too weak to ride home. They were all flushed and excited: yet it was all utterly innocent. It was as if they had all ravished her: they adored her. Yet they weren't even physically aroused. She had become for them a water-pixie, a mermaid, and all the next week Paul dreamed Botticelli-like fantasies about her. It was a joyous, childish sexuality, idealistic, even fairy-tale.

Next morning at the Crypt, Monck asked him with a wicked tongue-in-cheek look: 'Well, did you enjoy your day off with Bobbie?'

'It was marvellous.'

'I told her,' he said with another arch look, 'there was safety in numbers. She, poor thing, knows how to look after herself. But I was wondering if you did.'

'Oh, it was all very innocent really,' said Paul. 'We got very childish, you know, paddling and running about. Like puppies.'

'That's what she told me, before she caught the train to London this morning. "Moncklet—it was so lovely yesterday. They were such funny boys. And it was just a childish day by the sea."'

Paul noticed that he was talking about his own childhood as if it had passed some time ago. But inwardly, he was still puzzled as to where to put his own newly found adult sexuality.

16

Because it was wartime, people would float in and out of a place like the Maddermarket Theatre—odd young men would appear because they had been posted to an aerodrome near Norwich, or because they were on leave from the Middle East, and then disappear as suddenly as they had come. Everyone in those days was accustomed to being suddenly presented with a temporary relationship and most were prepared to be friends with someone who, they knew, might vanish overnight, to a foreign country, or the north of Scotland, or even an 'unknown destination'.

In such encounters people were often deceived: there was no chance to discover the deeper aspects of an individual's character, and one simply enjoyed a friend's company at a superficial level.

'I am prostitute enough,' declared Moncklet, 'to greet every newcomer with enthusiasm—though I dread that one day someone will go off with the silver.'

Yet he didn't preach promiscuity. He said: 'One must go down the street and say "I'm not for you!" and "I'm not for you", and then . . .'—with an impish expression of delight and raised eyebrows— '. . . with *you*, it's different.'

His response was quite different, however, to the arrival of any evident and self-declared homosexual. Though he even warned Paul against the 'Buggers' Circle', he entered to some degree into the tacit freemasonry between homosexuals. And while Paul might have been 'safe' with Moncklet, he certainly wasn't with some of these. One of these encounters later on that spring was deeply disturbing.

A young airman called Richard Drake arrived one day at Ninham's Court sporting a paisley neckerchief in the opening of his blue battledress blouse. Paul had been sent back to his family for the moment so that the airman could stay with Monck, who was being as skittish as a girl about his visitor. Drake was helping with the stage managing.

'Poor Richard,' Moncklet exclaimed one sunny morning, 'wilting in a Nissen hut out at Coltishall in a marsh! He's so grateful for a bit of civilised life that he has washed all my chair-covers by hand for me.'

Paul had just arrived to take instructions for certain letters, and the youth was wringing out the plain linen chair-covers with his hands, his sleeves rolled up revealing a metal chain on one wrist. He had curly fair hair and a long pale face with hollow cheeks.

'Hallo!' He shook hands with a wet hand.

'They were *filthy*,' Moncklet sighed. 'What shall I do? Everything is going to pot since my dear old Mrs Crowe got her fallen womb. The floors haven't been *scrubbed* for a month.'

He spat the word 'scrubbed' showing his prominent eye-tooth.

'We can do it this morning,' said the airman. 'Paul can help me.'

Paul found it very satisfying shifting all the furniture out of the way, lifting the mats, sweeping, and then scrubbing the yellow and pink bricks of the long living-room with its tall Elizabethan windows. These were not leaded, but had panes in them at least four feet tall. The room looked bright and fresh when they had finished and the bricks had dried. They talked all the time about the theatre: Richard had been an actor before being called up, and had tried to produce plays in the RAF.

'But it's *hopeless*,' he declared. 'They only want rubbish, thrillers and that sort of thing. And the *material*!'

He made a droopy gesture with his right hand, and it struck Paul how effeminate he was. He would, he thought to himself, make a good wife for someone, and thought it the more as Drake made a fish dish with cheese sauce for Monck's early supper. Paul wondered what Drake's relationship with Monck would be. Surely the little man wouldn't just have him sitting by his bedside, holding his hand and talking, which was how he often behaved to Paul? But what more active encounter could they have? He felt a little jealous; but he certainly didn't want to be drawn into the circuit. He put himself on the alert.

But he found Richard Drake very persuasive. Something in the man seemed to make persuasion necessary to him. He was full of energy, and this was attractive in him: he was always shaking his curly fair hair back over some busy task—filling the coal bucket, or washing-up with methodical rapidity. Monck loved this, of course, and he couldn't fault him.

'I suppose, dearie, you've put all the best cutlery in the ordinary kitchen basket?'

But no, Richard had even brushed out the baize-lined canteen and arranged the best knives and forks in their proper places, the right way up.

Drake was going to London for the weekend and persuaded Paul to accompany him. Paul was very much a schoolboy still, and the older serviceman opened up, in talking to him, a new adult world—of people in the theatre, of interesting bars and pubs. Monck looked doubtful when he first heard of it, but laughed it off, saying ominously: 'He'll have to learn to defend for himself,' a slip of the tongue of which Paul made a mental note.

'I know someone who'd *particularly* like to meet you,' said Drake.

Paul was flattered. How could anyone suppose that anyone in London would be pleased to meet him, a sixth former from Norwich?

'I'm going to Maurice Heal's on Saturday night for drinks. You and he would get on splendidly.'

'Maurice Heal? But he's very famous,' said Paul. 'He broadcasts a lot.'

'That's right. He's a very well-known barrister. And a very cultured man.'

'I'd love to meet him,' said Paul. But it seemed very much of a dream, to be introduced to such a high personage.

They hitch-hiked to London, travelling most of the way in a very fast sports car to Hendon. There they caught a tube train, where they peered out through the small diamond-shaped peep-hole in the shatter-proofed window: the glass was covered with a close-woven net to prevent splintering in blast. There were posters by Fougasse of Hitler listening under the bed to people giving away secrets, and 'Billy Brown of London Town' which advised the public not to pull off the net on the windows:

'I trust you'll pardon my correction:
That stuff's put there for your protection!'

148

People on the trains seemed tired and languid, their faces tense and anxious. On the platforms there were people already arranging their bedding on the wire and metal bunks, to spend the night on the tube train platforms. The air in the tubes smelt foetid and stale. Paul was afraid there might be a real blitz, and became apprehensive. What was he doing, messing about in London with this stranger?

They arrived at a big block of flats in Earls Court and walked up the dark staircase: there were only dim blue lights on stairs, because of the blackout. Richard Drake seemed very much at home in Elsworthy Mansions, and Paul was puzzled. The young airman pushed a brass bell-push, outside a stout-looking outer door, No. 7, on the first floor.

The door was opened by a small, balding middle-aged man with a moustache, in a brown suit with large checks in the pattern, to whom Paul took an instant dislike.

'Why, hallo Dickie!' exclaimed this older man, and put his arm round Drake's shoulders.

'Hallo, Ding-Dong,' said Richard. 'I've brought a young friend from Norwich, Paul, Ding-Dong.'

They shook hands.

'Paully, come in,' exclaimed the man addressed as Ding-Dong: no surnames seemed to be given. 'Come and have a drink.'

He led the way through a panelled hall hung with Hogarth engravings of the Rake's Progress, and through a massive pine door into a library. It was a long, handsome room, with oak book-cases round the walls, and others free-standing, jutting into the room. These seemed to contain mostly law books, but there were some literary works, sets of Gibbon and Dickens and modern works. Along the bottom of one wall was a full set of the *Encyclopaedia Britannica*, and one section of the bookcase near the fire was full of beige and brown luxury editions of art plates.

The firelight gleamed on the panelled walls, the red and blue leather bindings in their sets and rows, the gilt lettering and tooling on the richer bindings, and on the moulded ceiling. Round the fire, which was in a polished steel basket in an Adam fireplace, were leather armchairs, a big desk along the wall, and a table with a tray of glasses and decanters. The room was lit by brass study lamps with cylinders and screws that enabled them to be raised or lowered, and big green circular shades.

Standing in front of the fire on a dark red Afghan rug was a plump elderly gentleman with white hair, and a full, much creased and genial face. Paul recognised him at once, from photographs he had seen in the newspapers and magazines. Maurice Heal was a famous commentator on matters of law, political freedom and morality: and wine. Paul quailed a little; he could cope with Nugent Monck's provincial fame in the city of Norwich. He was rather daunted by an encounter with a national notability. This distinguished elderly man, with his old-fashioned dark grey suit, a waistcoat, a watch-chain, wore very finely made shiny brown shoes that glowed in the flames.

'Come in, Dick, and make yourself at home. Hallo, young man,' he added to Paul.

'This is Paul,' said Dick with, Paul thought, an odd simper.

'Hallo, Paul,' said the older man, booming rather. 'I expect you've heard of me?'

'Yes I have,' said Paul weakly, and blushed, shaking the plump smooth hand, and tripping over the mat which had tangled round his feet. He stumbled and lurched, and felt the elderly lawyer's arm quickly laid against his back. He was astonished to sense what felt like a pat on the bottom.

'Well, you find me in a different role,' said the great man. 'A quite different domestic role.'

The other laughed: giggled, rather, and Paul felt disturbed and apprehensive. They seemed to have some secret between them which he didn't share.

'I've read quite a few things you've written,' he said. 'It's always good to meet someone whom you only know in print.'

'Let's hope it's not a disappointment to come across me in the flesh,' said Heal, with a deep fruity voice. He had put on a strangely vivacious look, and a kind of leer which turned a face which on the whole seemed to display benignity and honesty into one of fleshy sensuality and cunning. Yet he was an attractive man.

'Come on, Ding-Dong, you're bloody slow with those drinks.'

Paul was handed a big, thin, beautifully cut tumbler with a heavy base, containing a quarter of a pint of whisky with lumps of ice in it.

'Cheers!' they all said. Paul drank a gulp of his, and, being unused to whisky, choked. Drake giggled again.

Drake explained how they were working as secretaries for Nugent Monck.

'Hem!' exclaimed Ding-Dong, grinning, his teeth showing, He had a way of twitching his whiskers which Paul found repulsive, and with the fire and whisky his face was going an unpleasant purple.

'. . . and we scrubbed his sitting-room out for him yesterday.'

'Dirty old man,' said Ding-Dong, who was becoming skittish, emphasising his light-heartedness by a strange little wriggle of the hips, and his short, clumsy legs. Paul felt he must be a military man, in mufti, and he wondered how he came into Richard Drake's picture.

'I didn't get your name,' said Paul, suddenly, boldly.

'Ding-Dong,' said Ding-Dong.

'I mean your surname.'

'Oh ho,' said Ding-Dong. 'No names no pack-drill, eh? No,' he said, suddenly cautious. 'We don't go in for names.'

'You see,' said Richard quickly, 'Ding-Dong is something, *actually*, awfully high in the forces—you don't mind me saying that, do you, Ding?—and it won't do to fling names around *socially* . . . Maurice, of course, well everyone knows Maurice, Maurice the Moralist . . .'

The plump pale notoriety guffawed.

'And he must be regarded as above contumely . . . no one would believe anything queer about him.'

Ding-Dong was laughing with a strange staccato bark, throwing down whisky and spluttering.

'I see,' said Paul. 'Only, rather I don't see how it matters, so long as everyone keeps out of mischief.'

He was warming a little with the whisky, and Ding-Dong was watching the boy hungrily.

'But that's just it, Paully dear,' said Ding-Dong twitching his whiskers, 'we don't intend to keep out of mischief—not at all, at all.'

Suddenly, Paul found his purplish, dark face pressed against his, and the man's wet lips under his moustache seeking his mouth, to kiss him.

Paul Grimmer was no great prude, but he felt immediately

sick, and his youthful virginal repulsion was mingled with a shocked sense of betrayal. He had supposed he was being introduced to a great man of thought and culture, but now he suddenly realised he had been lured into a homosexual retreat—a boy procured for boy-lovers. He pushed Ding-Dong away sharply, and as he did so he saw Maurice Heal's face turn from benign gentleness into a frightened but also vicious hostility.

Ding-Dong, actually thumped quite hard on the chest, choked a little, and then became red and enraged.

'Damn puppy,' he said. 'The damn puppy actually struck me. What the hell do you think you're doing, sir?'

'I must go,' said Paul.

'Go! I'm damned if you'll go: you'll answer for that, sir.' He was looking round, as if for a weapon, a stick or something.

'I'm sorry, Richard,' said Paul, whose heart was beating, and who found it hard to breathe, 'I shouldn't have come here. There's some mistake . . . You've assumed something about me, and it's wrong . . .'

The great man was quite flustered, his hostility now turned to a kind of gentle cunning.

'Can't be helped, Dick, can't be helped. Everyone makes mistakes . . . Look here, stay for another drink, er . . . what's your name . . . Paully, won't you?'

He took Paul's glass from him.

'I shouldn't waste any more drink on him,' sneered Ding-Dong. 'I'm going to bloody well kick him out.'

'You don't need to,' said Paul. 'I'm going . . . I'm . . . I've not enjoyed it much coming here . . . to this great man's place,' he added spitefully.

He was nearly crying. Richard tried, in a girlish way, to defend his friend.

'Leave him alone,' he minced. 'Come on, Ding-Dong, make allowances, man. It just didn't work this time.'

'Bloody boy hurt my tits, punching me like that. At least he deserves a black eye before he goes.'

Ding-Dong flung himself at Paul, but Drake pushed him off, with his girlish wrists, and Heal, in the rear, muttered: 'Oh, come off it, Ding-Dong, the whole thing's a balls-up. Don't be absurd, man, good heavens!'

152

At last, the two younger men were outside, Paul gasping and tingling with fear and rage, and the heavy door slammed behind them.

'I'm ever so sorry,' said Richard.

Paul realised the man was a kind of pimp, bringing likely boys to Heal and his man-friend for seduction. He must have supposed that because Paul worked for Monck he would oblige. But Paul was sickened by the undercurrents of cruelty and aggression, the meanness and hostility. He recalled Moncklet's sour warning: 'Never trust a bugger!' His heart was beating, and his sweat was drying cold. They had actually tried to keep him there! He shrugged.

'Now where the hell do we go—it's past midnight already?'

But Drake knew of a little hotel nearby: he would do, thought Paul. He was sick of his companion: a predatory sod, a pansy. The horrible compulsiveness in these homosexuals!

All through the night, as he tried to sleep, the airman became desperate in an attempt to seduce him on his own behalf. He whispered, he pressed his face to Paul's hair, thrust his hands into his bed, lay on top of him, until late in the small hours, cajoling and wheedling.

'But it's such a little thing to ask!' he whined.

At last, in desperation, Paul flung his whole weight behind a punch into the man's face, in the darkness.

'Fuck off, you bleeder!' he shouted.

For a moment, he thought he would be murdered. But then he heard the man shuffle away in the dark, sniffing as if blood was trickling down his nose, gasping thickly: 'Bastard!' He heard the door of the double twin-bedded room close, and leapt out of bed to lock it. Let the man sleep where he could. At last, his heart calming a little, he dropped off to sleep. Richard Drake spent the night on the floor of the hotel bathroom, his pillow a bloodstained bath-mat. But Paul Grimmer was half-way back to Norwich, hitch-hiking, before he woke up. And that day Drake had to rejoin his unit.

17

Annie was fascinated.

'But supposing you had let him kiss you? What would have happened then?'

'Oh, I suppose it would have become some kind of masturbating or other, revolting session.'

'But he's ever so famous, Maurice Heal, Paul. I heard him on the wireless last week. I can't imagine him actually . . .'

She shook with laughter, with her eyebrows high with incredulity. In a strange way, the episode made her even more fascinated by Paul. She had a great sense of fun, and even when they were making love, hugging one another half-clothed in a wood, Annie would suddenly burst out with laughter, and lean back and look at him, and say: 'Fancy! I'm being kissed by someone who has been kissed by Maurice Heal!'

'I was *never* kissed by Maurice Heal,' Paul would say, rather sulkily.

'Well *nearly*,' teased Annie. 'It's as near to fame as I shall ever get,' she added ruefully.

'Oh, do shut up, Annie, and concentrate.'

'Yum!' she would say, putting her big laughing mouth to his.

But she would grow fat, when she was thirty, and she had such a jumbled taste in clothes. He loved Annie in a way, loved her for her generosity, her warm-heartedness. But deep within himself there was a reserve, part snobbish, part realistic, in its recognition of differences of interest. There is a capacity in youth for self-interest which can be cruel—cruel in its pursuit of what is right for the deepest part of one's soul, one's essential freedom. And youth will look forward to a change in situation that brings its own changes: Paul knew that when he went to Cambridge next autumn it would be all up with Annie. And in any case, just now, he was sick of sex.

·   ·   ·   ·   ·

After all that, Paul stayed at home again for a bit. But that didn't work, either. He was still struggling, wondering how to find a balance between his own uncouthness and the world the other side of the theatre, the world of apartments filled with works of art, of a life like Elsa's where elegant meals were enjoyed by people of cultivation and manners. But then, of course, he had found limitations in that world too. There was the older woman pressing her body to yours: the notoriety wanting to go down on his knees to your youth. So Paul Grimmer found himself completely lost, looking out one wet day at the grey streets from a bus joggling along Unthank Road to the Maddermarket Theatre.

He had banged the front door of his home, with its brown treacly varnish, and latched the garden gate, aware as he did so of movements at the curtains next door. There was no real community life in the little suburban street, though occasionally people asked about the next door children's welfare, or borrowed an implement or an ointment in an emergency. But the housewives watched all the time, peeped and watched, each closeted in her isolation and neurosis. People had been brought into these raw streets of semi-detached houses and they seemed to share so little. They collected round them evidences of prestige—a car, or two dozen roses, or a racing bicycle: and each family continually peeped, to see what was being unloaded from the van next door, or who was going out where and in what clothes. But the street was under the pall of a continual silence—no warmth of gossiping or conflicting voices, as in your village or city slum. The men went off on bicycles or in a car to work in the mornings, while their wives stayed behind, occasionally twitching the curtains, peeping at the world outside, or emerging one by one with their shopping baskets. The only link between them all was a grasping after a new kind of respectability, a sense of being above a certain kind of commonness: but the penalties, as the family doctors knew, were severe.

It was always a relief to Paul Grimmer to walk away from the quiet sleepy dreadfulness of those little streets, past the next row of houses, which were older and more substantial, down to the bus stop. At the end of the street, next to the untidy shrubbery in the garden of the Jenny Lind hospital, was a row of limes, which dripped their sticky fluids in summer and covered the pavements with slippery dead leaves in the autumn.

It was nowhere, that little area of suburban streets, neither vulgar nor pretentious, without shape, without form or drama. As the bus rolled down Unthank Road, the houses grew a little more pretentious, some of them having high privet hedges and timber trees, one even displaying brick gateposts and a drive. But it was still nowhere. The chemist's shop over which he had been born was nowhere, and nor was the little rise beyond it called Park Lane Hill.

You weren't anywhere until you reached the Catholic cathedral, a dreary Gothic building constructed about 1905 in all the academic clichés of architectural Catholicism, conveying none of the splendours of European devotional building, not even in imitation.

Once past the Catholic cathedral, however, the bus was inside the old city walls, and one was really somewhere. There was St Giles's church at the top of the precipitate Cow Lane leading down to the slums of Pottergate. Next to the church was a marvellous second-hand bookshop with a tray of books outside and rooms of books for sale, going creaky floor by creaky floor right up into the roof. On one side of the street was an eighteenth-century redbrick building known as the Clinic, where he had been inoculated against diphtheria as a child, and on the other side the building with rather mean little marble pillars where the Masonic Club met. Further along was the forecourt of the Norwich Hippodrome, and half-way down Guildhall Hill a magnificent Regency courtyard on the left, housing a library behind handsomely porportioned windows.

Once he reached there, Paul Grimmer would feel he 'belonged', though, in truth, he had nothing really to do with the black-and-white speckled mediaeval Guildhall, with its flint-work and leaded windows. It was simply that it offered a setting which was dramatic in some way, though he couldn't be sure in what way. Walking up the somnolent surburban street he felt a dread of being nobody; diving down Love Lane off St Giles, he could dramatise himself, and think of himself as 'Paul Grimmer going about his business in the city' as he turned round the corner by the timbered Toc H building, and down the alley under the tower of St John's Maddermarket.

This week, however, he was a little thrown in his insecure self-possession by Moncklet's nervousness. Paul suddenly saw that the little man had his insecurities, at certain times feeling himself to

be something of a provincial nobody. The occasion at this parti-
cular time was the visit of a famous London actor, Esmé Percy,
to take the part of Don Juan in an excerpt from Bernard Shaw's
Man and Superman. As Monck's main helper at the time, Paul
was given the task of accompanying Percy and steering him
about.

This would have been difficult enough for a boy of seventeen in
ordinary circumstances: Esmé Percy was famous as actors go, but
wasn't in Paul's opinion, very good. He was too flamboyantly
homosexual, and his manner was too stereotyped, a continuous
humming drawl, full of 'ahs' and 'ums', accompanied by a few
hammish gestures and a good deal of fluffing of his lines. He had a
soft bulging face, blue and pink, with receding curly hair, and a
plump awkward body which rolled and stumbled, with short legs
and a tendency to tubbiness.

'I will see you onto the rostrum myself,' declared Monck. 'But
if I am called away, Paul here will see you onto the rocks, and help
you off, when the scene is ended.'

'Ready, Mr Percy?' Even though he insisted on 'Esmé' time
and time again, everyone in the theatre called him Mr Percy since
Moncklet had built up such a myth about him. He held Paul's
arm tightly in his soft grip.

'I am now,' he drawled in his languid but precise voice, 'climbing
the steps to the stage . . . I am now on the stage . . . I am moving
towards the rocks . . . My God! I'm sure that was a nasty bracket or
something sticking into me! I shall *fall*!'

'Paul,' cried Monck from somewhere behind, '*please* don't let
Esmé *fall* . . . It will ruin everything if Esmé *falls* . . .'

'No! Monck! I think I am all right. I think I shall make it! I am
thrusting myself up with one hand on the rock . . . I am swinging
myself round . . . I am seated on the rocks . . . now . . .'

And so began the scene. 'Music!' called Monck.

'Ah! you have not yet lost the sense of time. One soon does, in
eternity . . .'

Actually, though Paul thought the famous actor was boring in
his delivery, which was monotonous, he was amazed that anyone
could remember so much prose. But the Norwich Players stood up
to him well. Elsa took the part of the old woman.

'You were like all men. Libertines and murderers all, all, all!'

'And yet we meet here, dear lady.' Percy rather threw it away, indecisively.

'Stop!' called Monck. 'Dear Esmé, if you could please be a little more *sinister* with that line.'

'Oh, yes, I realise, Moncklet—it is very much like something *you*'d say.'

'And yet ... we meet *here* ... dear lady!' Monck put his head on one side, with his eye-tooth prominent, and a bitchy mockingness in his face. Percy did it even more maliciously. They went on.

'Happy! Here! Where I am nothing! Where I am nobody!'

The unfortunate man had one glass eye, and a huge Alsatian guide dog, to which he was devoted. His eye, apparently, had been bitten out by such a dog: but this one seemed to Paul the most difficult animal for pushing and shoving he had ever come across. It was devoted to the small plump and clumsy actor, but in such a way as to be always pressing towards him, at him, and over him, to make sure, as it were, he had still got him. The dog was called Giorgio, and everyone was exhausted by the attention this animal required. When Percy had to go on the stage without him, the big black dog would nearly go frantic, and eventually had to be shut up in a property cupboard, where it howled and scratched miserably.

'I'm not very good with rocks,' Percy declared, 'especially not in your awful darkness, Monck.'

Since *Don Juan In Hell* takes place in Hell, the light had to be dim and blue, Moncklet said, while the walls and rocks were nearly black. Percy would lament in almost total darkness. Paul thought it the most boring theatrical experience he had ever had.

'Not at all: you are a lady: and wherever ladies are is hell.'

It was all talk: the two old homosexuals loved the destructive talk and the endless series of stagey situations.

She: '. . . even *here* you pursue me.'

He: 'I protest I do not pursue you. Allow me to withdraw.'

She (*seizing his arm*): 'You shall not leave me alone in this dreadful place.'

Paul heard it all, all through rehearsals and all through the week, but he saw very little, since he was crouched backstage, waiting to rush on at any moment when Esmé Percy's legs should give way or he should trip over. Percy must not *fall*. Strangely enough, his moment did not come until the Saturday matinée, at the moment when Don Juan is expatiating on the eye.

'Just as life . . .' declared Esmé, waving his arm more emphatically than usual, after a good lunch at Gundry White's where he had taken Monck for 'old time's sake' . . .

'after ages of struggle, evolved that wonderful bodily organ, the eye, so that the living organism could see where it was going and what was coming to help or threaten it, and thus avoid a thousand dangers that formerly slew it, so it is evolving today a mind's eye that shall see, not the physical world but the purpose of life, and . . .'

—for some reason, perhaps because of the wine, Percy dried up. 'Thwarting and baffling,' called the prompter, but in his efforts to hear, the plump old actor began to slide off the rocks, calling: 'Paul! I'm falling!'

At the same moment, Peter Taylor-Smith, searching for a prop for the next show, opened the door of the property cupboard and Percy's big old black dog bounded onto the stage, knocking his master flying. The plump little man rolled down the plywood and canvas rocks on to the apron stage, calling out: 'My eye! My eye! I've lost my eye! Giorgio, you fool!'

'Lights!' called Moncklet. 'Lights up! Esmé's eye! Save Esmé's eye!'

Paul held onto the actor's belt, while the big dog, excited and confused, alternately barked, nipped Paul's arm and licked his master's face, almost choking him. Paul had a horrible fear the wretched animal would bite out the other eye. People in the little auditorium were at first amused, thinking this was all part of the play, but then gasped as Percy's glass eye flipped out and rolled across the stage into the stalls, while the man clutched at his face. And now there were gasps of consternation and dismay, and a rattle of seats.

'Don't stand on Percy's *eye*. Please don't stand on the *eye*! *Please* remain seated,' cried Moncklet, spitting into the beams of the floods. 'Please keep your feet *off* the ground and look for Mr Percy's *eye*!'

Then the blue jellies were all pulled up and the houselight in

159

the centre of the ceiling went on. A dusty glass eye was eventually handed up to the producer.

'Please keep calm!' he cried, agitated and running up and down the apron stage.

'I'm terribly sorry, ladies and gentlemen,' declared Monck, seeing that Paul had the little old pro on his feet. 'There will be a short break, while Mr Percy repairs and recovers himself, and then' (he recovered himself) '. . . all *hell* will be let loose again after about ten minutes.'

Laughter and cheers greeted this as Paul heaved Giorgio off the stage and into the Green Room where Percy was pushing back his glass eye, which had been washed for him by Cecily.

'It was that fool of a boy,' he was saying. 'He just let me roll into the front row.'

Paul was quite hurt.

'I'm sorry,' he said. 'What was it *I* did wrong?'

'Esmé,' said Monck, 'I am so *very sorry* that such a *dreadful* thing should happen in my theatre . . . some damned fool opened the door of the prop cupboard, and Giorgio simply leapt out like a mad thing. You were *already* falling, and then you completely lost your balance. Paul, of course, could do nothing, since the dog laid hold of his arm.'

'Dear Moncklet: don't mention it. I *do* apologise. I really was so put out.'

They dusted him down, and after apologising once more to Paul, off he went again in the dark and began drawling away: 'No, I sing, not arms and the hero, but the philosophic man: he who seeks in contemplation to discover the inner will of the world . . .'

Monck crept up to Paul in the backstage darkness, while the boy was in fits that he should tumble, too.

'Are you all right?' he hissed.

'Fine,' said Paul. 'But I'm sorry if I've disgraced you.'

'Nonsense!' said Monck. 'The ridiculous ass fell off himself. Of *course* you could do nothing. And as for that *revolting* dog! I admire Esmé,' he whispered, his hiss growing powerfully sibilant, 'but alas, I shall *never* have him in my theatre again!'

18

After an evening in the theatre it was too much to walk the two miles back home. But he was needing a holiday from the Crypt after Drake. So Paul took a room in a flat in St Giles, just round the corner from Ninham's Court. There, he hoped, he would finally have Annie in his bed all night. He rented the room from Tom Sayle, a large raw-boned man who was a conscientious objector working on forestry. Sayle was another homosexual, an aggressive and athletic one, with a large ugly head, straw-coloured hair and glasses, and an ugly feminine mouth, weak and sensuous, with pig-bristle stubble on his chin. His flat was large, with a sitting-room, four bedrooms and a kitchen, on the first floor of a rambling Georgian house. Paul hardly knew him, but made his arrangements through a strange friend he met at the discussion group, Abel Kerr, a fat timber worker, a pacifist.

The flat was dully decorated in brown paint and porridge colours, but reasonably clean and roomy. Tom wore a housewife's pinafore when he cooked or cleaned, and tried to see that his tenants kept their rooms clean too. He was a Journalist. Paul began to feel that everyone having anything to do with the arts or intellectual life was a homosexual or something odd. Sayle let three bed-sitting rooms, one to a balding middle-aged dwarf, also a homosexual, with teeth like a horse's in a large head like a child's. Dirty Don, as he was called, had enormous feminine hands with long bony fingers which caressed everything about him with the suggestion of an old man's impotent menace. This creature was repulsive and probably, Paul thought, a spy or crook, though he always boasted of being in the aircraft industry. His eyes were icy, watery and blue. His legs were pathetically short, and his feet large, curving upwards in their huge brogues like those of a stage comedian, a clown or Grock. The other tenant was Tom's friend, Abel. He seemed to have a friendly nature but his palms tended to be sweaty and he was untidy with his body in such a way as to be often offensive as he belched or slapped one's knee too hard in mirth so that it stung. His clothes were loose and unwashed. Paul liked him at times: at others, when Abel brought in fish and chips and ate them nosily, fragments of batter sticking to his bushy brown moustache, Paul wondered how he could ever bear to be under the same roof with such a repulsive man. Kerr was round-headed and already going badly bald at twenty-five, though his beard was very strong and his fat sunburned cheeks were blue with stubble. But the pacifist's need to argue his case at the Music House discussions had brought them together.

They all shared the sitting-room and a large kitchen with a big window over a yard at the back. Paul's room had a gas fire and was furnished with two ugly armchairs covered with worn corduroy and imitation leather. Around the walls Paul had pinned his poor reproductions of Braque and Picasso. There were also one or two daubs in yellow and bright blue done by Kerr who fancied himself as an artist. Paul's was the least well furnished of the rooms. Besides the armchairs it had a hard ramshackle single divan bed, one wooden chair, a tea-chest covered with a table-cloth for a table, and an alarm clock. But he only paid fifteen shillings a week for the room, and he was glad to have his freedom so cheaply. There was a bathroom, dark and chilly, with a large old-fashioned geyser which they worked as if driving a tram, with levers and huge taps, while the meter clicked and wheezed like a harmonium underneath it. While the geyser was running they were supposed to open an attic light with a cord, but if they did the rain came in, or wind which made the geyser blow back with a terrible roar. So they let the fumes accumulate and hoped for the best, entering the bath, even after the geyser had been extinguished, in a poisoned trance. Tom Sayle spent the whole of Friday evening in the bathroom cleaning himself with obsessional attention and noisily singing old music-hall ballads. He picked his ears and navel with pieces of cotton wool twisted on matchsticks, which relics he often left lying about afterwards. Then he could be heard working away at his chest expander, the springs clashing and humming. From this ritual he would emerge with his straw mop of hair standing on end, his body scented with talcum and geyser fumes, full of aggressive physical force.

At the end of the second week Paul threw a house-warming party. He had invited Annie to his room at once, but she had refused. At last they realised that it was she who wouldn't 'go the whole hog' as she put it. Her Catholic upbringing now came to tell, and she flatly refused to make the 'final surrender'. In the end, to get her there at all, he had thrown this party, hoping that perhaps she'd stay behind afterwards, and give in to him in bed at last.

They drank cider and some draught beer brought up in jugs. Abel Kerr was there, fat and sagging in his worn cords, and a tall smooth, dark young man called Brian Bodley who vibrated nervously and talked incessantly. Bodley was another from the discussion group, a windbag whose endless flow had driven many away from Frost's circle. Paul had to ask Sayle to the party, because he needed to borrow his tumblers. Sayle was in a fluffy and aggressive mood, with a bright glint in his glasses and a pair of green corduroy trousers over his great hams. Officiously he took over the party, and threw open his own room, which was next to Paul's, which Paul resented. He didn't want to seem too great a friend of Sayle's. It was all getting out of hand. Bodley brought an awkward girl from his office; he worked with a firm selling stationery, and wore a neat black suit that looked rather crumpled and shiny, like used carbon paper. The awkward girl was blonde and her hair looked greasy. She was in a shapeless green wool frock with soft leather shoes each of which had a big frilly leather tongue. She was pop-eyed and adenoidal. Paul thought her the most unattractive girl he had ever seen. Her nose was long and coarse: but Brian Bodley basked in her admiration, and she seemed to think him great and wise. There was no sign of Annie yet: Paul strained to listen for the rusty rattle of the doorbell.

Would Annie come? The siren had just gone, but she wouldn't, he knew, be deterred by air raid warnings, having a young woman's courage and indifference to danger. Of course, if anything started she might dodge in a shelter somewhere. There was no air raid shelter at the flat; in bad raids they crouched under the stairs by the dustbins in the dirty hall, where Tom Sayle's tall gent's bicycle stood. Paul peeped down there now. The bell croaked. He opened the large brown door, studded with many old holes of past chains, hinges and other fastenings, and there was Annie.

He kissed her large smiling mouth. Annie wore a scarf, a hairy yellow pullover and brown woollen trousers. Paul was disappointed: he wanted her to dress in her feminine way, as she had for him when she came to join him at fire-watching. But he could see she had dressed to meet the 'Bohemians', as she called Tom and Abel. Yet she looked well and, in her style, arty and provincial. He was annoyed with her at once, because she seemed less interested in him and his new room than in the whole set-up, Abel and Sayle included, and was in a rather silly party mood.

'And where the hell are the boys?' she cried, going up the stairs with a filmic kind of posture, acting the kind of tarty, gangster's moll woman that she wasn't at all like.

He was surprised to find himself critical of Annie. But they were both becoming tired, he realised, of their skirmishes in shelters and cinemas, but were not yet ready for anything more domestic Paul was only aware of the clumsy patches of powder on Annie's cheek, and saw that her sandals weren't chic—they were heavy and like a child's shoes, quite belying her sophisticated 'entrance'.

She felt him cold and critical.

'Don't you like me like this?'

'I like you anyhow.'

But it sounded the lie it was.

'Are they all there?'

'All? Well, there's Sayle and Kerr.'

'Oh I like Tom Sayle.'

'And a chap I don't know called Brian Bodley.' Paul lowered his voice. 'Can't *stand* him.'

Annie piped up in an affected way, annoyingly loudly: 'Oh I know him . . . he's nice. He's ever so clever.'

Suddenly Paul had an inward surprising sense that Brian Bodley and Annie could get on very well together, both being essentially 'provincial' as he called it. Yet Annie was so warm-hearted, whereas the carbon paper man . . . Paul took himself up in his own mind. He was getting so critical. He couldn't stop knocking his friends. Friends! Was that all Annie was?

She walked excitedly up the stairs in front of him.

'Perhaps I should have carried you over the threshold,' he said after her.

But the remark was unfortunate. It only revealed how far they were from 'living in sin' as she called it. She gave him a look which displayed resentment at his possessiveness, apprehension that he might try to go too far, and a deeper reaction against their very intimacy. She was going to pay him out for the way she supposed he looked down on her intellectually, by playing merry hell with Tom, Abel and Brian. She'd pay him back for those headaches!

He could see too, that at a deeper level, at the level of her creative womanhood, Annie felt let down: there, last spring, among the buttercups, he should have possessed her, and should by now have offered to marry her. 'I lost pretty Nancy, by courting too slow!' Monck had teased him, when he discussed it with him, quoting from an old folk song. But with the university and then National Service coming, what could he do? Better not to be attached to anyone. But now he had no excuse, and Annie found that all he wanted to do, having read the poets, was to 'infuse her', she said, 'with his venom'. So there was trouble coming, and he felt it. Yet he was proud, too, to have his own woman in his own place, such as it was.

As he poured Annie out some cider the all clear went.

'False alarm.'

'It must have been a fault of identification. I'm told those towers at Trowse are to do with this. There's a device called a black box. Each of our planes has one, and returns a radio beam. Then they know it's a friend. The enemy, of course, don't have them.' Brian Bodley was holding forth, in his clever-dick way, in a fluting, know-all voice.

Annie encouraged him.

'A plane crashed into one of those towers. I saw the poor fellows being got out of it: we were on a bike ride, my sister and I. I love that poem, don't you, from the film: "Johnny in the clouds . . ." '

'Isn't that secret?' Paul asked Brian, interrupting.

'What?'

'About the radar station.'

Abel Kerr laughed derisively.

'I thought you were a bloody socialist, Paul?'

'So what?'

'Well, do you believe:

"There are some secrets
Should never be told," '

he sang mockingly.

Abel belched. 'The more secrets you tell the sooner the war will be over. Kill the cold war by keeping your mouth open!'

Paul was confused. Annie came to his rescue, and, to his delight, turned on Brian.

'I don't see how it helps if you are a pacifist to go in for, well, careless talk. Like if you know there's going to be a bomber raid, and you talk about it. Perhaps a friend will be in a bomber raid, and you talk about it. Perhaps a friend will be in one of the bombers, and . . .'

'That's how one gets corrupted. It's their war, but they play on our loyalty to our friends. I always make a point of talking carelessly,' said Brian. 'Suppose I went selling stuff to a fighter station: I see some papers lying about, secret ones. I read them of course. Very interesting. Would I be bound to keep the things to myself?'

'It's a kind of being . . . well, a traitor, that's the word. That's what it is!' Annie flared up, her large amber eyes innocently angry. 'You wouldn't do such a thing if you'd lost a brother in the war or something.'

'Have you?'

'No, but my brother's out there in the desert.'

'Why do we always have to talk about the fucking war?' Tom Sayle gleamed at them, clean, bristly and congenial. Yet they felt the strange denial there was in him, that he was a man, and that the war existed. They all felt the same: nothing they said or did really mattered. The war went on, like the weather. Much of its reality, such as the threat of coastal invasion, they had to deny, in order to keep on trying to live through it normally at all. Paul tried to answer.

'We've got to make our minds up. You've made yours up about National Service: I haven't, not yet. But it's not only that—you've got to make your mind up on all kinds of things—careless talk, defeatist talk, pro-Hitler talk, anti-Jew talk. I don't see why being a left-wing socialist has got to mean you give away military secrets, or talk against the war.'

'It's a question of the means of production. Hitler has taken them over. So have we, virtually. Things have got to go like that: the war will bring it to pass. After the war we shall find ourselves in a collective economy, willy nilly.'

'What's the point of fighting the war, then?'

'It's to protect our interests.'

'You're cynical, aren't you? I thought it was for principles.'

' "*Your* courage, *your* resolution, *your* efforts will bring *us* victory." The upper classes gave themselves away on their first poster. Yet they'd all like to do what Hitler's doing to his opponents. It's a phoney war, isn't it?'

Paul was furious with this man, whose words seemed to mean nothing to him. His neat, carbon paper suit! Gab! Paul wanted to disagree with everything he said, though he had to confess he inwardly agreed with some of it, the socialist part. It was all talk anyway. Abel and Tom disliked political argument because when it came up they could see before them the long and painful demand to justify their position as conscientious objectors —it would be yet another taste of the dismal experience of the tribunal, and this they hated to remember. As conscientious objectors they had spent a great deal of care on their arguments in preparation for the tribunal, only to be met there with the fatuous old arguments about duty and nation. Paul admired them for their principles. They could defend their position—much better, reflected Paul, than some of those who had found 'cushy' jobs in service units, or had wangled themselves into civilian jobs which exempted them from military service. Little deformed Don milking the aircraft factories—always pushing pound notes round at cafés and pubs for his bum-boys! But the conchies had suffered, and evaded arguments with bubbling amateurs like Bodley. Paul tried to direct the conversation in another direction.

'Where were you at school?' he asked the bright young man.

'Oh, I was at Mount Pleasant and then Brackendale, and went as far as School Certificate. But then I took a commercial course. I suppose since you are going to Cambridge you despise that.'

'I never think about it.' Paul felt that made it worse.

'Oh, but do you think about what's happening to you in your own education? How much you'll be taken in, indoctrinated in bourgeois attitudes to life? Cambridge is nearly all public school. There's a real class tie-up.'

'I shall join the Socialist Club.'

He was glad Roy Short wasn't there, to hear him asserting his anticipated membership of the Socialist Club against these people.

Paul pretended to be amused, but was really angry. Brian Bodley was attacking him because he was envious of him. Bodley had had to give up trying to get to a university. So he must disparage the whole thing.

'Of course you get a broad outlook on life. But it's all charged with upper-class attitudes—can't help yourself. I had a cousin at Trinity and you can't tell him anything.'

'You *can* tell me anything.'

'Well, let's have a republic then!'

'It wouldn't bother me that much, only it doesn't seem worth the effort of bringing it about.'

'There you are, you see. You really resist ideas.'

'Is that an idea?'

'What?'

'To bring about a republic.'

'It's a crucial part of my plan.'

'Your plan?'

'My plan to save England.'

'Oh, jolly good.'

'I'm not a socialist. I'm an anarchist.'

Brian Bodley polished his spectacles with a bright silk handkerchief. His plain blonde companion had said in an undertone: 'I agree. Oh yes, I agree.'

She said this whatever he said. He had all the accoutrements of being really grown-up—a cigarette holder, a cigarette case, a chromium-plated lighter, a fountain pen, a wrist-watch and 'radical', oh-so-radical, opinions. He displayed them all with as much conviction as if he were middle-aged: yet he was only eighteen. Then he had the girl, too, like a personal adornment, to say: 'Yes, I do agree,' very much under her breath. Yet he was such an *enfant terrible*, verbally demolishing 'bourgeois society' over a glass of gassy cider. Now Bodley turned, mercifully, to Abel's paintings.

'You've been influenced by Braque, of course.'

'Oh Christ,' said Kerr and went off into Sayle's room. 'Of course!' he shouted, farting loudly, with an obscene gesture.

Annie, who was warming up to a party in her gawky loose-limbed way, rather boyishly followed him. They put a record on the portable gramophone and danced.

168

'We–e–e want
A little white room
With a window by the sea!'

Paul felt lost. He couldn't dance well, and didn't want to be possessive. He didn't want to talk to the unstemmable Bodley. Nor did he want to accept that the only thing left for him was to talk to Tom Sayle, especially since there was no other man in the room for Sayle to make a pass at. Four more glasses of beer and Sayle would be uncontrollable.

'Just behind the steeple,
Not a sign of people
Who–o–o wants
Pe–eople?'

The nostalgic song evoked in him always the cinematic dreams of the love he would like to know, of living away with a woman, a weekend by the sea, a honeymoon intimacy by the fireside, a household. He looked round him at the dingy apartment: here he had hoped to entertain Annie alone in a new private little world. But now look at it! The first environment that was really *his*: he couldn't help comparing it with Moncklet's lovely house. A cigarette abandoned by Brian Bodley burned its way in the paint along the top of the spotted cream mantelpiece. Paul stubbed it out, with an angry distaste. He could feel Bodley's damp spit on it, and the burnt part was hot and stung his fingers. He went out to wash his hands in the kitchen. On the landing he passed Bodley with his blonde: he was demonstratively kissing her with his hands pawing all round her body. Sayle came into the kitchen pink and angry.

'Wants to take her in the bathroom. I told him not in any bloody room here. I won't have it, I *won't*. Not in my bloody flat.'

'A bit early, isn't it? I mean the party's only just started.'

'Bodley's a ram.'

You can talk, thought Paul. But he was glad Bodley had been frustrated: it was supposed to be his party. Yet with that plain girl! With God all things are possible, he thought, and smiled. He wished he could bring that out, Monckishly. But they were all such hoydens. He wished they would all go home, including Annie.

169

Where was Annie?

Brian Bodley was now on Paul's bed in a clinch with the plain blonde. Her woollen frock of a pathetically faded green drooped on her submissively relaxed, shapeless body. Paul watched her, and felt how sad it was that she desperately wanted the man to caress her because she was plain. He took in the cruelty of the clever Bodley to take advantage of this. Flushed, she began to groan: it was too much for Tom. Aggressively he took over a folder of drawings and prints.

'Brian, I wanted to ask you about these. Do you think they're worth anything?'

There was no holding Brian back from such an invitation to give his expert opinions, which he would give on any subject. He dropped the girl and began to talk. Olga lay abandoned on the divan, looking peevishly flushed round the mouth and deprived. Paul hated his party now: to feel responsible for such grossness in such ugly people!

But then he saw Annie. She was lying on Abel Kerr's lap her head back, and the man's mouth full on hers. Abel's hand was under her pullover, and moving over her breasts. Then he began to explore her thighs. Annie didn't look at Paul, though he paced over to the window, deliberately, agitatedly. His girl, his lovely, warm-hearted own Annie was gone, in a glazed gaze of lust. She was breathing loudly in passion, in a possessed way such as Paul had never seen in a woman—certainly it was not a state he had ever generated in her. Kerr laughed, as if at her abandonment, and sank his hairy mouth on hers again. She wrapped her arms ecstatically round his fat body and pressed her breasts to his hairy open front.

Paul, stunned, had never seen a woman lapsed out so: certainly he had never known a girl to let herself go so under his own caresses. It seemed strangely animal and frightening. The lustful confidence of the man! His shamelessness! But more frightening were the feelings in himself. Had there been a bludgeon, or spiked fire-iron, or heavy beam within reach the boy would have brought it down with all his force on Abel Kerr's greasy balding head. His vision, already a little bleary with alcohol, dissolved, and only a distant distaste, a distant need to keep himself separate from them all, kept him in possession of himself. Yet he must find relief somewhere. His world, his love idyll, had dissolved, here in his own room!

The siren went again. But they all ignored it, the blonde in deprived anguish, Annie in aroused lust, Tom and Brian in intellectual combat as Tom interposed himself between Bodley and this woman who wanted him so immediately. Only Abel seemed, by his occasional indifferent laughter, and his hairy personality, to be himself in his coarse way. He was like a rutting animal, murmuring to the heaving Annie, detached and gloating.

Tormented, Paul stood for a moment, paralysed with hate. She's rotten, his soul shouted within him. Yet he knew she wasn't: she was kind-hearted and young. And at this his soul shouted the more deafeningly—it was that kind-hearted youngness he had wanted to be their unique possession. Now it was all over. Tears burst from him.

'All so ugly!' he cried, unnaturally loudly in the kitchen. He had to do something, to relieve the agony of his jealousy.

He picked up a heavy full tin of Cerebos salt and hurled it through the landing window. The window was a large one, some six feet high with eight panes. Sayle had had two huge frames made to black it out, but they still stood on the landing, and the window was bare. The Cerebos tin knocked out the centre crosspiece and the rest of the window collapsed. The whole made a satisfying crash.

'Christ, what's that?'

Abel was the first out. He found Paul sobbing.

'Have we been hit?' said a breathless, Norfolk voice.

The voice was Annie's, strangely familiar, at the moment when it had seemed to Paul that she had gone away from him for ever. But he could not move. His arms were cramped by misery in front of his streaming face.

'What—did you do that, smash our bloody windows just because I was loosening up your girlfriend?'

The indifferent sensuality in Abel spoke jeeringly. Paul tore into his face with his fist, making Abel's plump nose go awry, and dark red blood spurt out into his moustache hairs. Tom Sayle clasped Kerr from behind. The timber men were strong, and Paul was scared now of their revenge. Annie, come to suddenly, was screaming. Brian Bodley was talking about something MacDougall or someone said about sexual jealousy.

Paul almost jumped over the toothy dwarf who was coming up the stairs. Dirty Don was grinning maliciously and wagging a long finger of his large lady-like hands.

'You'll have to pay.'

'I'll ... be ... glad, to pay, and get out of this, and you ... scrabbling about in the cupboards at night, trying to get through into my room.'

Paul paused and panted. He felt mad.

'You ...'

He gasped. His hands hurt.

'You dirty buggers.'

Sayle laughed. Somebody threw a bottle. It smashed under Tom's bicycle. Paul crunched out over the splinters, kicking the dustbin over with a crash. People were gathering in the street.

'Paul! Paul! I didn't mean it. It was all a mistake. Can't you believe it? I ... I was ... a little squiffy, that's all, Paul. Don't you trust me?'

But he shook her hand from his cuff speechlessly, and walked out into the night. As he got near his home the heavy guns near the coast opened up and he spent a restless night with his mother trying to sleep in the air raid shelter in his home garden. There were no bombs dropped in Norwich, but attacks were made on airfields round about. Occasionally in the night he dreamt of bottles being hurled down to burst at his feet, as he tossed on the wire bunk underground. The stars paled at last in a misty dawn.

'Why, you'd better stay at home for a bit, boy. You look all out o' condition!' his mother said. She sensed there had been a crisis. She never liked Sayle, though fortunately she had never seen Dirty Don. Next day she went with him, to collect his bits and pieces from Sayle's flat, in a taxi.

'Brought your mother?' Sayle sneered. Paul was clipped.

'How much?'

'Oh, three or four quid'll cover it.'

His mother paid the man out of her handbag. Paul noticed that her hands were trembling. He felt he was a child again and couldn't cope at all.

A few weeks later Paul met Annie again. She wore a hat and coat, and had her hair up. She looked grown-up, womanly, and he approached her respectfully, though he despised her now too, and bitterly hated her disloyalty to their shared secrets of the box office and the riverside. But they had a cup of coffee together, while Annie pursued her bright chatter that he now found so provincial. Yet her large brown eyes sparkled and he liked her again, warmly.

'Paul, you know . . . you know, what we could never do ?'

He was startled, and had a cold premonition of what was coming: Abel had exerted his potency, then, had he ?

'It's happened to me now. And I'm going to marry him.'

'Oh.' Not, surely, the sweaty, farting Kerr ?

'The first time he took me out, funny, wasn't it ? You and I— our love was never . . . consummated, was it ? Yet, well with this one he took me straight to bed.'

Paul's eyes filled with tears, and then he laughed. She was so naïve and generous and floppy. Floppily provincial. He felt jubilant at having escaped her—escaped the deeper tie. My God! In twenty years!

'What are you laughing for ?'

She looked hurt.

'I'm thinking of you married to Abel Kerr. Well, remember our sweeter moments, Annie, dear.'

It was her turn to throw up tears.

'I will.'

She bit her friendly loose mouth.

Paul put his hand on her shoulder. She pushed him away.

'Only it isn't Abel, you silly man, it's Brian!'

'Brian! Oh Christ!'

He got up, really distressed, and looked at her face.

'You don't mean it.'

'I do!'

'Bloody Brian Bodley!'

She was angry now, a loyal fiancée.

'He just took me to bed, just like that. He's really grown-up. And he's *clever*.'

Paul was deeply hurt, jealous and angry.

'Well, cheerio,' he sneered. 'I hope you'll be happy,' he added, with a scoffing grunt.

Annie was going off, crushed and defiant.

'My God,' Paul said loudly. 'I hate that bastard!'

She stopped, bewildered. She wanted Paul to like the man she had decided to marry. Paul felt that if he said more she might cling to him, or leave him unkindly. There was no cause. They'd get on all right. Could he claim he loved Annie?

He went hurriedly up to her.

'I'm sorry to be bitter, Annie, but I'm badly jealous . . . though I know it's all over between us. I'm glad, now . . . I couldn't claim you. I didn't claim you enough. But you see, I've got to go away to Cambridge and then the Army. We'd have parted anyway, wouldn't we, Annie, dear?'

Annie, tearful, nodded.

'My father liked you,' he added sadly. 'He'll be upset.' It seemed a silly thing to say now.

Paul felt a surge of tenderness for her. As he watched the rather ambling figure go, in her unfamiliar hat, he was glad he had met Annie.

But he was amazed at the speed with which he had lost her.

'Mrs Bloody Brian Bodley!' he swore to himself vindictively.

19

Paul went back to the Crypt again to live, feeling altogether defeated in his attempt to be independent in any way. He busied himself in work, reorganising all the little man's files, which were a muddle. Moncklet could never find a bill or a letter, shoving them all into a drawer. Only in the theatre, in his art, was he professional and exact. Monck was very grateful. Archly, he declared: 'Never an ill wind! If you hadn't broken with Annie I would never have had my files spring-cleaned.'

'I can forget her in the day,' said Paul. 'It's at night it all comes back.'

'Ah, yes,' said Moncklet. 'It takes a long time to forget the bodily comfort . . . but I must play the part of Pandarus: "If she be lost, why, we will recover another." '

'That seems cynical to me.'

'She wasn't intelligent enough for you, Paul.'

'Funnily enough, we both knew that. It used to give her headaches to think of it. But she was warm-hearted, Moncklet.'

'I'll grant you that. She brought me a pot of honey once, when I was ill, when you were away at Oxford having interviews. She is *kind*.'

'Too warm-hearted for bloody Brian Bodley.' He sighed.

'He'll cut his throat in the church,' said Moncklet, quoting Laertes.

'I wonder how long it will take.'

'For some people—all their life.'

The little man trotted off into the kitchen to peel potatoes, and Paul turned to read through a bunch of letters he was finding it difficult to classify. It was odd for Moncklet to go off with such a cloud over him, he thought: he watched the little man's retreating back, thinking that there were areas of his experience of which he knew nothing and which he would never penetrate. But he could

175

detect a deep sorrow somewhere there: it was out of this that there came his funds of sympathy—so that one could always go to collapse, there at Ninham's Court, in a crisis.

Paul was surprised by the persistence with which Roy Short kept asking him to go alone with him down to the Music House. One Saturday morning the next spring he came to the Crypt quite clearly determined about this.

'When are there no people there?' Short asked, looking inquisitively into his face with his sidelong short-sighted eyes.

'I've no idea,' replied Paul. 'The discussion group is Wednesday evenings as you know and I think there's concerts sometimes on Fridays. I suppose there are committee meetings on odd days. Why do you want to know?'

'I'd like to go in and have a look round when there's nobody there.'

'Whatever for?'

'Ha! Ha!' replied Roy, skipping and cracking his fingers. Then, with a particularly meaningful look, half in play, half in an odd sinister seriousness, he asked: 'Have you got a key?'

'N . . . no,' said Paul. 'I do know how to get in, though.'

'Let's go!' said Roy, striding off, drawing Paul along by his sleeve.

'I still don't know why you want to go in there. You see, it was something of a favour to be allowed in, because I'd said to Frost I'd love to play that grand piano in there. He spoke to Melchett Pike, who's secretary of the Music Society, whom I don't even know, and he said it would be OK. I don't know that I ought to let anyone else in.'

'Don't be so dog in a manger,' said Roy, pretending to be hurt. 'Melchett Pike is a horrible reactionary pansy,' he added, cracking his fingers angrily. 'You can't refuse to let me in! It's obviously politically important we should look thoroughly into this institution.'

He made an ingratiating bow at Paul, and acted a fawning smile. Paul could see that the man was exerting his influence over him, as his sometime head boy and as one who liked his company. There was something that alarmed him about Roy's obsessional need to get into the Music House, and his angry disdain for Pike and the Society.

Roy presented it to him as a boyish lark, just to go in and have a root round the place. Roy was like that. He had a kind of playful delinquency, which, when it saw an open door, urged him to go in and see what was going on. But just as he would be the first to go in, he'd be the first to slip out, leaving Paul, who was so naïve, to be caught and explain why he was in there at all.

Roy had done something similar one day as they were passing a wholesale chemist's near St Andrew's Hall: walking down an open space called The Plain, they suddenly saw, through two doors which happened to be open, tall flaming burners and men in white coats working over glass flasks bubbling on tripods, with huge stills looming behind them.

'Oh look!' exclaimed Roy. 'The Alchemists.'

' "Sutton's Analytical Laboratories",' read Paul. ' "Danger. No admittance to unauthorised persons." '

'Huh!' exclaimed Roy, going boldly in. 'I bet they're doing something appalling like testing chemicals on rabbits, or trying pesticides on guinea pigs!'

He walked in confidently as if on business there and Paul, puzzled, followed him. Roy peered at the rows of brown bottles and brass stands holding up complex structures of glass pipes, and then as rapidly slid out, seeing a man in a white coat with a bald head stepping towards them. But Paul did not see him go, and was chatting happily, in their play-acting way, aloud to himself.

'. . . of piss and eggshells. Hey! Look at that row of poisons, arsenic, mercuric chloride, strychnine . . . enough to poison the whole of Norwich.'

'Oh,' he said, 'sorry,' as he turned to bump into the overalled chemist.

'Have you any business in here?' the bald elderly man said sharply.

Paul was confused. He couldn't see Roy anywhere.

'I came in, following my friend . . .'

The man caught his sleeve.

'Mr Blakemore!'

'Coming!' from the end of the benches, where a tall yellow flame flickered, lighting up the big laboratory room, all shadows and strange shapes of jars and drums of chemicals. There were real old distilling retorts, like small elephants' heads, as in old engravings of alchemists' shops.

'Whatever's the matter?' exclaimed Paul, rather nonplussed.

'Can't you read?' said the elderly man, in a blunt and unpleasant voice. The other came up, a young man whose white overall was stained with yellow spots. The older man held Paul's arm tightly.

'Just see if he's whipped anything,' he said. The other began to pat Paul's pockets.

Paul protested.

'There's absolutely no need for that. You've no right ... of *course* I haven't taken anything. I only wandered in after a friend...'

'Where is your friend?'

'I don't know. He must have gone out again.'

'There's a clear notice out there, young man. We didn't put that up for fun. We've had several lots of drugs stolen recently...'

'Oh, I see,' said Paul. 'Well, I'm sorry ... I wouldn't have come in myself.'

He was furious with Roy, but his plump friend only laughed. Paul found him several hundred yards away, doubled up with laughter, pressing his hand on his stomach.

'Ha! Ha! Caught by the Alchemist! Wonder he didn't turn you into an alligator!'

'Oh, bugger you, Roy. They went through all my pockets. I was worried in case they got the police in. I think you ought to have stood by me.'

'Me?' said Roy, 'I only peeped in. *You* went sniffing into the poisons.'

> "I sent you of his faeces there calcined:
> Out of that calx, I have won the salt of mercury ..." '

For Roy his knowledge of literature and history was always a kind of weapon against 'them' and his attitude to the world was this combination of playful egoism and contemptuous hostility. As they walked through the city to Castle Meadow, Paul felt increasingly uneasy at being persuaded to let Roy into the Music House. He knew it was often left open. At the Maddermarket they locked up at night, of course; but during the day, and all through the three weeks' rehearsals, the theatre stood open and unlocked, people drifting in and out. They took great care of some things, like ancient musical instruments and rare books. But there was a pleasant lack of suspicion, and everyone was trusted.

Many of the expensive-looking jewels were paste, made from cheap costume jewellery bought in chain stores. But some of the swords, period waistcoats, embroidered gowns, hangers and belts and some jewels were valuable, even priceless. It wouldn't have been difficult to make quite a haul from the theatre, if some unscrupulous person had tried. But, despite the poverty all round in the sordid streets by Guildhall Hill, there was little danger of burglary in those wartime days.

Paul felt a great love and loyalty towards the theatre and Monck's house, where the books alone were so valuable, not least because some were signed and inscribed by famous authors. To him all that was inviolable, and he had extended the same feeling to the Music House, because it was a centre for culture and intellectual exchange. He was disturbed to think that Roy intended some mischief. But the man had a strong political philosophical line.

'Honesty is a bourgeois concept: all those things in museums and places, they've all been stolen anyway: we must give them back to the people. The bourgeoisie steal things and then erect their own property interests into absolute moral laws. It's absurd. They must be *smashed*.'

So he admonished Paul, all the way along London Street.

At last they reached the arched door leading in to the Music House. Paul lifted a stone urn at the side of the threshold, and there was a Yale key. Roy guffawed.

'Pretty elementary that,' he said, cracking his fingers. 'They can't really care much about what they've got in there!'

It was strange being in the building alone with Roy in such a mood. Paul felt furtive, as he heard their voices echoing in the big empty rooms. He had come in once before alone, to play the big Bechstein: but the echoes had overcome him and he had fled, feeling uncomfortable. How could he justify his presence there, when he played so badly? The huge instrument seemed to amplify all his clumsy faults, and he felt shy and inadequate, even in front of no one but the dim shadows in the ancient stone and timber rooms. Now he felt even less justification for being there, especially as Roy poked around, opening and shutting doors and peering in the cupboards.

'Why should Melchett Pike have all these symphonies?' Short suddenly asked, having opened the gramophone cupboard.

There were rows and rows of albums on the shelves, in black and maroon folders with gilt lettering.

'I think they belong to the Music Society,' said Paul. 'They have sessions listening to them on that.'

He pointed to a tall gramophone horn, some six feet high, shaped like a tuba straightened out, and made of papier mâché.

'What a ridiculous cult! How crafty-weedy!'

'I don't see why you say that.'

'Sitting round that great pooping thing, gloating on symphony after symphony, weeping into their hankies. What miles and miles of nice sound! No one could ever listen to all these. There are hundreds. He ought not to have so many. No one ought. Look! They're all marked with his name.'

'Well, why don't you join the club? Isn't it good of him to let people use them?'

'Huh!' exclaimed Roy. 'I shall join it, like this. I shall take two symphonies, and you'll take two.'

He yanked out two albums at random.

Paul hesitated, appalled. Roy seemed to need to take something out of the heart of the Music House, to spite the man he barely knew. Whatever did he want? Paul had a feeling of foreboding, and felt a cold quiver of fear.

'You mean . . . borrow some, to listen to?'

'People in the club can, can't they?'

'I don't know. I've never joined. And you're not a member either. You have to pay a guinea a year.'

'I'm making myself an *honorary* member. Pike has no right to hoard all these symphonies like this. He's a rich queer pig. Here you are: you take these two, and I'll take these.'

'I don't think we ought to.'

'Ha! Ha! I'd love to see his face when he finds they're missing.'

Paul put the albums down, rather flutteringly.

'I can't,' he said.

'Can't what?' said Roy, with a contemptuous point. 'I *order* you to take them!'

'I can't steal other people's things.'

'What rot! How silly you are! Laws about property are only the erection of class interests into universal rules. "Steal." What rubbish!'

'It's wrong!'

'Only because your mother says so. We . . .'

Roy did a strange little dance, in his stiff and plump way.

'We float *above morality*.'

He did a mock glissade towards Paul and dug him quite painfully in the ribs.

'Nietzsche said so. We must find a new basis for our morality. So we must despise all bourgeois morality as mere epiphenomena of a corrupt society, we must experiment: I *order* you to take two symphonies. And I will take two.'

Paul found himself unable to throw off Roy's influence. He made it such a game, such a childish cheeky game. It seemed absurdly solemn to resist. And Paul didn't want to break up their friendship. Perhaps he could find some way of returning the albums. So they slipped away, carrying two symphonies each, locking the door and leaving the key under the urn again.

On the bus, Roy pushed his two albums on Paul's lap, and made to get off.

'Keep these for me for a bit,' he said, laughing at Paul's discomfort. 'Ha! Ha! Goodbye!' He made another balletic gesture.

So, feeling overcome with the wrongness of what they were doing, Paul hid four albums of classical symphonies in his bedroom. He didn't even have a gramophone on which to play them.

He had forgotten all about the incident when, one Saturday morning two months later, there was a knock at the glass-paned front door of their semi-detached house. Through the crinkly glass he could see the outlines of two men in hats. His mother was out shopping for the weekend.

He opened the door. The two men were strangers to him, though he thought he had seen one of them at a gramophone session at the Music House. Paul blushed. One young man wore a brown pork-pie hat. Both were conservatively dressed in dark raincoats and ties with blue and grey stripes. Paul didn't ask them in: indeed, he kept the door only half open to them.

'Are you Paul Grimmer?' one of the young men asked, a boy with a pink and white face, with a slight blue shadow of beard and eyes with long dark lashes. They both watched his face steadily, and Paul became uncomfortable.

'Yes,' he said, with a rising sound, to emphasise his incredulity at being visited by two strangers.

'We're sorry to bother you, but there's a bit of a mystery at the Music House.'

'A mystery?' His voice sounded cracked.

'Some gramophone records have disappeared. We've been checking over and they've gone.'

'Disappeared?'

He would have to be careful what he said. He looked past them, at the bees working the white Alyssum in the cracks of his father's concrete paths. It was so familiar, the little garden and its fence in late summer dryness: the intrusion into it of this thing that was so wrong for him seemed foreign. It would be so easy to say: 'I borrowed them.' But he must surely talk to Roy first. Inwardly, he was confused. But he must hide that. He was aware of being suspiciously silent.

'Well?' he said.

The men moved their feet, looked at one another. The fresh-faced one licked his lips and put his hands in his raincoat pocket.

'We are asking various people . . . you see . . . they might have borrowed them . . . without telling the secretary . . .'

'You know, they're Pike's. They're quite valuable, really, about five pounds each.'

'We don't want any more to disappear.'

'Oh dear,' said Paul who had recovered his composure, 'how awful. Well, I'm afraid I don't know anything about it.'

They looked surprised. What did they know? The fresh-faced man turned slightly minatory.

'Well . . .' he said, turning and sighing. 'We shall have to get it investigated.'

Paul thought of the albums, pushed under his bed upstairs. Blast Roy, he thought. Here were some youths, missing records from their music club: what the hell had this to do with 'bourgeois epiphenomena' and experiments in revolution? He felt sick: but now he couldn't give way. He would have to think of some way out.

'Sorry,' he said, making to close the door. One of the men turned back.

'You're quite sure you and your friends haven't borrowed a

couple of albums just to play over at school or something? We don't *want* to go to the police.'

Paul shook his head, rather numbed, sullen. The man shrugged his shoulder. Grimmer realised that they knew very well he did have them. But he couldn't give them up: he couldn't explain. What maddened him most was that he couldn't face explaining how he had been so absurd as to have Roy land the theft on him as a game, and that it was really nothing to do with him at all, nothing of his.

Paul Grimmer was furious when he came to himself after this visitation. He knew he had panicked and that it would have been much better to have made a clean breast of everything. But he could not do that with any conviction. The whole thing was so alien to him: it was no part of his philosophy to steal or to justify stealing. He never wanted anything of anyone else's: he was never covetous, except of other people's cultivation and he knew the remedy for that.

He walked through Christchurch Road and took a trolley bus to the top of St Stephens. There he walked along the old flint wall of the city, with a row of houses built on it, to Short's. His friend kept him on the doorstep: he was still in his dressing gown, though it was mid-day.

'I want to talk about these gramophone records.'

Short blinked sleepily, and said, languidly: 'What records?'—making an angry face at the same time, mouthing 'Shut up!'

Paul suddenly saw an advantage: Short didn't want his mother to know. She was always very quickly aware of trouble: Paul could see her ruddy face and watering eyes moving out from the kitchen towards the hall.

'You know perfectly well what I mean.'

Short looked him steadily in the face, very short-sighted, and angry now with Paul's 'tactlessness' as he would put it.

'I simply don't know what you're talking about, you horrible man.'

What a baffling, almost hypnotic will the man had! Paul felt blocked, his fury mounting within him. Short's mimed 'Shut up' revealed clearly enough that he did know: yet, for his mother's benefit, he assumed an outraged innocence—and now this bold mask was to be preserved against him in her hovering presence.

'Why don't you ask him in?'

'I don't want to come in,' said Paul, 'I'll talk about it here and now.'

Short tried to slam the door: Paul stuck his foot in it. It hurt badly, but he kept it there.

'Are you boys quarrelling?' asked the mother, becoming ruddier than ever, and beginning to smoulder over her eldest son, whom she worshipped. 'Whatever is that about?'

'Go away, mother,' said Short coldly.

She turned with a snort, and went back into the kitchen.

Roy Short stopped pressing the door on Paul's foot, and cracked his fingers instead.

'A couple of friends of Pike's came to ask me whether I had them,' said Paul. 'And I said I hadn't.'

'More fool you,' said Short in a low voice. 'You *have* got them, *four* albums, in *your* room.'

'And *you* landed me with them,' Paul said, astonished at his coldbloodedness.

'I? I have nothing to do with them at all.'

'But . . .' spluttered Grimmer.

'Prove it,' said Short. 'Ha! Ha! I know nothing whatever about them. Do you mind if I shut the door?'

'Bloody Hell,' cried Paul. 'And it was your idea.'

'You don't have to accept my ideas. If I tell you to put your head in the fire, etcetera.'

'You *ordered* me to take them.'

'Why should you take any notice of what I say?'

'I shall take them back.'

'Do.' Short gave a maddening smile, with his big regular teeth. 'Very sensible.'

'What was all that about . . . about teaching Pike a lesson, for being rich and beastly, for being a Wagnerian fascist?'

'You don't understand. It was just a hypothesis . . .'

'A hypo . . . a hypothesis . . .' exclaimed Paul. 'What the hell do you mean?'

'Do you have to stand there a-arguing?' came Mrs Short's plaintive Norfolk voice from the kitchen. Neither took any notice.

'I am curious,' said Short, awake and self-possessed now, 'I

184

want to see this place, you take me. It's like a play. Pike is a fascist, I say to myself, because he likes Wagner and Strauss and lectures on the greatness of the Siegfried music. Let us see how we can make him uncomfortable: so, we find his place is crammed with gramophone records. I propose to you that we punish him, and you readily agree. Mission accomplished. What happens next is none of my business.'

'But it was your idea!'

'Ideas—I lay no claim to ideas: if people take them, it's none of my business. Much of life is acting. I acted that part: you fell in with it. I'm a nihilist, I told you: we turn the screw here, we turn the screw there, discrediting society, discrediting reactionaries, discrediting bourgeois values and concepts.'

'A very egoistical nihilist!'

'So what—the damage is done, as far as I'm concerned. So long as I *survive* to do more mischief—that's all that matters.'

'But what about *me*?' Paul shouted, pushing his face in at the door, and pointing to himself.

'Don't shout! There you are.'

'But I am a friend of yours . . .! Or *was*!'

'Not any longer, I think, or you wouldn't be shouting at me like that.'

'Fah!' said Paul, really baffled, not knowing what to say.

'Do you mean "Pshaw!"?' asked Short, insultingly, showing his big white teeth in a grin.

'I really must shut the door now. It's cold. I really don't know anything about those records, you beastly man. You'll just have to deal with it yourself.'

The door shut in his face. For some time Paul stood there, imagining himself picking up a brick and hurling it through the window. In the end, he didn't do it for Mrs Short's sake: she had been kind to him and given him cake. Instead, he turned round and got a bus home. There, he wrapped the four albums in a piece of brown paper and took another bus to the city. He walked down King Street, only to find there was no key under the urn, and the lock had been changed: the Yale lock was a bright shiny new brass one. He was in despair, and expected any moment to be caught red-handed. No one, certainly, must see him. His heart beat loudly. And then he noticed that the door was not shut at all, it was ajar. He pushed his shoulder to it, and it yielded. In the dark interior, he saw a bentwood chair. Hastily, he placed the four gramophone record albums on it, and fled.

His relief, as he walked back to the open space by the Corn Hall, was enormous. He felt like the angel, the greeny bronze angel on the war memorial there, putting the sword away. He was free: he had put it all right. So, that was the end of it.

But what, he thought, as he walked along Castle Meadow under the great mound—what was it that was so wrong about it all? He really had only intended to keep the records for a short while, falling in with Roy's idea of making use of them. The summer had dragged on, and he had forgotten them. Was he just afraid of being caught and prosecuted? No, the worst thing about it all was the action was not and had never been his: it was totally a wrongness imposed upon him—by someone he'd thought was his best friend. He had often admired Roy, even felt a great fondness for him, not least for his play-acting. But how, in this closeness, had the man forced him to be so false, and made such pointless use of him? Would others do that? How could he know? He walked down through the Arcade to the marketplace, where he bought a pound of Cox's orange pippins and sat eating them thoughtfully on the bus home.

It struck him, suddenly, during a concert in the Guildhall, that he had never even heard those records. He had been watching the percussionist, trying to relate the structure of the music to the man's movements, the way he struck his tubular bells, tuned and beat his kettle drums, and the way he moved about his corner of the orchestra space. Thought and emotion transformed into movement, the lonely performer following the composer's intentions, pacing about like a wild cat in his cage, attending to the sounds in the air.

Nothing from the albums he and Roy Short had 'borrowed' had ever come alive like that. What was it that Short had wanted, as he had declared in his covetous, hostile way: 'Pike doesn't need all those records!'? What had he taken? Discs of black, brittle plastic. The cardboard sleeves bound in maroon cloth, the gilt lettering. There they had lain under his bed for weeks in limbo, suspended, until the awkward and embarrassing moment when he had at last put them back through the door of the Music House.

186

What had he stolen? He had never enjoyed them: he had taken nothing from Pike, nothing that ever came to life, in his ears, in his consciousness. Four albums of inert bakelite, or whatever it was, and dusty cardboard, had been moved from the Music House clubroom to his bedroom study. He had stolen no meanings: he had not even worn the grooves of the recordings so much as by the millionth of an inch.

The thought left him perplexed as to where meanings resided. Now he was caught in the toils of moral meanings. He couldn't stop thinking about it. Yes, the albums were Pike's property, and he had no right to take them. But this was confused in his mind with Short's meanings. There was a meaning in Short's stealing that he could not fathom. Short, with his irascible and possessive mother, cracking his fingers as he did with some deep inner rage unbeknown to himself, had wanted, somehow, to get the goodness, the sweetness out of the ancient Music House, out of Pike and the slightly homosexual entourage that worshipped music through his club. He had taken the albums out of the cupboards with malicious glee—loading Paul's arms with them. Then he had lost all interest.

But Paul had only the husk, the drab objects. He didn't even have a record player. The unlawful possession he was accused of was the possession of nothing. And, in any case, how could one ever be accused of stealing music? It was free—free as the air. Am I stealing music now? he thought, as the orchestra threw itself into a great *tutti*, the drummer playing his sticks like someone beating metal on a bench. The soundwaves fly out in their great circles: a little wave comes into my ear—I feel Beethoven's passion, and take it into myself. Is that stealing? Do I steal when I come out of an art gallery, and carry the impressions of Constable and Corot in my memory? Steal meaning?

Meaning, he decided, was above the mundane dimensions in which theft or lawful possession are concerned. One couldn't be accused of stealing meaning. So was he blameless?

It was a strange mood in which to go up to Cambridge. With a start, he suddenly realised there might be some kind of police investigation: he had heard rumours from some of the people at the Maddermarket, and others whom he met from the discussion group. Was he under suspicion here in his home city?

20

Paul should have been withdrawing himself from Norwich and preparing himself to go up to Cambridge. Moncklet, rather grim-faced and wearing his dark grey trilby, a blue woollen scarf and overcoat, stumped out dragging him by the arm to buy him a teaset.

'You can buy a perfectly good tea service at Woolworths,' said the little man, 'only it will have to be pale blue or cream. You will have to decide which to have: cream is such a disgustingly non-descript colour that you had best have pale blue. Both are thirty-two shillings and sixpence. You are not worth it, but you must have something to eat your breakfast with. You'll never get up in time to go to Hall for it.'

So the tea service, wrapped in newspaper, went into the second-hand cabin trunk which Paul was taking to Pemning. It was now September, and term began on the fourth of October.

But instead of cutting himself off from Norwich, Paul Grimmer fell in love with a girl in the Public Library. He had met her before, at a party. Like several of the brighter grammar school girls, she had a part-time job at the library desk, stamping books. There, under the bright lights, a girl could display herself to the adult world dressed in her best and wearing make-up, taking the tickets out of the world's books, and stamping them with a date.

Annie had not been an intellectual, by any means, he laughed to himself: she used to look at the pictures in his books, but the text daunted her. Once, when they had been at a party, he found himself arguing fiercely with Joan Banham about an interpre-tation of *Hamlet*. Annie had sulked, because he had paid the other girl so much attention, with her dark close-cut hair, the fine bones in her face and the dainty gold sleepers in her pierced ears.

Now she seemed a gate-keeper on the path to the higher culture. Suddenly it became of great importance to him to go to the Central Library when Joan was there. She was on duty, he found, on Monday, Wednesday and Friday evenings. So he became an avid borrower, three times a week, and he found most interesting those shelves from which he could watch her moving at her work, hoping for a glance in his direction.

She was a small girl, sharp and vivacious. Her father had been a civil service officer out in India, and there was something Eastern about her—a certain look in the eye, the movements of her fine doll-like fingers. Her neat, quick hands seemed to him like those of a Japanese servant girl as she quickly snapped the tickets out of the manila pockets of his books. She had a neat little smile too, rather supercilious, with a dimple at each end of it and a tiny crease line round the corners of her mouth. Her little mouth made into a Cupid's bow with bright red lipstick was quick and precise.

'More James Joyce?' she exclaimed. 'I can't think how you understand it.'

'I don't,' he said. 'Not all of it.'

It was *Anna Livia Plurabelle*, one of the small sections of *Work in Progress* published from time to time by Faber.

'Probably a good thing.'

She was a little puritanical. She sometimes wore a small silver cross hanging at her throat.

'I'd like to try *Ulysses*: can you get me it?'

'It's kept here on a special shelf. It's in, I think. Shall I go and ask?'

'Why can't I just take it?'

'Why can't you?'

She took the large green volume and peered inside at the front cover. She wore spectacles and was a little short-sighted.

'I don't see any reason, if you've got a spare ticket, unless . . .'

She suddenly looked at him, and went a little pale.

'What?'

It was at once clear to them both that she had heard he was a thief. Her eyes were full of trouble now. She displayed herself —even though she was only seventeen—as quick-acting, as self-acting, and decisive. But here was a problem: she wanted to impress him by her librarianship play. But suppose it was true that he stole gramophone records ? She wouldn't want to impress him, nor would she want her library career spoilt, for a cad. In her home they still used the word 'cad'. But she couldn't believe this young man, with his earnest green eyes, was a 'bad 'un' as her father would put it. So, recovering her composure, she looked deeply, straight into them. Paul felt a quiver in his belly, so penetrating was her look. He turned his eyes aside, to examine her thin gold sleepers. She grew cool again.

'There are some things you just can't say to people, aren't there ?' she said.

The blood rose in his throat, and he couldn't speak. He looked round, carefully making sure no one was in ear-shot.

'Yes,' he croaked. 'I . . . I think I'm in love with you,' he added huskily.

'Oh!' She was really surprised. 'Oh, but that wasn't what I meant at all . . . I wasn't referring to that sort of thing . . . Oh, dear . . .' she became quite confused.

'I'm sorry,' he said. 'It just seemed the next line in the play.'

She laughed, a musical little flute of a laugh, which she suppressed with a kind of sneeze, and a hand over her mouth.

'No . . .' she went on. 'I had just heard . . .' She gave him a darting, penetrating glance, of great intimacy, '. . . that you weren't trustworthy.' She gave a breathless laugh, quite a spasm, at her audacity.

'Me!' he said, really outraged. 'Oh, that!' He looked really miserable. 'I'll explain it all to you, one day.'

He took the book, and turned. Then he held it out. 'Are you going to let me have it ?'

She smiled. The smile meant to convey that she believed in him, against rumour. He took it as a response to his declaration of affection, accepting it. He leaned forward, feeling faint, the bright lights, books, tickets, papers, posters of the library cubicle swimming in his eyes. With a little tinkly laugh, she drew back and, brusquely, stamped his book with a click of her rachet stamper, slamming its cover to, and pushing it towards him.

The production of *Twelfth Night* had been postponed, and there had been a crisis over who was to play Viola. Joan, who had always wanted a part in the theatre, had applied for an audition for the role, and had been accepted. Moncklet was obviously taken by her rather boyish figure. Paul was to play Fabian, a dull part, the last work he would do at the theatre before going up to the university. At least it enabled him to be there, tormented as he was by jealousy of Benny, the middle-aged teacher who was playing the Duke.

Paul was always amazed at the way people transcended themselves in the little theatre, even before they applied greasepaints nine and five to their faces. Monck's artistic firmness was the clue: from the young people who took the youthful leads, little more than children and dizzy with the musty smells of the wardrobe, the Leichner and the face-powder, he insisted on clarity. They could speak verse if it was natural to them with a slight Norfolk accent: but they must be clear. And there must be a good reason in the art for anything they did, in posture or gesture.

'I wonder why you did that?' the little man asked suddenly, as Joan made an awkward pause. Paul was there, watching.

'I thought she might have suddenly behaved like a woman and gestured to him to sit down, when it was for him, really, to indicate that to her.'

'Good ... yes, we'll keep that. Only when you *do* sit down, perhaps you could cross your legs very self-consciously—because this would be something that wouldn't come naturally to a girl then.'

Under Monck's coloured lighting, the young, hardly out of school, became the noble youths of Padua or Illyria—not least because Peter's costumes, many of them museum pieces were so historically accurate. Monck had been studying Veronese with enthusiasm again, and his ambition in this play was to have every scene a tableau from paintings of that period, both in his scenery and the costumes.

Joan was almost transparently pale as she held her doll-like face to the Duke's and spoke of:

'A blank, my Lord, she never told her love
But let concealment, like a worm i' the bud
Feed on her damask cheek . . .'

In the shadowy interior of the empty little auditorium, she

brought out with clarity all the strange ambivalence of sexuality in the part:

> 'I am all the daughters of my father's house.
> And all the brothers too . . .'

Paul found himself, even at rehearsals, much moved, and he was transfixed by Joan's acting, the yearning seriousness she conveyed and seemed to glow in. He turned to the little man, who was stroking his bald forehead thoughtfully between his thumb and forefinger. Moncklet's grey eyes were full of water: and he even gave a grunt of satisfaction.

'She'll be good,' he said, between clenched teeth, as he often spoke during rehearsals when he was moved. 'Don't *tell* her,' he hissed, 'or she'll get conceited and spoil it. But she'll be *good*. We shall have the clergy in tears.'

It was his ambition always to have the clergy in tears: if those petrified hearts could be moved, he believed, the play was a success. Having delivered the line, Monck wandered off from the auditorium into the foyer. Paul watched him, through the crack of the door as he stood alone, looking round proprietorily. He had no idea Paul could see him. Suddenly Moncklet saw a big crumb which had dropped from a sandwich lying in the middle of the foyer on the coir matting. He picked it up delicately between thumb and forefinger, looked round for somewhere to put it, and finding no waste basket or ashtray, ate it. Paul felt a strange pang at the little man's solitariness, alone with his standards.

But Paul told Joan about Monck's delight in her as they drank their coffee out in the courtyard, under the stars. It was still warm in late September, and the night over the city was heavy with autumn. The leaves on the few trees in the plague-fat churchyard were going flame-colour already. He was in state of intense excitement about this girl, and how she had entered into Viola's statuesque concealment of her love. He was possessed by a fantasy evoked by the tightness of her jerkin under which the shape of her small breasts was emphasised, however much she was supposed to be a boy. He had a fantasy of the jerkin being undone, and the breasts being revealed as evidence of her femininity. And over the vision played the words of her aside, like a tremulous melody:

'A little thing would make me
tell them how much I lack of a man . . .'

In the dark, her face was thoughtful and tired. But her eyes lit up in their reflection from the open door onto the courtyard.

'Moncklet said you were good.'

'Did he!'

'I wasn't to tell you. I thought you were wonderful.'

Suddenly he put an arm round her and drew her to him. Clumsily, he pushed his lips onto hers and kept them there for an instant. Her lips stayed reserved under his, but the close pressure of her breasts against his chest sent hot shivers through his body. He realised that the way she had suddenly looked up at the stars had drawn him: he couldn't resist her. She didn't resist him, but she gave a light laugh, rather scathing in tone.

'How easily is a boy bewitched,' she said. The schoolgirl had suddenly come out in her again. So the physical contact reduced the encounter to something banal. He was bewildered. But Joan wasn't angry, and accepted his hand when he took hold of hers. It was simply that the fascination, the vibration between them under the stars, was a 'literary' one. It belonged to the excitement of books, of poetry; of memorable words, and the sweet cheat of the theatre, the lovely cadences of the songs, 'Come away, come away death . . .' sung to the plucked twang of the spinet, and her statue-like face under the soft lilac lights.

He wrote her a poem:

To J.B.
Night Breeze in the City
Cold heavy air from the sky and the stars,
Sharp glints of frost in a purple-black tomb,
Drifts from the shadows and plays in bright bars
Of cold yellow light in the darkness and gloom,
And plays in her hair, and freezes in flight
Our tremulous words to fine silver lace,
And bears them like delicate moths in the night,
And rustles her coat and brushes her face . . .

But he could never finish it. Why not? It was one of those experiences which end (he told himself) with dots or a comma. It was really too 'sixth form' for words.

It all belonged to a mind experience that was something both coming into being and also belonging to a past stretching back to the Italian Renaissance, dimly grasped. But the lovely fantasy could not yet be lived fully in the body, not while they were still only seventeen. So it perished like a moth, between his lips and hers. After that, they only talked when they met—about theatre, and *The Wasteland*, Ernest Hemingway and Salvador Dali. They didn't even hold hands.

But bodily, it had a strange effect that fascinated him. He was much afraid that after Annie had left him he would go back to masturbating. But he didn't. The old Adam of his body didn't taunt him: instead, he gloated on fantasies of Viola, who was greater, in her Elizabethan doublet and hose, than the Joan of the library and he pursued her, in imaginary Illyria

> 'Unstaid and skittish in all motions else
> Save in the constant image of the creature
> That is belov'd . . .'

But, outside, the world was still undeceived. One day when they were alone outside in the theatre courtyard, taking tea between matinée and evening performance, both in doublet and hose because Peter had been fiddling with the costumes, repairing them, she said: 'Paul, listen to me seriously.'

'Right!' He threw a ham Hamlet-like pose, his arms folded, his one foot forward.

'How knobbly your knees look in hose!'

She giggled in her schoolgirl way.

'Do be careful,' said a flutey voice. 'Do be careful with the *hose*!' It was Peter. '*Please* don't go near any rose bushes.'

'There can't be any rose bushes for miles,' Joan called out.

'Well, you know what I mean.'

The male seamstress sighed and went in, all the cares of ten pairs of tights on his grey head.

'Paul, you know I'm trying to get into the Civil Service.'

'Yes.'

'When this play ends, you are going away.'

'Yes.'

'It has been . . . lovely . . . being friends with you . . . only . . .'

'What?'

He felt cold inside: she had turned pale and was being determinedly serious, her eyes dark and the little line round her mouth hard.

'We shall have to stop. I shall tell you why. I am not supposed to tell you this . . .'

'What ?'

'You know my mother likes you, but my father doesn't ?'

'Well ?'

He was a little angry now, the spell was falling from them so quickly, as if the autumn was breaking up suddenly, the coloured leaves being stripped from the trees by a cold harsh wind. She whispered almost.

'He told her something, swore her to secrecy but she told me, for your sake, knowing I'd tell you. There will be a court case. The police are going to prefer a charge. They were urged to drop it, but Rickson and his henchman at your school pressed them the other way.'

'How ?' The word leapt out angrily in the quiet courtyard. She looked worldly wise now with her small features, her eyes dark and intent.

'Oh, I can't tell you . . . it's all Masonic tie-ups and people meeting one another at do's, influential people in the city. It's political, too, in the background: you and Roy Short and your attendance at People's Convention meetings. But . . . '

'We must break up. There isn't a future for us, anyway, is there ?'

He felt alarmed for her, perhaps having her career spoilt, because of this association with him, this little Maddermarket dream!

'Well, you see, they're very careful about letting people into the Civil Service nowadays. I'd tell them to go to hell . . . I'm sure it would come out all right for you . . . but . . . if I loved you deeply, it would mean putting my career aside. I'm not prepared to do that yet for someone, for anyone. But I'm very fond of you, Paul . . .'

He kissed her cheek. She was crying a little. We must look funny, he thought, in Elizabethan costume, hugging and crying. Joan gave a little sob and drew away.

'This is a bit silly,' she said, in a low, cold voice.

'Yes,' he said. 'Let's start now. It's going to be hard, once this show is over. Well, let's be hard.'

'No,' she said. 'Not hard for you. You're going to Cambridge at the end of next week. I ... I think it may be hard for me ... for a bit.'

'Did you? Do you ...?' he blurted out. She nodded, a strange little nervous, shaky nod.

'Now ... what a pity!' He actually stamped his foot. 'But look,' he said, taking her arm gently. 'I'm very grateful to you, for letting me know that secret, if that's what it is. And for being so sensible! That's it,' he added, pulling her to him. 'You're so *sensible*.'

'Oh God,' she said, turning away, ironical and disparaging of herself.

He thought sadly about her all the way across the lonely stretches of Thetford Heath in the pouring rain a week later, when his father and mother drove him in their little Austin Ten to Pemning College, with his cardboard boxes full of books and china and his trunk of clothes. He said nothing to them about the gramophone records and the possible theft case. They knew nothing: he hoped his college wouldn't know. Norwich might have rumours: surely Cambridge wouldn't have? Would he be able to start afresh? Would it follow him? A certain misery fell over him as they unloaded his bits and pieces on the gravel path at Pemning and carried them up the rather resonant stone staircases to the room where his name was freshly painted over the door, in white letters on shiny black.

All the first week at Pemning he found it hard to sleep, and often woke in the grey wet dawns. The man he shared his room with would be sound asleep, breathing deeply, and Paul would be alone with his own tiresome thoughts, unable to escape from the treadmill of self-accusation and fear. He had been summoned to appear for an interview at the police station.

It was still warm weather, and one morning he made his way through the city to the river, down the passage between Trinity and Trinity Hall, before sunrise. Already, the tall walls of Tudor brick were reverberating to the clatter of milk churns and the banging of pans in the college kitchens. A friend of Roy's in the

Socialist Club had told him about a punt he could use, moored by the little boat-shed at the back of the colleges. The pole was lying inside, chained to the bottom boards with a bicycle combination lock: he had written the code in his diary, when he met the man at a party. To unchain the punt itself there was a trick: the padlock wasn't really a lock at all—one simply pulled the staple out. It was all as the man said. Only the punt, its green paint peeling and its wood going rotten in places, was half full of water, and it took ten minutes of bailing with a yellow enamel saucepan to empty it, sloshing the dirty bilge-water into the river. The splashing noise in the morning mist set the ducks off quacking under the hanging fringes of the weeping willow.

At last he was away, the metal end of the pole crunching into the gravel bottom five feet below him. He was alone on an empty river, gliding along beside the lawns below Wren's long Trinity Library of yellow and pink stone. The sun, rather rosy in its rising, was just beginning to touch the tops of the roof lanterns on the long Gothic New Court, on chapel campaniles and spires.

Such a moment, when there is no one about, catches all the mystery of Cambridge. He felt the detachment the little river provides, the opportunity to stand back and see the colleges gliding by, as if moving through their own time, but having their own unity, belonging to the same stream that flows from Ancient Greece, through the Renaissance, diverted at the Scientific Revolution, to flow on now, through the age of technology. But what does technology lead to, he thought sourly? That the river is more sewage than water, while at any moment any of the buildings might be swept away like smoke? Yet in the air were still the memories of Plato and Aristotle, expressed physically by those bookcase ends inside that great Library. And of Newton of course, in the notebooks shown there in a glass case, in which the great mathematician recorded the purchase of a chamberpot, 2s. 1d.

The real Cambridge was as evanescent as the pink light in the air touching the misty towers. And he felt now that he belonged to it, in that floating-past way. Sitting face to face with Halley-Whicker, his tutor, talking to the old man in his College rooms, he did not feel he belonged. The man's long sallow face and his big eyes, made grotesque by his thick lenses: that wasn't 'Cambridge'.

Nor was the average lecturer's drone. Sitting on the hard benches in Mill Lane, he felt alien, unable to follow the bearded mumbling from the old men in gowns. But pushing the heavy punt down river, watching the sun rise over the mellow brickwork of St John's, he knew he belonged to something he could only call 'Cambridge' in spirit, and that would always remain 'Cambridge' for him. Yet whatever was there to belong to, escaped him. Once he had punted under Magdalene Bridge and along beside the laundry which was beginning to puff steam and hiss at the river, he began to lose the idea altogether—and by Jesus Lock he was simply on a fen river, slowly unloading towards Denver Sluice, merging into East Anglia's flat alluvial plain. He seemed to have lost 'Cambridge' there.

He turned the old punt back because it was taking water fast: it turned slowly, and with its long straight planks to the current, drifted almost down to the lock before he could get a good push on the deep bottom, and urge it back towards Magdalene. Would he re-enter 'Cambridge' now?

Cambridge, he thought, as he slid under the cast iron Magdalene Bridge, painted green, is somewhere between here and Coe Fen. But what 'Cambridge' was he could not say: it had a meaning, but the meaning could be in someone's head; if it existed at all, it was a meaning sustained in the minds of a few persons, perhaps expressed by them, and so recreated in other minds. But there was nothing else. All the little snobberies of Cambridge families and academic officers—all that was nothing: mere social 'side'.

The sun was well up now, but between the tall buildings of John's and under the Bridge of Sighs, it was cool still and he shivered. Somehow the way the buildings were constructed there, although he did not know it, brought to Cambridge some of that deathly splendour of the Venetian Canals: massive palaces from whose waterside entrances boats had slunk for centuries on sordid or deadly errands, or to wild and splendid occasions. The Bridge of Sighs, Victorian copy though it was, conveyed another idea, an idea from Europe, as it slid over his head—an attention to the Renaissance in Italy with its links with Greece, and the East beyond. In that strengthening morning light he felt illuminated, alone on the river, making his slow way along it, the water dripping from the pole down his arm, illuminated about the relationship between himself and the idea that was Cambridge; and relieved, too, from his feeling that as a 'scholarship boy' from Norwich he was only an outsider. He possessed Cambridge, and was as much part of its idea now as any of the present establishment of the little provincial town. The charming bridge into Clare, with its stone spheres: Gibbs Building and the massive towering chapel near it; the wooden Mathematical Bridge at Queen's, and the Fitzwilliam Museum, with its huge ornate classical echoes—he loved them all, and they all spoke to him, for the first time, in stone and wood, in form and compactness, of the flow of European ideas. To get along the Coe Fen stretch he had to punt round under the Granary balconies, and heave the flat boat up the rollers into the higher reach, a difficult task for a youth on his own. Two cows lumbered over the meadow, curious to watch him, grunting over the heavy slimy boat as it tried to roll down into water again. He felt he was striving between sinking back into the fen, into the land of meadows and cows, and rising to the higher aspirations of the colleges and museums. By the Fen Causeway Bridge he felt he had won; he had taken Cambridge in; but this was also the end of it, and so he turned back, at last, rather weary, chaining the punt back at its berth.

Was this all he was going to have of the place? Now the day was at its height, his dream faded, and he slunk home, feeling nobody.

Back at Pemning, he sat in his College room wretched and dazed, loathing his own weakness. How the whole thing gathered impetus, from the time one made the first error! He recalled the afternoon in which Roy had encouraged him to take him down to the Music House, and then, in reckless breach of the trust placed on him, had coarsely taken the albums, and had planted them all on him. He had been 'led into crime' absurdly, by his best friend, sometime head boy of his school. All Roy had said to the police had been: 'You awful man—how dare you accuse me of such a thing!' And, of course, nothing had been found at Roy's house. Paul wasn't going to give him away. But then they had presented him with Roy's name and he had had to make a statement. How absurd!

He felt contaminated by the interview in the police station. The detective, a nondescript long-faced man in a crumpled dirt-coloured suit, had smoked all the time, and had turned Paul's own words into policemanese. The place was a drab, grey building: 'We thought you'd better come along to the station.' Inside, the plain heavy desks, the dull cream-coloured walls, the posters about incendiary bombs and the grubbiness of everything, the heavy air of low wrong-doing.

'Yes, we'd better stick to the word "borrowed",' said the detective, laboriously writing with nicotine-stained fingers. He had a blunt London accent, not Cockney, but clipped and urban, Enfield perhaps. 'But your trouble is that you denied all knowledge of these record albums when Mr Pike and a friend called at your home on 25 August.'

Paul shrugged his shoulders.

'I panicked,' he said: 'and I wanted to see . . . my friend first. It was his idea, after all,' he said, with an ill-grace.

'You were in your own shoes, weren't you?'

'What do you mean?'

'You didn't have to do what he told you. It was your decision to . . . "borrow" . . . these symphonies, wasn't it? How do we know you aren't just trying to unload the blame onto him? He doesn't admit anything.'

'I fully intended to return those records,' said Paul. 'It never entered my head to keep them. I didn't want to take them in the first place.'

'Then why didn't you take them back before? After all, you had them for two months.'

'I didn't have a gramophone. I was hoping to listen to them on the school one, but somehow I never got round to it.'

'Who's going to believe that?'

'Are you saying I'm lying?'

'Well, it all looks very bad, and if there's a court hearing, I don't think things will go very well for you, I'm bound to say. You noticed, I hope, I had to warn you that anything you say may be taken down and used in evidence against you.'

Paul turned hot and uncomfortable at the mention of a court hearing. He would be tried in public like a common thief.

Did the college know? His standing there couldn't be worse. He had already plunged into left-wing political activity. His tutor had warned him at the middle of the Michaelmas term that he had been told he wasn't working hard enough. The dry, balding classicist with gold spectacles had been coldly disapproving: 'You know, you're here to work,' he had said, 'not to show Russian films and write pamphlets.' He was on a city scholarship, and Norwich would want to know how its money was being spent. 'You've also already deeply offended the Master's wife.'

Paul's jaw dropped.

'I've not written anything to her that could be thought offensive, have I?' he said defensively.

Dr Halley-Whicker smiled a thin, lean smile, turning his big anxious eyes on his undergraduate.

'That's just the point. She has very kindly asked the freshmen to tea, and you are the only man who has not replied. She didn't tell me this. I learned it in a chance conversation with the Master's private secretary, who told me she was very upset.'

'She came round to my room and I talked to her then.'

'That was kind of her.'

'It was at the beginning of the term, as soon as she'd sent the invitations out. I told her I didn't want to be lectured on moral rearmament.'

'That was hardly polite. You know she feels a great concern for the spiritual life of the men here: so does Admiral Churchyard.'

'Well, perhaps I'd better go,' he said grudgingly.

So he had sat uncomfortably through the tea party in the Master's Lodge, perching edgily on the sofa covered with flowered chintz beneath the paintings of seascapes, talking to the pop-eyed old Admiral with Lady Churchyard beaming at him as if he were a repentant sinner. He quoted Marx at her, making her bristle, despite her good Christian intention to love him. Her comfortable, fanatical evangelism, even unspoken as it was on that occasion, made him hate Christianity even more.

The nearest he ever got to religion was his discussions with Moncklet, who was an atheist. He recalled a letter he had received from the little man that week.

'The trouble with Marx is that he knew nothing about God. A greater prophet had remarked that "Man cannot live by bread alone". I have never read a reasonable account of Christ's temptations. He knew he had power but refused it (seeing how little the Caesars did with it). He saw that he must work with and through the individual. There were enough materialists in the world. "What does it profit a man if he gain the whole world and lose his own soul?" But the Roman Empire was as spiritually starved as ours ... No, I'm not becoming "religious", no more than *always*. The Holy Ghost, the Holy Spirit seems the most important person in the Trinity—we apprehend God through the Spirit. Christ lives as *Man*, not as God and it is the work of the artist to follow Christ's example and work through the individual—and that is the work of the Maddermarket which is not always understood. Not to produce pious, moral plays, but to be like Chekhov where there exists something more than the spoken words ... something in the pauses—that is not piety but humanism ...'

That letter meant much to Paul, though he was amused by the way the little man so naïvely identified with Jesus. But Lady Churchyard's propaganda for moral purity and 'rearmament' repelled him; it seemed to him dishonest, though he couldn't say why. All he could greet it with was a rather stupid, sulky resentment—rather like Roy Short's idiotic kind of delinquency.

A few days later he was summoned to his tutor again. Halley-Whicker did not smile, but looked at him rather coldly through his very thick lenses, which enlarged the whites of his big eyes.

'I was glad to hear that you went to tea with Lady Churchyard.'

Was that all he had to say?

'Well, I tried to be polite. But I don't like that kind of proselytising.'

'Why not?'

The academic raised his eyebrows rather wearily. I suppose they get sick of the rebellious young, Paul reflected.

'It doesn't seem to me ... honest.'

A ghost of a smile appeared on the older man's face.

'I wanted to ask you about your own standards of honesty.'

Paul felt cold, and blushed.

'I suppose you know what I am referring to?'

Paul nodded. The neat room, with its pictures of Roman and Greek sculpture and architecture, swam. Was this the end of

202

Cambridge? He cursed the egoistic Roy in his heart: what right had the ass to embroil him in an affair he simply couldn't explain away? Would he have to get his parents up to argue with poor old Halley-Whicker? There was a turmoil in his head, and he felt sick.

'I have had a visit from an old schoolmaster of yours.'

Paul was startled. 'Who?'

'A man called Softfoot.'

'Softfoot!'

'He came, I think, at the suggestion of your new headmaster.'

'I bet he did.'

'Softfoot said that at the request of Mr Rickson he had spent some time both in Norwich and Cambridge observing your behaviour.'

Paul went cold and tense. It must be the end, then. He nearly got up and walked out. Halley-Whicker went drily on, staring through his big lenses.

'It seems that the Norwich Education Committee has been very anxious about the way in which grants have been wasted by young men with bizarre tastes and wayward opinions in wartime. I may say this is not my attitude: I'm only reporting what Mr Softfoot told me.'

Was this a gleam of hope?

'I asked this man what the college had to do with all this. He asked me whether I thought you were working hard. As a matter of fact, I had also talked to Dr Beavis at lunch. Though this may surprise you, he said you were reading a great deal and were making intelligent comments at supervisions.'

Paul dared not move. He couldn't remember making any intelligent comments. Nobody ever said anything: old Beavis just droned on with his own fascinating and scurrilous comments. Oh, yes; he had said something about the texture of Keats, which had generated a benign twinkle, he recalled.

'I told the man from Norwich that as far as we were concerned there was no complaint about your work, though of course Cambridge did often overwhelm a young man with all kind of lures—into political or theatrical activities, or whatever . . .'

Halley-Whicker smiled and put his long-fingered hands together under his chin.

'This, in a way, is what the place is for. I think there are ways, don't you, in which schoolmasters in provincial towns don't understand adolescents and young men?'

'Yes,' said Paul, his mouth dry, with a sense of understatement.

'He asked me plainly if I thought you were going off the rails . . . I said no. I wasn't quite sure on what grounds I said no. But I am a classicist, you know. I always remember the way the authorities treated Socrates, and I have had a little contact with your one time eccentric headmaster whose Bible was Pericles's Funeral Oration. If I bring my classical interests to the predicament of a rebellious youth, I find myself defending the apparently indefensible sometimes.'

Paul felt he wanted to kiss the strangely dry classicist, whose fingers now displayed, however, a trembling nervousness.

'Then,' he said leaning back as if detaching himself from something rather contaminating, 'he told me you were being prosecuted for stealing some gramophone records. Can you tell me anything about that?'

'It was all a silly mistake,' Paul burst out. 'It was a practical joke a friend played on me, that went wrong. I had no intention of taking those records, and in any case they are now returned.'

'Well, as far as we are concerned,' said his tutor, 'this seems to have happened long before you came up. In any case, I was deeply disturbed about the motives of Mr Rickson and Mr Softfoot in raising this with me. I was not happy that they seemed to be trying to find evidence to deprive you of your grants, in order to pay off some old score, as I saw it, though I may be wrong. Though it is very wrong of me to say so, professionally, I didn't like the man.'

To read the classics, thought Paul, didn't exactly disqualify a man from understanding modern villainy. This short-sighted academic, with a high forehead and a bird-like manner, was really rather magnificent. Paul could see it was all what Short and his Left-wing friends would call 'bourgeois' and despise. But he could see it was based on a deep and ancient approach to human truth they could not comprehend, on which 'Cambridge', 'Maddermarket' and civilisation, as he dimly apprehended its nature, rested.

'All this would be no reason for depriving a student—even a rude and unruly student—of his Exhibition. But I fear that if there is a prosecution, and if it is successful, the Education Authority in Norwich may think differently, and the college could do nothing about it. I mean, your Exhibition is only £40 per annum, and we couldn't ourselves make it up to the full amount. I thought I should explain that. And explain also that, while we don't care for many of your beliefs and attitudes, in general we shall support you, perhaps rather more strongly than someone whose views we endorse.'

Paul could hardly get down the stairs.

Who was he now to talk about dishonesty? His parents would be distressed, the city would withdraw his grant, the college would send him down, and his career would be finished. And all for a couple of records that meant nothing to him: he hadn't even picked them out himself. Roy had simply taken them off the end of the row and shoved them into his arms, purely out of his strange envy of Pike. Paul sat now in his room staring moodily at the purring gas fire. On the hearth was one of the teacups Moncklet had given him half-full of stale tea. As if he had money to spare—and this was now the little man's reward. He had written to Moncklet, confessing to the whole thing, and pouring out his misery, not at being 'caught', but at falling into the absurd situation by a momentary lapse, a practical joke, or whatever it was. But why give Monck pain and dismay—after all his kindness?

'Paul—message in the lodge.'

Someone with his head round the door. The thin young man, rather bored with trouble, in his blue tweed jacket and blue Daks sports trousers, walked slowly down the stairs of the echoing new building and up the drive to the porter's lodge. On a piece of paper was Moncklet's telephone number and a request to ring at once. He walked round to the telephone booth by the junior combination room and asked for the number in the smoky little cabin, feeling cold and low. A smell of stale tobacco hung in the kiosk: on the wall were scribbled numbers and 'try Alice 59862'. Hearing the familiar voice, he pressed button 'A'.

'Hallo, Moncklet. I'm very sorry to bother you with all this. It's absurd, really.'

'I have been . . .' said the voice, with dramatic deliberation. 'I have this moment returned from a most exhausting session with the Chief Constable of Norwich.'

'God!' exclaimed Paul.

'No, not God, dearie . . . only the Chief Constable . . .'

He was obviously playing to someone in the room: but he was serious, too, rather fierce with Paul.

'I have given him my assurance that you will never do anything so foolish again. I showed him your letter.'

Paul gasped.

'I asked him—"Is this a letter from a thief?" I virtually went down on my knees to beg him not to prosecute you. I said it would ruin your career, which was already in jeopardy enough . . . And I *won*.'

Paul heard him draw in a big bit of spit: Moncklet was evidently passionately excited by the episode. What a marvellous old man he was! Tears came into his eyes. Why should he care for a youth who was so unrewarding?

'I told him you were a rebel . . . with your absurd student politics. Yet you were facing the prospect of National Service. In a year or two you could well be *dead* . . . What value was there in punishing you now for showing disturbed behaviour during the kind of adolescence boys were having nowadays? I said that, like all intelligent young people, you were likely to fall foul of authority through sheer bloody-mindedness and ignorance. But I thought the report to the police had been made hastily and not a little maliciously, and if this case was dropped I would vouch for your good behaviour. I am a *damn fool* to do it: but I feel I must . . . Are you still there?'

Paul was silent, his heart beating joyfully, but beneath a stunned dazedness.

'Yes,' said Paul flatly. 'It's so kind of you, Moncklet.' He was nearly crying. 'I don't know . . . I don't know what to say, except thank you. I didn't really want to bother you with it . . . I had no idea . . .'

'You will *not be prosecuted*: do you understand that?'

'It's amazing. It's . . . too good to be true!'

He saw the little man's hand waving in the Crypt air.

'Say *nothing* about it. It's very rarely that these things can be stopped once they've started. For *God*'s sake don't go blabbing around your friends especially not your absurd *Socialist* friends. Just be glad and be quiet . . . There,' concluded the little man, 'I'm quite exhausted and must go and lie down. Come and see me soon,' he ended with a rising cadence.

'Goodbye!' he exclaimed finally, in a high-pitched, dramatic voice that spoke volumes—of the sad valedictory wave of the hand that accompanied it, and the sense he communicated that one can only create something between one person and another momentarily, before one or the other is swept away into darkness.

But Paul broke in quickly before Monck put the receiver down.

'You know, the awful thing about it is that I didn't do it, well, not really, from my own volition, I . . .'

'Roy Short made you do it.'

'How did you know?'

'Well . . . you're a *fool* to let yourself be influenced. But I knew . . .'

'How?'

'. . . Shall we say . . . telepathy?' The voice went up, impishly. 'It's difficult to explain on the phone. Of course, he rationalises it and pretends it's "politics". But really he, wanted to get his revenge on Norwich. He *hates* the Maddermarket. You see, we never recognised his genius.'

There was a pause. Paul still felt some loyalty to his friend: strangely, it was the man's monstrous egoism that had attracted him, his ruthlessness. He himself had become a victim of it. Yet that was what was unusual about Roy—what was attractive about Roy, his unattractive selfishness. Even his hate had a strange compulsive lure. He must remember that, all his life.

He sighed.

'Yes, I remember now,' he said. 'He said he *ordered* me to do it, because Pike was a fascist. So, he said, any moral scruples were out of the question.'

'Tell me,' said the little man. 'Has he left Cambridge?'

'Oh, yes,' said Paul. 'He's gone into the forces. He's training for special air services, behind the lines, and so on.'

There was a sarcastic chuckle at the other end. 'He'll do well as a spy.'

'I'm terribly grateful, Moncklet.'

'I shall expect a bottle of wine when you call next. But don't *steal* it.'

At last the black receiver went down and he was back, alone, in the dead, cold phone cabin.

When he returned to his room, he read the rest of Moncklet's latest letter.

'There is only one way of making any dreams come true, and that is to do the work oneself. No one else will do the dirty work for you. The reason why I am a *failure* is that I am *lazy*. I cannot work for more than ten hours at a stretch (my working day at present is 11 am to 12 midnight. Last night I went to bed at 2 am and worked till I was *finished* . . .)'

Old men! Monck and Halley-Whicker: yet they were in touch with the springs, as his friends in his own age-group were not. The old men reached right back across the Renaissance to Ancient Greece, and to the truths in Sophocles, Aristophanes and Plato. Roy with all his sophistication was a barbarian. What was he, Paul, going to be?

A few weeks later he arrived at the Crypt, in Norwich, carrying a bottle of red wine. It was late afternoon and the light was going: in the long living-room were two old men of the theatre, Monck himself and Peter Taylor-Smith.

The little man was fussing about some tights again. They had holes in. Peter was unco-operative.

'It's no good, they must be mended.'

'Can't we get any new ones? It's absurd trying to mend these. They simply won't take any more.'

'No one has any. They're not making them. I've tried Gandolph's and Nathanwigs. We can't get any made: in any case we can't spare any more coupons for stuff—I need them all for the women's costumes.'

Peter sighed.

'Well, if you want your *Tempest* costumes, something must be done.'

Monck pushed his chin out determinedly.

'I shall go down to the theatre and see what Barbara says. I'm sure we have some more tights somewhere. Perhaps she's hidden some. Paul—stay and talk to Peter: and then when I come back we can drink your wine.'

Pulling his grey trilby right down over his eyes and turning up his overcoat collar so that he looked like a diminutive gangster, the producer stomped off into the drizzly November night. Paul felt a little taut in the presence of the older man who had caught him fire-watching with Annie on that night last winter. There was silence for a moment as they sat watching the flames flicker on the bricks of the uneven floor, and on the rugs.

'He'll not find any,' said the elderly man. He was a stiff, big-framed man whose hair was now white. He wore a brown corduroy jacket, rather worn, and grey flannel trousers with a yellow pullover. On one finger of his delicate hands was a dull silver ring.

'It's funny,' said Paul, 'when I come back here, I feel it's home.'

Peter gave a dry laugh.

'Well,' he drawled, 'we all love him really, I suppose, maddening little man.'

'He's been very good to me.'

Peter continued to gaze into the fire, his head bowed, looking patriarchal. He said nothing: Paul wondered if he knew about the records.

'It seems so difficult, at my age, to know whom to trust. But he's trustworthy.'

'Absolutely. You know,' Peter went on, 'I have terrible rows with Monck—you've seen us at it. You have too—like the row about that girl in the box office that time. But he never bears anyone any malice. Come to think of it . . .' The old man bent forward, took the little black poker and split a lump of burning coal. 'I don't think I bear him any malice at all, old cat as I am. He's absolutely trustworthy. It's his art, his learning, such as it is. He is utterly humble in the face of great art, painting, poetry, music. So, he's completely . . . authentic.'

'As most people aren't.'

'Well . . . one feels like that, I know. But at least you're not like me, terrified of senility, and really quite dried up emotionally. I'm dying really. It's then that someone like Moncklet is superb. I just know he'll not throw me out till I die . . . which won't be long.'

Peter's health was really good, Paul knew, from the woman who painted the scenery. He had been 'dying' for ten years, but still seemed quite strong. Yet his hands were going a little arthritic, it was true, and they were all afraid he would not be able to go on with his needlework on the costumes. But he would live at Scutcheons until he died: and the theatre would always find some work for him.

'But you've worked for the Maddermarket all your life,' said Paul. 'What I can't understand is why, when I can't see my own way, it's a sixty-year-old homosexual theatre producer who seems to offer me, in his trust, some point in my life, and a direction, a meaning, when no one else does.'

'Not even your ample girlfriend?'

Peter couldn't help being a little bitchy. He was comfortably settled in his chair and was being more sympathetic and outgoing than Paul had ever known him to be.

'She was seduced by a really revolting stationery salesman and married him.'

'Less stationary than you, obviously.'

'I never . . . we never made love fully.'

'Well,' said Peter, not unkindly, 'there'll be a time . . .'

There was a pause. Peter went on as if talking to himself.

'I've never had a woman in my life, neither physically, nor emotionally. You'll put me down as a queer, and dismiss me as an old dying queen—but it's very sad, you know. It's really something one yearns for, funnily enough. Moncklet's the same: you know, many of us believe there was some awful tragedy in his life, someone he desperately loved died when he was a boy, or something like that.'

'I've noticed that, too,' said Paul. 'He hints at it, very distantly, very rarely.' The room was growing dark, but they still sat in the firelight. 'Certainly I've caught some deep tragic sadness off him. Perhaps if people are deeply in love in adolescence, and then it's shattered, they never recover?'

'I think that's why—let's say—single people like us are sometimes good with adolescents. I've heard Dr Heilpern talk about it as a schizoid thing, like Hamlet. So many things happen to the young, they don't have a strong sense of identity: "This too . . . unsullied . . . unsolid? . . . flesh should melt . . .": people drift through their lives, half attach themselves, then cut away, or prove unreliable. So they feel fragmentary themselves. But where you and Moncklet are concerned, you see, it isn't just you and the little man. Whatever its faults, this theatre enterprise is a community. It's the loyalty to that which sustains us all: it takes time to see that. Home, school, these have their place. But young people revolt against them: they are "authority", and they have to reject it. But the arts provide a separate ground, where we can all live beyond ourselves, beyond our restricted personal means.'

'One tries so many substitutes,' said Paul. 'Political clubs, music societies, discussion groups. But then comes a moment when you feel "I don't really belong in this"—it offers nothing to be loyal to. The university isn't substantial enough, I find, not even one's own college: there's nothing there to be loyal to, except for one or two,' he added, thinking of Halley-Whicker. 'There are people, and an "idea", but not a community.'

'I'm surprised you should say that. It's been one of the great sorrows of my life that I never went to a university.'

'Oh well, one feels a loyalty to the tradition it stands for of the pursuit of truth. And to "English" as a subject, to English literature. So that's very much like saying you feel a loyalty to the Maddermarket. But what makes me feel at home, here, is a sense of belonging to something beyond the Maddermarket—a creative dynamic—something beyond us all, which keeps before us a goal of whole truth to be found; something which comes and goes, even, a meaning that's there, for a moment, under Moncklet's lights, and then gone.'

'Yet it's more impersonal, you see, than many things. That's Monck's achievement—his respect for every work of art, for standards, for symbolism. He lifts us all up towards those things, beyond ourselves.'

'So you still feel that, after all these years?'

'Indeed!'

'It's much more so for me, a mere Norwich boy. Cambridge doesn't do that: it's very snobbish, really, more provincial despite the university. I heard a don's wife say: "A rather rough boy, come up from the grammar school." That's me. It's a poky little provincial place really. And I feel nobody there. I suppose Norwich is the same if one doesn't know the city. But Monck's international, almost, you know, and even timeless: even though the play dissolves in time, and all his work is gone as the last switch goes out.'

The door clattered, and the little man came in, brandishing a bundle of pale beige-coloured tights, which he flung onto the back of an armchair.

'Talk of the devil,' said Peter drily.

'We were saying you were of international status,' said Paul.

'The devil is certainly international,' said Moncklet, 'and his loss is a universal catastrophe. I have found six pairs of tights in, of all places, the *wig*-box.'

'Oh!' cried Peter. 'You know, Moncklet, at the end of a show, people don't care where they put stuff. I always ask for tights so they can be washed. But they just fling them anywhere. I *am* sorry. I should have looked harder.'

> '. . . let our lives, our souls,
> Our debts, and careful wives,
> Our children, and our sins, lay on the King!
> We must bear all . . . er . . . er'
> '. . . O hard condition
> Twin-born with greatness, subject to the breath
> Of any fool . . .'

The two older men laughed: both had been actors in the hard days, and knew much of Shakespeare by heart.

'As a prize,' said the little man, 'I shall drink some of Paul's wine.'

And he trotted away for the corkscrew and some glasses.

21

He was late, and so he did not go in by the main entrance of the great grey cathedral, but rambled round the back, the south side, until he found a door. It was open, and he went in just as the congregation was singing a hymn. He blinked a little as he found himself in the immense stone place: and there, immediately before him, was a strangely theatrical catafalque, and on top of it a little coffin. He could see at once that it was Moncklet, for no one else would have had such a squat little coffin. At once the whole intolerable awfulness of death burst over him, like the great stone waves of the cathedral's masonry. The cathedral dissolved in his burning tears, and he sobbed aloud, suddenly and uncontrollably distraught, utterly broken down.

No one saw him. He stumbled out as he had come. He couldn't stay to hear the clergyman's words spoken over the coffin, over the plain feminine little man who had been an atheist, yet with such a deep veneration for the meaning of Christianity. It would be absurd for the Church to claim him: and yet he had loved its drama and meanings too.

But being suddenly confronted with his corpse like that brought home to Paul Grimmer how much he had loved Moncklet. Not only the grief threw him as he stumbled around the Cathedral Close, but the recognition of his love for a man, for that small wizard, with his capacities to transform the world into art, into meaning. There was the pyramid, the last drama, and the Church bowing down to him. He recalled all the sacrilegious things Moncklet had said about the clergy: and yet recalled his affectionate regard for Christ, with whom he intensely and wickedly identified. 'He was simply not understood,' he used to say.

Paul communed in his head, in his soul, with the impish little man, dead: they joked. He knew Monck had had a good death, an easy death, at sixty-four: he had been lunching with Bobbie and some friends, and suddenly said: 'I think I am going to faint.' He died at once in Bobbie's arms, without pain or distress: simply fell asleep. It was little cause for weeping, after such a life, after producing two hundred and eighty plays. But as he looked up at the great pointed spire it seemed to Paul bleak and ridiculous in its aspirations. It could not solve the problem: Monck, that lively spirit, was no longer in the world. There was only that strange leaded and tiled architectural finger, pointing to a heaven that never was, where the little man never went. He could feel nothing but mockery and bitterness, and a dreadful sense of loss, as he drove back to Cambridge.